DEATH OF A CHR

Hayley and Sergio
minutes sifting thro
Garth's
all of it
velope s
of Dece

She p
a look a

"Who

"Loc

Sergi
Garth had a key made recently."

"Look at the notation near the bottom. 'Warehouse.' Tiffany said Garth was paranoid about the local competition stealing his recipe files so he kept only one key to this place."

"Maybe he just lost his key and had it replaced."

"He would need the original key to make a copy. Were there any keys found on him?"

"A key to his car, one to his house, and one presumably to here."

"Well, did the key to the warehouse look shiny and brand-new like it was a fresh copy?"

"No, as I recall, it was all scratched up and the copper was fading."

"Then maybe Garth had a key made for someone else. And that person would have had access to the warehouse, and could have locked it when he or she left, leaving behind a dead body and food burning in the oven. . . ."

Books by Lee Hollis

DEATH OF A KITCHEN DIVA

DEATH OF A COUNTRY FRIED REDNECK

DEATH OF A COUPON CLIPPER

DEATH OF A CHOCOHOLIC

DEATH OF A CHRISTMAS CATERER

Published by Kensington Publishing Corporation

A Hayley Powell
Food & Cocktails Mystery

DEATH OF A CHRISTMAS CATERER

LEE HOLLIS

KENSINGTON PUBLISHING CORP.
http://www.kensingtonbooks.com

KENSINGTON BOOKS are published by

Kensington Publishing Corp.
119 West 40th Street
New York, NY 10018

All Kensington Titles, Imprints, and Distributed Lines are available at special quantity discounts for bulk purchases for sales promotions, premiums, fund-raising, and educational or institutional use. Special book excerpts or customized printings can also be created to fit specific ington special sales manager: Kensington Publishing Corp., 119 West 40th Street, New York, NY 10018, attn: Special Sales Department, Phone: 1-800-221-2647.

Kensington and the K logo Reg. U.S. Pat & TM Off.

ISBN-13: 978-0-7582-9451-7
ISBN-10: 0-7582-9451-4
First Kensington Mass Market Edition: October 2014

eISBN-13: 978-0-7582-9452-4
eISBN-10: 0-7582-9452-2
First Kensington Electronic Edition: October 2014

10 9 8 7 6 5 4 3 2 1

Printed in the United States of America

Chapter 1

"I hate Christmas!"

"You don't mean that," Hayley said, gripping her four oversize shopping bags while racing to catch up with Mona, who was veering toward the crowded food court at the Bangor Mall.

"Yes, I do!" Mona barked as she plowed through a family of four that had failed to get out of her way fast enough. She made a beeline for Sbarro pizza and slapped her hand down on the counter, causing the pimply-faced kid behind the register to jump. "Pepperoni slice! Scratch that. Make it a whole pie!"

"Thanks, Mona, but I'm not really that hungry," Hayley said.

"Good, because I wasn't offering. If I'm going to get through this day, I'm going to need a large pizza and a pitcher of beer. I am so sick and tired of these annoying holiday crowds swarming around here in a panic like rats on a sinking ship!"

Hayley noticed a little curly-haired blond cherub, around six years old, in an adorable reindeer jumper listening to Mona and fearfully clutching her mother's coat. "Mona, lower your voice. You're scaring children."

"Kids are the worst! Snot-nosed, screaming brats! You know Christmas would be so much better if it was adults only. Just some spiked eggnog, a warm fire, and a *Duck Dynasty* marathon on TV. Heaven!"

Mona suddenly noticed the pimply Sbarro employee in his creased paper hat just staring at her. "What? Do I have to come back there and knead the dough myself? Hop to it! I'm starving!"

The kid nodded, turned quickly, and accidentally knocked over a stack of paper cups because he was so nervous dealing with this possibly unstable customer.

"And no husband!" Mona barked. "He's more whiny and needy than my boatload of kids. Honestly, Hayley, just one year I'd like to spend the holidays putting my feet up and relaxing instead of brawling with some sumo-wrestling supermom who wants the last Power Wheels Barbie Jammin' Jeep for her spoiled-rotten spawn!"

"You really do paint a picture, Mona."

Mona eyed the pimply kid; his hand shook as he ladled tomato sauce onto the pizza dough and splashed it around before slipping on a plastic glove and dunking his hand into a vat of mozzarella cheese.

Hayley rummaged in her coat pocket, pulled out a slip of paper, and then began to peruse it. "Look at how much stuff I still have to buy. I knew we should have gotten our Christmas shopping done right after Halloween. I never learn. Every year I plan on going early to avoid the crowds on Black Friday. And then I never get around to it and I have to go on Black Friday, but this year I had the flu the entire Thanksgiving weekend and now I'm way behind on everything."

"Don't get so worked up, Hayley. You need to chill," Mona said.

With her mouth agape, Hayley glanced at Mona, but Mona missed the jaw-dropping irony of her statement. Mona was too busy pounding her fist on the counter and yelling at "Sbarro Boy."

"Did you go to Italy to pick up the pepperoni? How long does it take to get a pie in the oven?"

"Mona, if you don't stop shouting at the poor boy, he's going to have a nervous breakdown!"

Mona groaned and turned to the frightened teenager. "Sorry, kid, I'm like a growling bear when I'm hungry," she said, slapping a twenty-dollar bill down on the counter. "This is yours if I'm chowing down my pizza in the next ten minutes."

Sbarro Boy had that pie in the oven in nineteen seconds and was now grinning from ear to ear.

Hayley studied her list. "Gemma wants an iPad mini and Rihanna concert tickets. Dustin wants one, two, three . . . six video games for his Xbox. There's no way I can afford all of this."

Mona dipped into her coat pocket, pulled out a pen, and thrust it in Hayley's face.

"What's that for?"

"Start crossing stuff off. Seriously. Why put yourself through this? Your kids will appreciate whatever you can afford to give them."

"You're right. I don't know why I feel the need to go overboard every year."

Hayley's cell phone chirped. She pulled it out of the back of her jeans and looked at the caller ID. "Oh, God. It's Danny."

"Don't answer it," Mona warned.

"I have to. The kids are going to go visit him during February vacation and I sent him their flight info this morning before we left for Bangor. He just needs to sign off and pay me back half the cost."

Danny Powell was Hayley's ex-husband. He moved to Iowa after they divorced and was now living with a girl half his age named Becky.

Enough said.

"I swear, every time you talk to him, Hayley, he makes you feel bad. Let it go to voicemail."

" I really could use his help buying a couple of things on the kids' Christmas wish lists."

"Have you *met* your ex-husband? Now you're just hoping for a friggin' Christmas miracle."

Hayley smiled and clicked on her phone. "Hi, Danny."

"Hey. Listen, this isn't going to work for me."

"What?"

"These tickets you bought for the kids to come see me during their February break. Three hundred apiece? What were you thinking?"

"They were the cheapest I could find."

"That's because you have them flying out on a Saturday. Weekends are always more expensive to travel."

"I couldn't book them for a Friday because I work, Danny. I'm out of vacation days and I can't afford to take any time off right now."

"How is that *my* problem?"

Unbelievable.

Hayley took a deep breath. "I understand how pricey it is. I was barely able to scrape together my half, Danny."

"It's too expensive. I can't pay you right now."

"I thought you were working extra shifts at Walmart during the holiday season."

"Yeah, but I got bills to pay, Hayley. You know how much it costs to heat our house in Des Moines during the winter?"

"No, I don't, Danny. Because it's just fun in the sun here in Maine!"

Hayley heard girlish giggling on the other end of the phone. "Who's that?"

"That's just Becky. We're having a Christmas party here for a few friends and she got into the holiday punch a little early. Happy hour somewhere in the world, right?"

"Merry Christmas, Hayley," she heard Becky sing before she erupted into a fit of giggles.

"Tell her I said 'Merry Christmas' back." Hayley sighed.

"Are you talking to the girlfriend?" Mona asked.

Hayley nodded.

"Hey, Danny, what'd you get Becky for Christmas this year? A Crown Disney Princess Tea Set?" Mona yelled before snorting at her own joke.

Hayley quickly covered the phone with her hand. "He can hear you."

"Good. Mission accomplished," Mona said, laughing.

"Is that Mona?" Danny said.

Hayley could picture her ex scowling. He never did like Mona. Mostly, because Mona always despised him and never wanted Hayley to date him, much less marry him.

If Hayley had only listened to Mona in high school!

But then again, he did help her bring two of the most amazing kids into the world—just one mother's opinion.

"Well, you tell her I'm taking Becky to Bermuda for Christmas!" Danny shouted. "That's right! We'll be lounging by the pool while she's trying on that pair of itchy gray wool socks her deadbeat husband buys her every year."

"Wait. What? I thought you just said you were broke."

There was a long, uneasy silence.

"Danny? Are you still there?"

"Yeah, I'm here."

"You're going to Bermuda?"

"Now don't jump down my throat. We got a good deal. And I bought the package before I knew how much the kids' plane tickets were going to cost."

"*That's* why you can't pay me back?"

The only place Danny had ever taken Hayley when they were married was to a campground in Moose Head Lake one weekend. They had to leave that spot early, since it rained the whole time and a Maine black bear ate all of their supplies while they went into town to buy umbrellas and a box of wine.

Hayley didn't want to engage Danny any more than she already had. She took another deep breath and calmly held the phone to her ear. "Okay. I'm sure you'll pay me back, just as soon as you can."

"Absolutely. There's a girl at work who is about to drop a baby after New Year's and she's promised to give me some of her shifts while she's out on maternity leave so I can make some extra cash."

"Fine. Now would you do me a favor? Dustin really wants this new *Metal Gear* video game that just came out and I was hoping you might be able to—"

"No. I told you, Hayley. I'm broke."

"It's under thirty dollars."

"No can do. Sorry."

"What? Did you spend your last twenty bucks on a new thong for Becky?"

She just couldn't resist.

"You really should stop spoiling the kids, Hayley," Danny said.

"Please. Not this again."

"You do this every year. Every December, around this time, your bank account is empty and yet you just can't help yourself. You max out your last working credit card buying all of this junk the kids don't need just so they have a nice Christmas. And we both know why."

"I don't need a lecture from you, Danny."

"You overcompensate because you feel guilty."

"Somebody's been watching *Dr. Phil* again."

"It's true. You divorced me, and now the kids are the victims of a broken home, and you can't live with yourself, so you go all out to make up for it during the holidays, just to alleviate some of the guilt."

"'Alleviate'? I didn't know you played Words With Friends."

"You can make fun of me all you want. We both know I'm right."

"Have fun in Bermuda," Hayley said, pressing the red end button on her smartphone screen.

She turned to Mona.

"Come on, Mona. Let's go. We have some serious shopping to do."

"Don't let him get to you, Hayley."

Hayley fished a Visa card out of her bag. "I think this one may have some credit left on it."

"You're going to regret this, Hayley."

"Gemma needs some new ski boots. Let's start at Dillard's."

"What about my pizza?"

"Get it to go."

Mona knew there was no point in arguing; Hayley was on a mission.

Hayley knew that when she was driving back to Bar Harbor in Mona's truck, the flatbed filled with shopping bags, she would realize Mona was absolutely right. Once again she had allowed her husband to get underneath her skin because she knew on some level he was right, and she just played into his hand by spending far too much money on the kids.

Was it so wrong to want them to have a merry Christmas?

She would just pray that there was no expensive emergency between now and the time Sal doled out her year-end Christmas bonus at the *Island Times,* where she worked.

But unbeknownst to Hayley, there was indeed going to be an emergency. A *really* big one. And it wasn't going to involve a threatening phone call from a creditor.

No. This emergency was going to involve a dead body.

Chapter 2

He kissed her softly on the lips.

Her body shivered as he gently placed a hand on the small of her back, drawing her closer to him.

She was light-headed from the spiked eggnog they had been drinking and she giggled like a schoolgirl as he brushed his lips against her.

She hated that she laughed while he was pressing himself up against her, but romantic moments like this—especially ones as passionate as this one—always made her nervous. And she had a bad habit of laughing, which invariably broke the sexual tension.

But he didn't seem to mind.

He had told her on numerous occasions that he loved her laugh.

She tried desperately to rein in the giggling, but she couldn't help herself.

A chortling sound escaped her lips.

Oh, God. How embarrassing.

With one hand still resting on her lower back, he raised the other behind her head and tenderly pulled her face toward him until their noses touched. Then, more forcefully, he buried his mouth over hers. They embraced tightly, groping, tearing at each other's clothes.

She ripped open his red-and-white-plaid shirt.

Luckily, the buttons didn't pop out.

There was a t-shirt underneath.

This was going to take a little more effort.

He released her long enough for her to get a good grip on the undershirt and yank it up over his head.

She sighed at his rock-hard abs.

For such a busy man, he sure did have a lot of time to work out at the gym.

She ran her fingers over the soft mat of hair that spread across his chest and then followed it down the treasure trail on his torso.

He pushed her down to the floor, crushing a half-wrapped cardboard box.

Nothing breakable was inside. Just a dress shirt for her son. So there was no need to stop at this point.

This was so much better than that *Fifty Shades of Grey* book she had been forced to read in her women's book group last summer.

This was actually happening. And there were no whips or chains involved.

She had never been big on props during love-making. Just the essentials. Like a condom.

The lights from the Christmas tree illuminated his smiling face as he lowered himself on top of her and he slowly, methodically unbuttoned her blouse.

Maybe Mona was right.

Spiked eggnog.

Josh Groban singing "Silent Night" through the iPod speakers.

Their thrashing bodies knocking a few low-hanging bulbs off the tree.

Christmas was so much better when it was adults only!

He had reached the last button on her blouse and was working at unsnapping her bra now.

That's when she heard a cough. From upstairs. One of her kids was awake and moving about. Probably heading to the bathroom.

Hayley quickly thrust a hand out and nudged Aaron away from her as she strained to hear what was going on upstairs.

The mood was definitely broken.

"What's the matter?" Aaron asked, still shirtless and looking incredibly hot.

"I think I heard one of my kids."

"So?"

"Well, I don't want them wandering downstairs for a midnight snack and seeing their mother having sex underneath the Christmas tree."

"Okay. Let's go upstairs to your room and

lock the door and we'll be as quiet as little mice. Although I'm not sure how capable you are of *not* making noise."

"What do you mean?"

"Are you forgetting what happened on top of my office desk last week when you forgot yourself and started moaning and got all of those poor dogs in their cages out back barking like crazy?"

Aaron was the local veterinarian.

Hayley had been dating him for months.

Her kids loved him. In fact, her daughter Gemma worked part-time at his office as a receptionist a few days a week after school to learn the ropes, since she was planning on going to veterinarian school one day.

But the fact that Gemma and her youngest child, Dustin, were both fans of the handsome vet, with the rock-hard abs, still did not make her anywhere near comfortable hosting him at her house overnight. It certainly was not because she was a prude. Far from it. However, her ex-husband Danny's accusations that she was guilt-ridden over the divorce might have held a kernel of truth. She didn't want her kids getting attached to another father figure until she was absolutely sure. Her last relationship, with Lex Bansfield, a caretaker at one of the opulent seaside estates, had dissolved after his boss passed away and he moved out of town to find work. But right around the time she met Aaron, Lex showed up on her doorstep with plans to open his own contracting business in their hometown of Bar Harbor. He had expected just to pick up right where they left off. Hayley had to break the news that she had met someone else. So ever since that tough conversation, the two of them had kept a respectful distance. Mindful of the fact her kids had fallen in love with Lex and were heartbroken when they split up, Hayley wasn't willing to put them through that again. Not until she was 100 percent certain that Aaron was the one.

Gemma was already a goner. Working for Aaron had cemented her opinion of him. She adored him. Dustin, though, was a tougher nut to crack. He was never one to be effusive; but after a night on the couch with Aaron, laughing at a Cartoon Network Adult Swim show he shouldn't have been watching, he shrugged and told his mother, "I guess he's all right." Which, when translated from Dustin-speak, meant, "The man is a god!"

The toilet upstairs flushed and Hayley heard feet padding across the hardwood floor and then a bedroom door closed.

She waited another few seconds and then patted Aaron's chest with the palm of her hand. "Okay, the coast is clear. Kiss me."

Aaron grinned as he reached for his shirt. "Sorry. You've already got me all worked up, and if we keep kissing, then I'm not going to be able to stop myself. I know you're still not cool with me staying over, so before I drink too much spiked eggnog and can't drive myself home, I better hit the road."

"Aaron, I'm sorry—"

"No need to apologize. I totally get it. I know you're just being protective of your kids, and that's one of the reasons I love you. So until you feel they're ready for me to stay overnight, we'll just have to keep driving my doggie patients crazy at my office."

Hayley smiled and then leaned in and kissed him.

He cupped her face with his hands and returned the kiss.

She sighed.

God, he is sexy.

Aaron climbed to his feet and threw on his t-shirt. He draped his plaid shirt over his arm and walked to the front door. Hayley followed him until he stopped and turned around.

"You never told me what you want for Christmas."

"Santa already brought me the only thing on my list."

"Now you're just playing with me," he said, kissing her one more time before heading out the door. "I'll call you tomorrow."

Hayley slowly shut the door behind him.

She wasn't playing with him. She meant it.

This guy could be the one.

If she didn't screw it up.

Hayley decided she would finish wrapping the rest of the presents she and Aaron were supposed to be wrapping before they had gotten side-tracked. Then she'd haul them upstairs to the closet where she stored all of the kids' gifts she had bought.

She picked up a ribbon and had barely gotten it around the first box when she heard someone rummaging around upstairs.

It was coming from the closet at the end of the hall adjacent to Gemma's room, but she knew it wasn't Gemma.

It was Dustin.

Trying to get a sneak peek at his Christmas gifts.

She had warned both her kids that she had memorized the return policy on all of the gifts she had bought for them in the very likely event that one of them, mostly Dustin, didn't have the patience to wait until Christmas morning to examine his booty.

Hayley chucked her shoes and soundlessly ascended the stairs in her stocking feet until she reached the top step and had a clear-eyed view of her son on his hands and knees, foraging through the closet.

Hayley cleared her throat.

Dustin yelped and jumped up, knocking over a few boxes stacked in the corner. He whipped his head around to face his mother. "What are you doing up here? Shouldn't you be downstairs with Dr. Aaron?"

"He just left."

"I thought you two would be so busy sucking face right now that—"

"I wouldn't hear you up here breaking my rule of not going into that closet?"

"Yeah. Sort of. I didn't see anything. I swear."

"That's not the point. You tried to. I caught you red-handed."

"Okay, you can return anything you want. Except the new Batman game. If you were like the best mother in the world and already bought me the new Batman game, *please, please, please* don't take it back to the store."

"Only if you're back in your room and in bed in the next twenty seconds."

Dustin hurled himself out of the closet, slamming the door behind him, and raced down the hall to his room. He jumped into his bed, wrenched the comforter up over himself, and closed his eyes.

Hayley couldn't help but laugh to herself as she went to close his door. But then something dawned on her. "What do you mean 'sucking face' with Dr. Aaron?"

Dustin opened his eyes.

"Oh, come on, Mom. It's not like Gemma and I don't know what goes on between you two after we've gone to bed."

"What do you think goes on?"

Dustin puckered his lips and made kissing sounds. "A little of this. A little of that."

"Okay, maybe some of that, but nothing else. Do you hear me?"

"Are you serious? That's all you do?"

"Yes."

"Seriously? Come on, Mom, you've been dating for months."

"I mean here. In this house. That's all we do."

"So you do the rest somewhere else?"

"I really don't want to have this conversation with you."

"Well, I'm sorry, but you started it."

He was right.

Why on earth did she call him on the kissing comment?

"The dude is a good guy. Gemma and I have no problem with him staying over, if you want him to."

"You two have *discussed* this?"

"Yeah. *Duh.* We're totally cool with it. And you better do it soon, or otherwise he may think you're not serious and move on. Let's face it, Mom, there are a lot of younger, prettier women in town just waiting for the two of you to break up so they can pounce on him."

Hayley glared at her son, who quickly caught on to his faux pas.

"The 'younger, prettier' part didn't come out right. Please don't take it out on me Christmas morning."

I'm taking relationship advice from my teenage son? How awkward is that!

However, Dustin was a smart kid, and maybe he did have a point.

Definitely not about the younger and prettier women in town, though. No, the part about letting Aaron know I'm serious about him.

After all, Aaron had been so patient with her. So loving.

Maybe the nine months of keeping it casual was enough.

She had just gotten the green light from her kids.

Perhaps it was finally time to take it to the next level.

Island Food & Spirits
by
Hayley Powell

Lord, where does the time go? It seems like just yesterday when I took down our Christmas tree. I blinked and now Christmas is looming right around the corner again. Every year after the holidays I swear to myself that I am going to be more organized when Christmas comes around again. But here it is December already and I am totally unprepared.

I was finishing up a little late-night present wrapping the other evening and I thought back to a Christmas Eve many years ago. The kids were very small and just beginning to understand that Santa Claus, a fat man in a red suit, with a white beard, would be swinging by the house in a red sleigh with a team of reindeer to bring them a present or two if they behaved well and went to bed before Mommy's prime-time TV shows came on. Okay, I may have made that part up. But you get the idea. Once the kids were sound asleep, my husband at that time and I were able to relax and enjoy his mother's famous Christmas Eve eggnog cocktails!

We must have made a few strong batches that night because I remember my ex being very sweet and charming. I was actually enjoying his company. That is, until the moment he jumped up and announced that he was going to dig out his old Santa Claus costume that he bought for our first Christmas together and dress up and surprise the kids. You're probably asking yourself, *Why did he buy a Santa outfit before you had kids?* Let's just say that's a whole other story! And no, I don't have a "thing" for older men with white beards! (But I do get a thrill whenever I see a man in uniform, even a Santa suit!)

My gut told me to stop the madness. The kids were already asleep. It was late. But Danny was so excited about his brainstorm. Unfortunately, he never had the best judgment, especially after a few rum-spiked mugs of eggnog. There was no stopping him as he raced out of the room. I just sat in my favorite recliner, turned up the Christmas music, and poured myself another eggnog.

I must have nodded off. The next thing I knew, I was jolted awake by loud sirens and someone shouting my name and banging on the front door. Disoriented, I wandered to the door and threw it open. I found myself staring into the concerned face of the Bar Harbor fire chief as he was shouting about how some "dumb-ass" was climbing up on my roof!

At first, I just stared at him, not comprehending anything, but then I stepped outside and spotted the ladder leaning against the side of the house. Hearing "dumb-ass" should have been my first clue. It was Danny. The fire chief grabbed my arm and dragged me over to the driveway in the freezing night air as the two parked fire engines continued blaring their sirens and flashing their lights.

This, of course, led to half the town showing up in their pajamas to get a front-row seat for the drama. Everyone was staring up at the roof. I hated to look, but didn't have much of a choice. There was Danny in his Santa suit hanging onto the chimney for dear life and crying like a baby while a fire truck ladder was being raised to reach him. Note to self: *Next year, don't put so much rum in Danny's eggnog.*

I just wanted the frozen snowy ground to open up and swallow me whole as a brave fireman climbed the ladder and wrapped a rope around Danny's waist so he wouldn't slip. Then the fireman led him safely to the ladder and down to the ground, which Danny promptly kissed while saying a silent prayer.

Seriously, the idea of Danny Powell praying? The man hadn't stepped foot inside a church as far back as I could remember, not even on our wedding day, since he insisted we should be married by a justice of the peace. Then, to make matters even more humiliating, the gathered townspeople began clapping and cheering for our brave firefighters. A photographer from our local newspaper at the time snapped pictures and Danny smiled and waved like a fool, bowing so low his fake beard fell off.

I slipped back inside my house as fast as I could, hoping no one would notice me. I ran upstairs to check on the children, who were shockingly still sound asleep, having completely missed the circus outside caused by their father.

Danny swaggered through the front door like he was a rock star, looking back, loudly thanking everyone, and wishing them all "Merry Christmas."

Sure enough, Danny's Christmas Eve rescue picture was front-page news the following week. The kids were thrilled their father was so famous and he regaled them with the tale of his Christmas Eve rooftop adventure. I was furious he had embarrassed me in front of the whole town, but he made it up to me. He put on the Santa suit once more and we recreated that first Christmas together as newlyweds. And that's all I'm going to say about that.

This week I'm sharing my ex-mother-in-law's Christmas Eve Eggnog

Cocktail recipe. Now remember, the amount of rum you use is entirely up to you. However, if you have a husband who might like his eggnog a little too much and comes up with a few crazy ideas, feel free to pull back on the rum or leave it out altogether!

Christmas Eve Eggnog Cocktail

<u>Ingredients</u>

4 cups milk
5 whole cloves
½ teaspoon vanilla extract
1 teaspoon cinnamon
12 egg yolks
1½ cups sugar
2½ cups light rum
4 cups light cream
2 teaspoons vanilla extract
½ teaspoon ground nutmeg

Combine your milk, cloves, ½ teaspoon vanilla, and cinnamon in a saucepan, and heat over low for 5 minutes. Slowly bring the milk mixture to a boil. In a large bowl combine your egg yolks and sugar. Whisk until fluffy. Whisk the hot milk slowly into the egg mixture, then pour back into the saucepan and cook over medium heat, stirring constantly for 3 minutes or until thick. Do not allow to boil. Strain and remove the cloves, and let cool for about an hour. Stir in the rum, 2 teaspoons vanilla extract, and refrigerate overnight before serving. When ready, grab some mugs and throw on some Christmas carols and let the holidays begin!

I remember that Christmas money was especially tight that year, but as luck would have it, the grocery store had a sale on Turkey drumsticks! You can be sure this particular recipe will satisfy the turkey lover in your household!

Roasted Turkey Drumsticks

<u>Ingredients</u>

4 turkey legs
¼ cup margarine or butter, softened
1 teaspoon salt
¼ teaspoon pepper
1 teaspoon poultry seasoning
1 teaspoon dried thyme
½ cup turkey or chicken broth

Preheat your oven to 350 degrees. Rinse and pat dry your turkey legs and place in a roasting pan. In a bowl combine all of the ingredients, except the turkey/chicken broth, and rub all over the legs, coating nicely. Pour the broth in the roasting pan and cook in the preheated oven for 1 hour 30 minutes to 1 hour 45 minutes, or when a meat thermometer reaches 175 degrees. Remove from oven, cover, and let rest for 10 minutes. Then let the feasting begin!

Chapter 3

Sal charged out of the back bull pen at the *Island Times* newspaper into the front office, where Hayley was at her desk and on the phone with an advertiser.

"Hayley, what day is this?"

"Monday, Sal," Hayley said before returning to her call. "So you'd like to buy a full half-page in ad space?"

"When's the office Christmas party?"

"Hold on just one moment, please," Hayley said, cupping the phone receiver with her hand. "Tuesday."

"Tuesday, as in next week?"

"No, Tuesday as in tomorrow night."

"Damn!"

"Sal, please! I'm on with the Congregational Church. They want to buy an ad for their upcoming Nativity pageant."

"Sorry for my language, Reverend Staples!" Sal bellowed into the phone.

"It's not Reverend Staples. It's his secretary."

"Oh, well, then who the hell cares? It's not like *she* has the authority to get me in trouble with God."

"Can I call you back in about five minutes, Denise?" Hayley asked. "Thanks."

Sal waited for her to hang up the phone before he offered Hayley his biggest, widest smile. "I've got some good news for you, Hayley."

Hayley looked at him skeptically. "I'm listening."

"I'm giving you a promotion."

Hayley could hardly believe her ears. "A promotion? Really?"

"That's right," Sal said, crossing to the coffeepot and pouring himself a cup. "I am making you *senior* office manager."

"*Senior office manager?* But, Sal, I'm the *only* office manager. Wait. Does this mean you're going to hire someone to help me? Like a junior office manager? Oh, Sal, that would be fantastic!"

"No, there's a hiring freeze. There's no junior anything. I just want to recognize the bang-up job you've done around here and give you a fancier title and some more responsibilities."

"And more *money*," Hayley added emphatically.

"Yeah, we can talk about all of that after New Year's. But in the meantime, I just want to bring you up to speed on the senior office manager's duties. Answering phones, handling the classified ads, press releases, obituaries, stuff like that."

"I already do all of that, Sal."

"Oh, and, of course, the senior office manager is in charge of the annual Christmas party."

"Hold on, Sal—"

"Congratulations, Hayley!"

"Now, wait just a minute—"

"I don't expect anything too elaborate, given the fact the party's tomorrow night."

"Your wife always plans the Christmas party. What's changed?"

"Nothing. I just feel that it should be up to you as senior office manager to decide what we do for the party. I'm giving you free rein. Anything you want to do."

"Sal . . ."

"Okay, we've been fighting a lot lately. She let her lazy college dropout nephew move in with us for a few days to, in his words, 'get his head together.' Well, that was six weeks ago and it's put a real strain on our marriage. We've barely been speaking to each other. Last week, when I asked her how the party preparations were going, she told me to go straight to hell. So I figured I would handle it, because—let's face it—how hard can it be? But then it just kind of slipped my mind and I was just checking my calendar and realized—"

"Senior office manager? Really, Sal? Is that what you chose to go with in order to lay this whole party off on me?"

"I really do value you and what you do around here, Hayley. If I could make you a senior vice president of whatever, I would. I would do anything to keep you happy, but newspapers aren't what they used to be, and our online traffic has been down ever since the *Herald* became Bar Harbor's answer to *TMZ*, focusing on sleazy town gossip, and basically doubled their readership in four months. . . ."

"You're really going to stick me with planning the Christmas party at the very last minute, Sal?"

Sal took a deep breath and then let out a whoosh of air. "No, you're right. It's not fair to place the burden on you. This was my screwup. I'll handle it. I'll just cancel the party this year. I'm sure everyone will understand."

Sal lowered his head and slinked away.

Before he left the front office, Hayley stopped him. "Sal, wait. Okay, you win. I will take over the party. I've heard great things about Garth Rawlings. He catered a dinner party I attended a few months ago and his food was delicious. Maybe he can whip up a few hors d'oeuvres for us at the last minute."

"Whatever you think is best, Hayley. I trust you. Just make sure everybody has a good time, since the Christmas bonuses are going to be so low this year," Sal said before escaping to his office.

That's just what Hayley did not want to hear—a paltry Christmas bonus.

She was counting on a decent amount in order

to pay off her credit card bills and maybe have a few dollars left over to get her hair done in case she was invited to a swanky New Year's Eve party.

A girl can dream, can't she?

She glanced at the clock: almost noon. She had thirty hours to pull together a memorable Christmas party. If anyone could deliver mouthwatering holiday treats, it was Garth Rawlings. Why he didn't have his own show on the Food Network was a mystery.

Hayley reached for the phone just as it rang. She picked up the receiver. "*Island Times,* this is Hayley."

"Hayley, this is Tilly over at the hospital. I'm afraid I have some bad news."

"Oh, God, what? Is it one of my kids?"

"No, oh, gosh, I'm sorry, I didn't mean to scare you. It's okay. Nobody died. There's just been an accident."

Hayley gasped. "One of my kids? Which one? What happened?"

"No, your kids are fine. Boy, I really should have thought this through before I called you. My gut told me to stay out of it and now I know my gut was right because I've upset you, and—"

"Tilly, please tell me who's been hurt!"

"Lex Bansfield."

"What?"

"They just brought him in. Apparently, he was hanging garland from a streetlamp at the corner of Cottage and Main. He slipped and fell off his ladder. They think he may have a broken collarbone, and his right leg was twisted and all banged up. Well, I know you two have been on the outs—"

"We're not on the outs, Tilly. We just don't see each other anymore."

"Yes, well, he's all alone here, and I don't know why I thought to call you and let you know because my gut told me not to. . . ."

"I know all about your gut, Tilly. I'm glad you called me. I'm on my way."

Hayley slammed down the phone, jumped up from her desk, grabbed her winter jacket off the coatrack, and flew out the door with one thought in her mind.

Lex was injured and she had to be by his bedside.

Chapter 4

By the time Hayley got home from the hospital, it was already approaching the dinner hour; she had yet to even think about what she would serve her kids. Leroy, her adorable white Shih Tzu, with a pronounced underbite and boundless energy, greeted her at the door, with his tail wagging. Blueberry, her recently adopted cat, an oversize Persian fur ball, with an infinite amount of attitude, was sitting menacingly in the hallway just off the kitchen. With his tail flapping up and down, he glared at Hayley, perturbed his own dinner had yet to be served.

As she yanked open the refrigerator to take a quick inventory, Gemma came bounding down the stairs, squealing with delight. Blueberry skittered out of the way just in time to avoid Gemma's sneaker nearly crushing his tail. Gemma raced into the kitchen, her arms waving in the air.

"Mom! Mom! You're never going to believe what just happened!"

"What?"

Gemma stopped suddenly, a disappointed look on her face.

"You mean that wasn't a rhetorical question? You actually want me to guess?"

Gemma nodded.

"Um, okay. You got an A on your geometry test."

"No. Come on, Mom. Be serious. Guess something that's, like, actually in the realm of possibility. By the way, I flunked it and you have to sign the test to acknowledge I showed you the score, and I have to take it again next week before the Christmas break. Now guess again."

"You flunked? Gemma, if you ever want to get into vet school, you're going to have to do better. . . ."

"Stay on topic, please, okay, Mom?"

"Fine. But we're not finished discussing that test. Okay. Let me think. That cute boy in gym class that you've been texting all of your friends about finally asked you out on a date."

"No. And thanks for reminding me about his total lack of interest in me. Good job, Mom. Now I'm completely depressed. Way to go."

"Okay, you know what? I'm not going to guess anymore. Why don't you just tell me?"

"Reverend Staples called a few minutes ago and he's decided to cast *me* in the Congregational Church's Nativity play. I tried out for one of the

Three Wise Men, but he didn't think I was right for that part."

"He probably saw your geometry test."

"Mom!"

"Just kidding. So, who are you going to play?"

"The Virgin Mary!"

Wow. I did not see that one coming.

"Gemma, that's fantastic. I'm so proud of you!" Hayley hugged her daughter tightly.

"Mary's, like, one of the leading roles!" Gemma shrieked. "The show is totally centered around her. She's the most important character in the whole play."

"Well, yes, honey, but God and the baby Jesus are pretty critical too in the scheme of things."

"What are you talking about? They have no lines! I have pages and pages of dialogue I have to start memorizing. I just hope they get someone really hot to play Joseph."

Gemma sailed back out of the kitchen and up the stairs, nearly plowing over Blueberry again. He had ventured gingerly back into the hallway, still annoyed that his ceramic bowl, with kitty paw prints on it, was still not filled with food.

Hayley went to the cupboard and foraged for some special-diet canned cat food when the back door to the kitchen swung open and Aaron walked in, rubbing his hands to warm up from the cold.

Hayley smiled at the sight of him. "What are you doing here? I thought you had to work late."

"I was supposed to neuter Alma Henderson's

Maine coon cat at five-thirty, but he somehow got out the back screen door and ran away before she could get him into the pet carrier. Probably knew what was coming and got the hell out of Dodge."

Hayley laughed. "Do you want to stay for dinner?"

"I was thinking of taking you and the kids out for pizza at Geddy's."

"Well, Dustin's having dinner over at Spanky's house, and Gemma is confined to her room cramming for a makeup geometry test, but she doesn't know it yet. I've got some leftover meat loaf and makings for a side salad she can have."

"Perfect. You prepare that for her and I'll call and make a reservation at Portofino for two. Candlelight dinner. Bottle of wine. I'll even let you spoon-feed me the tiramisu."

"Now that's quite an upgrade from pizza."

"Sound good?"

"Sounds wonderful. Oh, wait. I have a meeting later tonight, around nine, with Garth Rawlings, the caterer. I'm going to hire him to prepare a few appetizers for our office Christmas party tomorrow night and wanted to go over everything with him at his office."

"Okay, so we skip the tiramisu. But the bottle of wine is nonnegotiable."

"Deal."

He kissed Hayley on the lips. "You smell so good."

"That's probably just the wild cherry Little

Trees air freshener I hung from my rearview mirror this morning."

"Don't kill the mood," Aaron said, tickling her with his hands.

Hayley chortled and tried to pull his hands away, but he was having too much fun. He tickled her some more until her whole body was spasming. Then he locked his arms around her waist and pulled her into him, kissing her again, just as the phone rang. After it rang several times, it became abundantly clear Gemma had no intention of answering it from upstairs.

"Be just a minute," Hayley said, reluctantly extricating herself from Aaron's grip and picking up the phone. "Hello?"

"Hayley?"

She instantly recognized the voice.

Lex Bansfield.

"Lex, how are you doing?"

Aaron bristled just a bit at hearing Lex's name. He was acutely aware of Hayley's past history with him.

"My pride's hurt more than anything else. I just wanted to thank you for stopping by to see me this afternoon. It meant a lot," Lex said.

"Of course. When I heard you were hurt, I knew I had to see you to make sure you're okay. Is there something you need?"

There was silence on the other end of the phone.

"Lex?"

"I'm kind of embarrassed to ask. I know how busy you are."

"You know you can ask me anything, Lex."

"I had a bit of a tantrum earlier here at the hospital. Not proud of it. It was about the food they tried to serve me for dinner. Some rancid piece of overcooked meat and a tiny cup of something they called 'vegetable medley' made up of cold peas and stale carrots. Oh, and green Jell-O. Can you believe it, Hayley? Green Jell-O? Seriously, I haven't eaten crap like that since the third grade. I sent it all back to the kitchen and now I'm starving. Guess I didn't think things through."

"Do you want me to pick something up for you at the Shop 'n Save and bring it over to you?"

"Actually, I remember you keep cartons of your homemade turkey chili in the freezer out in your garage, and I was hoping, if you weren't too busy . . ."

"You know I completely forgot about that."

"I still dream about that chili."

"Well, I can defrost some in the microwave and bring it over to you in about a half hour."

Hayley glanced at Aaron, who was quickly summing up the situation in his mind and was frowning.

Hayley averted her eyes. "Hang on. I'll be there soon."

"Hayley, I know I'm not your responsibility, and I probably shouldn't even be calling you, since we're no longer—"

"We're friends, Lex, and I don't want to hear another word."

Hayley hung up.

"You're going to make him dinner?"

"No! Just warm up some of my chili. It's already made. I feel bad for him, Aaron. He's laid up in the hospital, and you know how awful the food is there. It's not like he has any dietary restrictions, so I thought it would be a nice thing to do."

"Well, I'll go with you to the hospital, and after you drop off the chili, we can go to dinner."

"Then we'll be rushed because I have to meet Garth at nine."

"Another time, then," Aaron said, turning to leave.

"Aaron . . ."

Aaron turned back around. "No, it's fine, Hayley. Really. I get it. He's your friend. I have no problem with you doing him a favor. No problem at all."

Nice words. But his face, however, told an entirely different story.

Chapter 5

"Now, given the time constraint, Hayley, don't expect too much from me. I was thinking, though, I could throw together a few apps tomorrow, like my very popular smoked trout and garlic cream on rye toasts and amaretto-bourbon punch," Garth said as he stood at a large wooden table in front of a giant stainless-steel oven in the warehouse at the far end of town that he recently converted into a kitchen/office.

"Garth, that sounds absolutely delicious," Hayley said, practically drooling.

"And maybe a baked Brie with pecans, with my homemade crackers, of course, and some ginger nuts, my artichoke turnovers, and rosemary vodka tonics. Oh, and I could roast some chestnuts because, after all, it is the holidays."

"My mouth is watering, Garth," Hayley said, petting the head of Garth's beloved bloodhound, Bagel, who stood at her side. The dog was also drooling, with most of it landing on Hayley's L.L.Bean boot.

"He likes you," Garth said, grinning.

"He's a real sweetheart," Hayley said, still rubbing the top of Bagel's head. The dog's jowls were flapping, and his mouth was slobbering. "I sure do appreciate your helping me on such short notice, Garth."

"Don't worry, Hayley. I will take your little office Christmas soiree and turn it into a magnificent night to remember. Did you know I catered the Rockefellers' Fourth of July party last summer on their estate?"

"No, I didn't know that."

"And Martha Stewart was there and she said my crab cakes were the best she'd ever had the pleasure of eating. I'm not lying, Hayley. *Martha Stewart!*"

"Well, it looks like I came to the right place."

"Normally, a little nothing event like yours would be way too small potatoes for me. Did I mention I flew to New York last Labor Day weekend to deliver personally my homemade out-of-this-world Jamaican jerk sauce to Anderson Cooper for his backyard barbecue? I'm not lying, Hayley. *Anderson Cooper!*"

"Wow, that's amazing," Hayley said, having no idea what else to say.

There was a mouthwatering aroma in the air wafting from the giant oven behind Garth.

"What is that yummy smell, Garth?"

Garth winked at her, thrilled she had noticed. "Just a little treat I'm preparing to take home to my wife tonight for a little late-night snack. It's my world-famous Grand Marnier soufflé with crème anglaise. Play your cards right and I'll give you a taste once it rises."

Hayley had to admit she was dying to try a bite—mostly because she was ravenous from having to skip out on dinner with Aaron.

Suddenly there was a loud banging.

"What is that?" Hayley asked.

Garth rolled his eyes, annoyed and frustrated. "It's coming from next door. I swear those guys are going to drive me into an early grave."

"What are they doing?"

"Nailing plywood together or something equally stupid and useless. The owner of this building put up a wall so he could divide this warehouse space into two sections. That way he could charge two rents for one space, essentially doubling his money. I needed a lot of space for my ovens and freezer, and this space was perfect, but I had no say in who would rent the other half."

"Who's in there?"

"Some contracting business. All day long, drilling and sawing and hammering and sandblasting. I've complained a hundred times and the owner doesn't do a damn thing about it."

Garth turned to his see his giant stainless-steel industrial oven shake. His eyes nearly popped out of his head as he rushed over and opened the door to check on his Grand Marnier soufflé.

"Oh, dear God, no! They've really done it this time! They've caused my soufflé to collapse! Those savages!"

Garth pulled the soufflé dish out of the oven and slammed it down on the wooden table; then he flew across the warehouse and out the door. Hayley heard him pounding on the door to the contracting business. After a few seconds the door opened, followed by angry shouting and a slew of four-letter words. Most of these were coming out of Garth's mouth.

Bagel seemed completely undisturbed by the yelling. His eyes were fixed on the soufflé sitting on the edge of the table. He was undoubtedly trying to figure out a way to get the soufflé off the table and onto the floor so he could lap it up.

Hayley walked over and poked her head out the door to see Garth wagging a finger at three men. They were all in plaid work shirts, torn jeans with paint stains, and tan work boots. She instantly recognized Billy Parsons, a local handyman in his early thirties. Billy was a real charmer, with a scruffy beard and easy smile, who had rescued Hayley with his home repairs on many occasions. Just behind Billy was a teenage kid around Gemma's age, whom Hayley didn't know. He was cute and wiry, with tousled brown hair that fell just below his eyes. He hung back a bit, more than a little intimidated by Garth's loud bellowing. The tallest of the three was Nick Ward, midforties, gruff, beefy, dark eyes, and a permanent sneer on his face. He worked on Lex's crew when Lex was a caretaker at the Hollingsworth summer estate before the family patriarch, billionaire frozen-food magnate Arthur Hollingsworth, died, which prompted Lex to move away from Bar Harbor for a short time looking for work. Nick was clearly the leader of this pack and was not afraid of going toe-to-toe with Garth. He was also gripping an electric drill and held it aimed at Garth's stomach like a pistol.

"You can call the cops all you want, Rawlings, but we have a permit to conduct our business here—and that means using our equipment, so get used to it!" Nick hollered.

"But it's after nine in the evening!" Garth wailed.

"Exactly. We thought you'd be long gone by now. We were trying to be courteous," Nick growled.

"Maybe we can work out a schedule with Mr. Rawlings so we're not using the power tools when he's cooking in his kitchen," Billy offered, trying to be helpful.

"That's not our problem! We're behind enough, as it is, and the boss is going to be laid up in the hospital with some broken bones for a few more days, so I'm in charge. As the acting foreman I'm telling you right now, keep your mouth shut, Billy!"

Hayley gasped.

Of course.

Nick Ward had lost his job at the Hollingsworth estate right around the same time Lex had and had been unemployed for months. It made perfect sense that he would go to work for Lex again after he blew back into town. Hayley had heard Lex was starting a contracting business, but she had no idea they had set up shop here.

Garth was practically blowing smoke out of his ears—he was so angry.

Hayley felt uncomfortable just standing there by the door.

Garth and Nick were nearly bumping chests, like a pair of hairy Neanderthals grunting and pushing and trying to mark their territory.

The testosterone levels were off the charts.

"I'm going to go now, Garth, and let you guys talk this out," Hayley said. "Everything you mentioned for the party tomorrow sounds scrumptious!"

Garth didn't hear her. He was yelling at Nick, threatening an expensive lawsuit and severe bodily harm. Nick just kept sneering, almost enjoying the arrogant chef's meltdown.

Hayley rushed past the angry scene and slammed into someone, knocking them both back.

"Oh, I'm sorry. Are you all right?"

"Yes," the woman said. She was young, early twenties, with bright red hair and the cutest dimples Hayley had ever seen. She was bundled up in a lime-green parka and had her arms folded to keep herself warm.

It was Connie Sparks, the daughter of Phil and Liz Sparks, restaurant owners who flew south for the winter. Connie worked as a waitress for her parents during the busy summer season and then spent the winters painting pictures of wildlife on canvas at the family cottage.

"Connie?"

"Oh . . . hi, Hayley," she said, shifting uncomfortably.

"What are you doing here?"

She hesitated, which Hayley found odd.

"I . . . I . . . uh . . . I'm here to see Garth. That's right. I'm planning a little holiday party for a few friends and I want to hire him to bake a Christmas ham or something."

"Well, you can't go wrong with Garth, that's for sure," Hayley said, noticing how Connie refused to make eye contact with her.

By now, the argument next door had dissipated and the prizefighters had apparently returned to their corners. Garth passed by, stopping suddenly at the sight of Hayley with Connie conversing outside by the front door.

"You two know each other?" Garth said, eyeing both of them.

Connie nodded and then added hastily, "Yes. And I told her I'm here to hire you to cater my holiday party I'm planning to throw at the cottage. Isn't that right, Garth?"

"Yes. Well, don't just stand there. You'll catch a cold. Come on in. Hayley, I'll call you tomorrow and we can discuss my fee and what time you want the food delivered."

Hayley nodded.

Garth and Connie exchanged a cursory glance before he hurriedly ushered her inside the building. He briefly turned back to look at Hayley and she swore she saw a flicker of fear on his face.

Fear was certainly not a word she would ever associate with the "Great Chef of Bar Harbor," Garth Rawlings.

Something strange was going on between those two, but she couldn't quite put her finger on what.

Chapter 6

Hayley set her alarm clock to go off an hour earlier than usual because she had made the decision the night before to prepare Lex a hot breakfast and drop it off at the hospital before work. She knew it was probably a bad idea, given that she and Lex were no longer together. Truthfully, the last thing she wanted was to send her dashing ex-boyfriend mixed signals. But after delivering a heaping bowl of her turkey chili to his bedside the night before, she felt bad for him. Lex was confined to a lumpy hospital bed, unable to move, stuck watching *Steve Harvey* and *Judge Judy* on TV all day. The least she could do was cheer him up with some of her home-cooked food. After all, breakfast was the most important meal of the day, and she was just being a concerned *platonic* friend. If Liddy or Mona were laid up, she would do the same for them.

So there was nothing to feel guilty about.

Besides, Aaron would never have to know.

She foraged through the refrigerator to see what she had for ingredients, convinced scrambling some eggs and frying a few strips of bacon would be good enough. However, she quickly found herself going all out, toasting pecans to add to a pancake batter and slicing fruit for a caramel-apple topping. Well, to be fair, it was the holiday season, so eggs and bacon just seemed so bland.

She squeezed some fresh juice, brewed coffee, adding some cinnamon, and sealed the pancakes in a Tupperware container; then she bundled up in her winter coat and carried everything to the car.

When she arrived at room 502 at the Bar Harbor Hospital, she could hear Lex inside complaining. The remote he was trying to use to raise his bed up so he could watch television wasn't working properly. Nurse Tilly was stabbing the buttons on the remote with her index finger, but nothing was happening.

"I'm going to get a crick in my neck if I have to watch the damn TV like this," Lex bellowed.

"Maybe it just needs a new battery. Let me go check and see if we have any. If not, I can run to the store after my shift is over."

"What time do you get off?"

"After lunch, around two."

"I'll need a heating pad by then to dull the pain!"

Hayley sailed into the room with a big smile on her face. "Lex Bansfield, if you don't stop abusing the overworked nursing staff, there's going to be a mutiny, and somebody's going to break your other leg."

Lex's face lit up. "Hayley, what are you doing here?"

She set the Tupperware container down on the tray table next to the bed and took the juice and coffee out of a paper bag. "Rescuing Tilly. I have some extra batteries in my glove box in the car. I'll go get them. And the reason he's being so impatient is because the *TODAY* show is on and he's got a big crush on Savannah Guthrie."

Tilly giggled.

"Tilly, if you don't mind, would you call the cafeteria and tell them they don't need to bring breakfast to room 502? Mr. Bansfield is already taken care of."

"Yes, I'll do it right now," Tilly said, grateful for finally having an excuse to escape Lex's grousing. She flew out the door.

Hayley lifted the top of the Tupperware container to reveal the pecan pancakes with their caramel-apple topping.

Lex inhaled through his nose to take in the intoxicating smell. "Last night your kick-ass turkey chili and this morning pancakes. What have I done to deserve such a feast?"

"Well, don't get used to it. It's only because I feel sorry for you."

"I have no problem being pitied if it means I get to eat your cooking."

Hayley snapped the top back into place, sealing the food inside the container. "But before you take one bite, you have to promise me you will stop being the patient from hell. I know this is hard for you—and you hate being inactive and unable to work—but these nurses work their tails off and do the best job they can, so give them a break, okay?"

Lex nodded, properly chastised. "Okay. I promise."

She reopened the container and handed Lex a plastic fork and knife. He dug in immediately, cutting a big piece of pancake and making sure to get a slathering of the caramel-apple topping before shoving it into his mouth.

Lex closed his eyes, with a euphoric look on his face. "Oh, man, this is better than sex."

Hayley smiled.

Lex opened his eyes again and winked at Hayley. "Almost better than sex."

He reached over and took Hayley's hand.

She felt slightly uncomfortable.

And yet, it felt good.

Warm memories of their time together flooded back.

Lex squeezed her hand more tightly.

He didn't want to let go.

"I'm already late for work. Sal's going to bust a gut if I'm not there soon. I better go," Hayley said.

Lex still held her hand. "Thank you, Hayley. You're a good friend."

He gently drew her closer to him with his hand, turning his cheek slightly to the right so she could kiss him.

She took the bait.

Hayley decided a friendly kiss on the cheek—between two good friends—was relatively harmless.

But then Lex blindsided her.

He quickly turned his face back so her lips landed on top of his.

He let go of her hand and cupped her neck, pulling her closer.

His lips devoured hers.

Her whole body tingled.

Lex had always been an expert kisser.

He was practically dragging her whole body into the hospital bed with him before she realized this had to stop.

Now.

But it was too late.

She heard the singing.

Coming from the doorway to room 502.

"'Hark! the herald angels sing, Glory to the newborn King. . . .'"

Hayley wrenched herself free from Lex's grip and spun around to see four Christmas carolers, all wide-eyed, watching what appeared to be Hayley mauling a hapless patient.

"'Peace on earth . . .'"

The singing trailed off.

There was an uncomfortable silence.

One of the carolers, a pudgy white-haired woman dressed like Mrs. Claus, complete with a red velvet dress and granny glasses, cleared her throat to break the silence. "Maybe we should come back."

The carolers shuffled off to the next room.

Mrs. Claus was actually Missy Anne Higgins, a retired widow who lived off her late husband's air force pension.

And Missy Anne was quite possibly the biggest gossip in town.

The news of what went on between Hayley and Lex in room 502 was about to spread faster than the zombie plague in that *Walking Dead* TV show Dustin was so obsessed with watching.

Island Food & Spirits
by
Hayley Powell

Last weekend, while I was whipping up a batch of my mouthwatering pecan pancakes with caramel-apple topping for my daughter and a couple of her BFFs, who were spending the night for her birthday, it totally brought me back to that fateful evening seventeen years earlier when my lovely Gemma first arrived in this world. Of course it couldn't have been a quiet, normal birth. No, she had to show up in true dramatic Powell-family style!

My ex-husband had decided that he would drive up to Ellsworth to do a little Christmas shopping after work one evening, which thrilled me to no end, seeing as he was thinking ahead instead of waiting until the last minute as usual. He had only been gone a couple of hours when I noticed how hard the snow was coming down outside. But living in Maine, he was used to driving in plenty of snow. Plus his truck had four-wheel drive.

My stomach had been a bit upset since dinnertime, which was to be expected, since I had devoured four good-size pecan pancakes with extra caramel-apple topping. I was eight months pregnant and expecting right after the New Year holiday, so I was having serious sweet and savory food cravings for the last three months. Normally, I wouldn't be eating so much. Yeah, let's go with that. I sat down to catch my breath and watch the weather on the news when I suddenly realized we were right in the middle of a severe blizzard warning. Six inches of icy snow and sleet had already fallen outside, and we were expected to get at least six to eight inches more. The wind outside howled and the snow was coming down hard and fast. Just like the pain that was building in my stomach. Probably just the baby kicking or moving around. I didn't want to panic, so I called my friend Mona, who was expertly trained in calming me down. After describing my increasing discomfort, she suggested I might be in labor. I laughed and told her she was crazy because I wasn't due for another three more weeks. Mona wanted Danny to take me straight to the hospital to be safe, but I told her he wasn't there. Suddenly there was a loud crash outside. I jumped and screamed. The phone went dead. I went to the window and saw that a giant tree had fallen on the power line right outside and everyone's electricity had gone out in the neighborhood.

I didn't bother to light any candles and decided just to lie on the couch and try to get comfortable with my aching belly and wait for the electricity to come back on and my husband to arrive home. The pain, however, kept getting worse. Maybe I *was* in labor. *No. Don't even think about that,* I told myself. How would I ever get to the hospital with no car and a raging storm outside? By dogsled?

I lay there for maybe twenty minutes, when suddenly my front door burst open and a bright light blinded me. A giant shadow covered in ice and snow came bursting through the front door. I screamed again. It appeared I was being attacked by the Abominable Snowman! As the monster stepped into the light, grabbing at my arm and yelling at me to stay calm, I realized it was Mona, her wet hair standing straight up in the air like frozen icicles.

She hauled me up off the couch and threw my boots on my feet. Wrapping my winter coat around me, she then half carried, half dragged me. She pulled me right out the front door, the whole time shouting at the top of her lungs about how she had already called Liddy, who was contacting the Bar Harbor Hospital to put them on high alert, and how Liddy was about to call the Bar Harbor Police Department and have them intercept Danny on his way home so he could drive immediately to the hospital.

I glanced around for Mona's truck, but it wasn't there. Apparently, she couldn't back her truck out of the driveway because of all the snow. Instead, she had jumped on her trusty snowmobile with her ice-fishing sled attached to the back and immediately snowmobiled over to my house. She ignored my protesting as she lowered me into the sled, threw a blanket over me, and screeched for me to hold on. Then she jumped on the snowmobile and we roared off like a bat out of hell, slipping and sliding all the way to the hospital while I held on for dear life to the sides, praying that I wouldn't fall out of the sled and deliver the baby in a snowbank on the side of the road!

As Mona sped into the hospital driveway, I lifted my head to see the sliding glass doors to the emergency room ahead of us. I prayed we wouldn't smash right through them. I saw Liddy jumping up and down inside by the admitting desk while waving her arms, frantically warning Mona to slow down. She mercifully let up off the throttle and began applying the brakes and skidded to a stop.

Behind us I heard police sirens blasting full force as a squad car squealed into the driveway, followed by Danny's truck. He had gotten a police escort all the way to town after crossing the Trenton Bridge.

The next thing I knew, Mona was running out the doors, pushing an empty wheelchair, and screaming at the top of her lungs, "Make way for mother and child!" as she pushed past poor Nurse Tilly and knocked her flat on her butt. I was still lying on my back in the sled, thinking to myself what could possibly happen next, when a flash went off in my eyes. It was a local reporter with the *Island Times* hanging around the emergency room on a stormy night, hoping for a story. I guess it was meant to be that I would wind up working for the paper since we always seemed to be in it.

After hoisting me to my feet and setting me down in the wheelchair, I was rushed inside, thinking, *Please don't let this be a false alarm after a fiasco like this!*

Well, it wasn't. Gemma Mona Liddy Powell was born at 9:53 P.M., three weeks early, with her beaming dad and proud godmothers by her side— and these women, to this day, still fight over who will raise her when I'm dead, which I hope isn't any time soon! A week later, as you can probably guess, the Powell family graced the front page of the local newspaper with the headline LOCAL COUPLE GET EARLY CHRISTMAS PRESENT!

Before we get to those pecan pancakes, I find it's always helpful for the chef to clear her mind with a cocktail first. A neighbor of mine gave me this drink recipe when I was pregnant with my daughter. It was very frustrating having to wait until I gave birth before I could try it; but when I did, it became an instant favorite. And since the odds of me getting pregnant now are about as high as me winning the Maine Mega Millions, there's no harm in warming up tonight with a lemon whiskey sour on a cold winter evening.

Lemon Whiskey Sour

Ingredients

1½ ounces whiskey
1 ounce freshly squeezed lemon juice
½ ounce simple syrup
Maraschino cherry for garnish
   (optional)

Place all your ingredients in a cocktail shaker filled with ice. Shake and pour into a cocktail glass and garnish with a cherry.

Pecan Pancakes with Caramel-Apple Topping

<u>Ingredients</u>

1 cup all-purpose flour
1/3 cup finely chopped pecans, toasted
1 teaspoon granulate sugar
1 teaspoon brown sugar
1/2 teaspoon baking powder
1/2 teaspoon cinnamon
1/4 teaspoon baking soda
Pinch of salt
1 cup nonfat buttermilk
2 tablespoons vegetable oil
1 large egg

Stir together the first 8 ingredients. Whisk together your buttermilk, oil, and egg in a bowl. Add to the flour mixture; stir until just moistened.

Pour about 1/4 of a cup batter for each pancake onto a hot, lightly greased griddle. Cook 2 to 3 minutes or until the tops have bubbles and the edges are crispy. Turn and cook other side. Top with the caramel-apple topping.

<u>Caramel-Apple Topping Ingredients</u>
2 (12 oz) packages frozen spiced
    apples, thawed
½ cup packed brown sugar
2 tablespoons butter
1 teaspoon vanilla
¼ teaspoon salt

In a saucepan, bring all of your ingredients to a boil over medium heat, stirring occasionally. Reduce heat to low and simmer, stirring occasionally, 2 to 3 minutes or until thoroughly heated.

Chapter 7

"Sal, you can't be serious!" Hayley said, staring at the hundred-dollar bill he had just slapped down on her desk.

"It's been a rough year, Hayley," Sal said, shrugging. "I have to cut corners where I can, and one way to do that is to scale back on the Christmas party. I'm sure people will be just fine with some spiked fruit punch and a few cans of Planters Mixed Nuts. It's really about being together to celebrate the holidays, right?"

"But you put me in charge. I already hired a caterer. I was expecting five times this amount."

"Then I'm afraid you're way over budget. Just call this chef guy and tell him this is the amount he has to work with," Sal said, not quite understanding the severity of the situation.

"But I'm sure he's already at the market buying ingredients!"

"Then why are you still sitting here, talking to me? You should be trying to get him on the phone."

Sal ambled back to his office as Hayley grabbed the receiver and looked up Garth Rawlings in her list of contacts on her desktop computer.

She punched in the number on the office phone. It rang a few times before Garth answered, distracted and irritated. "What?"

"Garth, it's Hayley Powell."

"Hayley, I can't talk right now. I'm going up and down the spice aisle looking for cayenne pepper, which I need for my sweet and spicy sesame walnuts, and I think they're out. Why would I expect this store to even carry the basic spices? Do you know how hard it is for a master chef to live in a rural, backwoods hick town?"

"I wouldn't exactly describe Bar Harbor as 'backwoods'—"

"They don't even have cayenne pepper, Hayley!"

"Point taken."

"Now I'm going to have to improvise and figure out a decent substitution. Can I call you back?"

"Garth, wait. I really need to talk to you. It turns out I don't have as much money to spend on the party as I originally thought."

There was dead silence on the other end of the phone.

"So you may have to dial it back a bit," Hayley said.

"How much are we talking about?" Garth finally said, his tone colder than an Alaskan ice cap.

"A hundred bucks," Hayley said, swallowing hard.

There was a click.

"Garth? Hello? Garth?"

She called him back.

It rang four times.

She got his voice mail.

She waited a minute and called him again.

This time he picked up.

"What?"

"I know it's not a lot of money, but how about we spend fifty of it on a nice fruit punch and the rest on one or two of your signature Christmas appetizers?"

"And what about my fee? I don't cook for kicks! What do I look like? A fat man with a white beard in a red suit? We're done here, Hayley!"

"Garth, please. We can work something out."

"Forget it! I am so tired of you cash-poor local yokels taking advantage of my talents!" he yelled at the top of his lungs.

There was a loud crash and sudden commotion on the other end of the phone.

"Garth? Is everything all right?"

"No, everything's not all right! You've wasted my morning and now there's someone here threatening to call the police."

"Police? Why?"

"It's your fault! You're the one who made me so mad I hurled my grocery cart down the aisle and hit the box boy stocking some Malabar Black Peppercorn Grinders on the shelf!"

"Omigod! Is he okay?"

"He got knocked down, but he's still conscious,"

Garth said before screaming, "Stop being a baby! It's not like you're bleeding or anything!"

"Garth, you need to make sure he's okay."

"Good-bye, Hayley! I never want you to call me again!"

There was another click.

Hayley sighed. She knew it was now her responsibility to prepare everything for the last-minute office Christmas party.

She mentally ticked off the ingredients in her cupboard and spice rack. She knew she had a block of Brie and some onions in her fridge. If she picked up a package of puff pastry shells, she could whip up some onion-and-Brie palmiers. She was also fairly certain she already had what she needed to bake her crispy ham and cheese balls. And if she could thaw some frozen crabmeat in time, maybe she could prepare some jumbo lump crabmeat and Boursin dip.

She checked her watch: 9:30 A.M.

The clock was ticking.

Sal would have to agree to give her the rest of the day off to cook. Otherwise, he would have to weather the blows from his disappointed and hungry staff and accept the fact that this year's office Christmas party was a major bust.

Hayley called Sal's line and told him she was running to the store. Then she grabbed her bag from underneath the desk and stuffed the hundred-dollar bill in her pocket when the phone rang.

The caller ID was Dr. Aaron Palmer.

She quickly picked up. "Aaron, I'm so sorry, but I can't talk right now. I'm having a bit of an emergency—"

"Mom, it's me."

Gemma.

Gemma was on a work-study program and spent two and a half days a week helping Aaron out by answering phones at his office. It was the perfect way for the aspiring young vet to get hands-on experience and extra credit, plus make a few extra bucks to go Christmas shopping.

"Is everything okay?"

"No! Guess who came in here today with her grandson's hamster!"

"Honey, I really don't have time—"

"Missy Anne Higgins!"

Hayley's heart sank.

"Apparently, the hamster isn't eating and her grandson is all upset that he's going to die, so she rushed in here, begging Dr. Palmer to save him!"

Hayley knew where this was going.

"Let me guess. She barely set the cage down before asking you if Lex and I are back together?"

"Yes! I said no, because you're not, right?"

"No, we're not."

"And that's when she said she was confused because she saw the two of you kissing in his hospital room. Which is a total lie, right, Mom?"

Hayley sighed.

"Mom?"

"Not exactly."

"What?"

"It's a long story. I'll explain everything later."

"Mom, you can't break Dr. Palmer's heart. He might not write me a good college recommendation if he hates you."

"Well, I'm happy you're not making this about you, Gemma. Now can I talk to him, please?"

"No. He's with a Napoleon Longhair cat with an ear infection."

"Okay, fine. I'll try him later. I have to go, Gemma. I have a lot to do today."

Hayley hung up and immediately fished her cell phone out of her bag.

She texted Aaron: **Need to talk to you. ASAP.**

Hayley then grabbed her coat and headed out the door. She was fairly certain she would not hear back from Aaron until he was good and ready. After hearing Missy Anne Higgins's breathless recounting of how Hayley and her former beau were lip-locked at the local hospital, Aaron would probably need some time to cool down.

Chapter 8

Hayley could barely keep her eyes open after she finished setting up for the party at the *Island Times* office. She felt as if she had been through the grinder competing on some Food Network cooking show where speed and endurance, as well as talent in the kitchen, were required in order to win the grand prize. Only, there was no grand prize. Just the satisfaction of knowing she had pulled off a successful holiday office party on a shoestring budget.

As the employees of the paper filed into the front office and poured themselves some fruit punch and dove into her assortment of Christmas appetizers, which she had slaved over in her kitchen all afternoon, Hayley surreptitiously checked her cell phone.

Still, no word from Aaron.

And it was already past 5:00 P.M.

She decided she had to put Aaron out of her

mind, at least for now, and focus on mingling with her coworkers. At least until she could put in enough face time so no one would be insulted when she slipped out early and went straight home to bed.

Eddie Farley, who headed up the paper's sales department, rushed up to her, his mouth filled with one of her onion-and-Brie palmiers. "Amazing, Hayley! The Barefoot Contessa's got nothing on you! These are amazing!"

"Thanks, Eddie."

He washed it down with some punch. "Punch is a little weak, but Bruce is taking care of that!"

Hayley glanced over to see crime reporter Bruce Linney emptying a bottle of rum into the fruit punch. He was already swaying from side to side, having stretched his late lunch with some fellow reporters into an all-afternoon happy hour.

Bruce put a winter cap with reindeer antlers sticking out from each side on his head and cranked up the volume of the Christmas songs playing on Hayley's computer. Then he began belting out "Christmas (Baby Please Come Home)" with Cher and grabbing any woman in sight as a dance partner.

At least, Cher was singing in tune.

It was going to be one of those parties.

"Congratulations, Hayley, I knew you could do it!" Sal shouted, trying to be heard over Bruce's earsplittingly awful singing.

He handed Hayley a red envelope.

Hayley couldn't help but smile.

It was her Christmas bonus.

"Don't spend it all in one place," Sal said, winking before shuffling off toward the punch bowl.

Hayley clutched the envelope.

Her heart was pounding.

She had been waiting for this check all year.

She hoped and prayed that her hard work would finally pay off and Sal would recognize and reward the crucial role she played as office manager and local food and cocktails columnist at the *Island Times.*

She knew deep down she was setting herself up for disappointment. She had heard all of Sal's excuses throughout the year. Traditional newspapers were on the wane. The competing daily, the *Bar Harbor Herald,* was enjoying a resurgence in readership. Local advertisers just weren't ponying up the usual ad rates anymore. And then there was Sal's ominous warning the day before, which downgraded her expectations. And yet she believed that in the end, somehow, she would receive a decent bonus.

Hayley resisted the urge to rip open the red envelope on the spot and stare at the check amount stuffed inside the jokey Christmas card.

That would be tacky.

But she couldn't wait until after she left the party.

She would die of curiosity long before that.

She remembered her winter jacket.

Hayley had moved it to the copy room to make more room on the coatrack for the employees' spouses, who were now showing up to the party.

That was her perfect excuse.

"Be right back, everybody. I'm just going to go put this envelope in my coat pocket so I don't lose it."

As she turned to go, Eddie Farley scooted up to her, waving his cell phone. "I've got everybody here tweeting about your out-of-this world apps, Hayley. I think hashtag Chef Hayley may be trending!"

"Thank you, Eddie. That's sweet," she said.

Twitter.

Tweeting.

Hashtag.

Trending.

It hardly made sense to her. Her kids tried to explain it to her, and she pretended to understand, but she really didn't.

Hayley slipped into the copy room and shut the door. She tore into the envelope and yanked out the card. She took a deep breath before opening it.

She closed her eyes and removed the check.

Visualizing a number in her mind.

She opened her eyes.

Barely enough to cover her next car insurance payment.

It was a crushing disappointment.

She was so dazed by the low number that she didn't even hear someone opening the door to the copy room and stumbling inside.

As a pair of thick arms circled around her waist, she snapped to attention and spun around.

"Hey, beautiful, Merry Christmas," Bruce Linney slurred, still swaying from side to side.

"Merry Christmas to you, Bruce," Hayley said, trying to free herself gently from his grasp.

"I'm sure there's some mistletoe around here somewhere. . . ."

Hayley noticed that he had replaced his cap with reindeer antlers with another cap wired with fake mistletoe dangling off the top of it.

Bruce's glassy eyes glanced upward at the mistletoe perched between them on his hat. "Oh, look at that. Now you have to kiss me."

He puckered his lips.

Unable to escape his grip, Hayley finally relented and turned his face to one side to kiss him lightly on the cheek.

"That's not a kiss! I want a real kiss!" Bruce protested, pulling her closer.

"Bruce, you're blisteringly drunk right now, and I think it might be a good idea if someone drove you home."

"Don't you feel it, Hayley? We've always had this sexual enemy . . . sexual enema . . . sexual Energizer . . . Bunny . . . ," Bruce said, struggling through his inebriation.

"'Sexual energy,'" Hayley said before instantly adding, "And, no, I don't feel it. Especially right now."

It was true that they had a history.

But anything beyond a mutual tolerance between them had long since evaporated.

"I do. . . . I feel it. . . ," Bruce mumbled.

Bruce had her backed up against the copy machine. He went in for another kiss and Hayley ducked out of the way. He lost his balance and fell forward; his lips landed on the glass of the copier. Hayley pressed the copy button and the flashing light blinded Bruce long enough for Hayley to dash out of the room and right into the belly of her boss, Sal, who was on his phone.

"Everything all right in there?" Sal asked, glancing at Bruce, who was covering his eyes with one hand while feeling around for a wall to steady himself with the other.

"Yes, everything's great," Hayley said.

She had zero interest in discussing Bruce's inappropriate behavior. He was hammered and would probably not remember anything in the morning. Hayley certainly didn't want to ruin the party by making a scene.

Her only thought at the moment, besides her paltry Christmas bonus, was leaving this party and calling the man she actually did want to kiss.

Dr. Aaron Palmer.

Her fear was, however, that he was no longer interested.

Chapter 9

"Hayley Powell, stop right there!"

The booming voice startled Hayley, who nearly dropped the avocado she was squeezing in the produce section of the Shop 'n Save.

She spun around, instantly recognizing the voice.

It was Garth Rawlings. He was dressed in all white, including a crisp white apron and a sporty little chef's hat. He was like a walking billboard for his catering business. He held a sack of sugar underneath one arm and was waving a bunch of bananas at her, which he had just picked up off the pile before spotting her.

Hayley was in no mood to be scolded again for causing him to quit on her, so she tossed the avocado on top of a bag of radishes and pushed her cart briskly in the opposite direction.

"Where are you going? I want to talk to you!"

Garth snarled, shocked that someone was trying to get away from the Great Chef of Bar Harbor.

Hayley knew it was pointless trying to outrun him, so she stopped and slowly turned to face the kitchen nightmare.

"Garth, I'm sorry about yesterday. I truly am—"

"What the hell are you talking about? What happened yesterday?"

"I could only pay you a hundred dollars and you hung up on me."

"Oh, that," Garth said, dismissing her with a wave of his hand. "Ancient history. I need to talk to you about tomorrow night."

"Tomorrow night?"

"Midnight Madness, my dear. Surely, you know it's tomorrow night."

Midnight Madness was an annual local event held every year around the holidays. All of the businesses in town keep their doors open until midnight, hosting locals and offering a variety of snacks, free champagne and wine, gift cards, and a lot of heavy discounts. It was a nice way of giving back to the community and to show their appreciation to all of their loyal customers. Hayley and her two best friends, Mona and Liddy, always made it a tradition to hop from one store to another, starting promptly at eight and taking full advantage of those plastic cups of wine along the way until the town clock struck midnight. Luckily, taxi driver Larry Shaw, who was in her brother Randy's class and had a huge crush on Mona when they were kids, was on call every year and ready to serve as their designated driver.

"Yes, Garth, I'll be out with my friends tomorrow night and we look forward to stopping by your warehouse to taste a few of your scrumptious delicacies."

She turned away from him and began perusing the butter lettuce being sprayed with water from tiny hoses lining the bin.

"Forget your friends. You're working for me tomorrow and tonight."

"I beg your pardon?"

"Do you have any idea how much you're blowing up on Twitter?"

"I'm what?"

"Well, not like 'blowing up' blowing up. I mean, not like some brainless twit of a pop star shagging a life-size stuffed animal on some music video awards show and now the whole world's talking about it. More like blowing up locally. I've noticed a lot of tweets from my Maine followers about how you killed it last night at your little office Christmas party."

"Really? People are saying they liked my food?"

"*Liked* it? They're fawning! Yes, *fawning*. And, frankly, I regret quitting on you because now I'm burning up inside with jealousy. Last night I sat at home watching my archrival, Gordon Ramsay, bitch-slap some incompetent sous chef while you *totally* caused a sensation with your jumbo lump crabmeat and Boursin dip!"

Garth shoved his phone in front of Hayley's face. She read the tweet on the screen: **Totally dying for Hayley's Crispy Ham & Cheese Balls. Check out pic of food table friend sent from Islander party. #yummy** Sent by a foodie in Hulls Cove.

"You just can't buy this kind of publicity. It's all about the buzz, Hayley. Please don't tell me you're going to open up a catering business to compete with me or I'll have a heart attack right here on the spot."

"No, Garth. I can barely get my column in on time these days, let alone think about opening a business."

"Big sigh of relief. Although I may still have that heart attack, because my wife says I put too much butter in my dishes and that I am close to sharing type two diabetes stories with Paula Deen. Now, about you working for me—"

"As much as I need a second job, I just can't right now—"

"Just two days. That's all I need you for. Two days."

"I really can't—"

"I'll pay you a thousand bucks."

Hayley nearly choked. She grabbed her chest and sputtered and coughed until her throat finally cleared and she was able to speak. "A thousand bucks? For two days?"

"Yes."

That much money would certainly make up for her lackluster work bonus. It would also go a long way in paying off that maxed-out credit card she had used at the Bangor Mall to buy her kids the Christmas presents on their lists.

"When were you thinking of having me start?"

"Today. Like right now."

"Are you serious?"

"I have three parties I'm catering this weekend and I'm way behind. I haven't even been able to think about Midnight Madness, and suddenly this morning I realized I have nothing to serve people who stop by my warehouse tomorrow night. So after reading the deluge of tweets singing your praises this morning, I got the idea to hire you to handle it."

"But I worked all day cooking for the Christmas party after you bailed on me yesterday, and I was there very late cleaning up after everybody, and I'm exhausted—"

"Twelve hundred."

Hayley's mouth dropped open.

She had no idea she was even negotiating.

And then there was Aaron.

He finally texted her late last night, saying he wanted to see her, so she had invited him over for dinner tonight, which was why she was at the grocery store before work, picking up some veggies for a nice salad and some fresh tomatoes and garlic for a simple pasta dish. If she was cooking all day and night for Garth's Midnight Madness spread tomorrow night, she would have to cancel.

"And I also have plans with Aaron, the man

I've been seeing, and I really don't want to cancel because a situation has arisen that I need to address with him, and, well, it's personal and I don't feel comfortable telling you—"

"Fifteen hundred."

Oh. My. God.

"Okay, yes! I'll do it! Just let me call my boss, Sal, and take a personal day and text Aaron to see if he's okay with me postponing."

"Great. We can shop together and I can tell you the kind of menu I'm thinking about, and then you can take the ingredients home and do all of the cooking in your own kitchen and bring it over to the warehouse tomorrow evening."

Hayley was bubbling over with excitement. Suddenly the idea of pocketing fifteen hundred dollars for just two days' work infused her tired bones with a renewed energy.

She knew Sal would be fine with her taking the day off. It was the week before Christmas and a slow time at the office. Plus she was ahead of schedule on all her office manager duties. Not to mention, Sal owed her for pulling off a memorable Christmas party. She could easily spend the rest of the day and night cooking and then punch in for half a day tomorrow before rushing home after work to heat up the food before Midnight Madness.

Aaron was not going to be so easy.

They still hadn't discussed what went down in Lex Bansfield's hospital room.

She grabbed her cell phone and began typing a text: Aaron, I am so sorry.

"Hayley! I need you over here pronto to help me pick out apples to roast for the Christmas ham!" Garth hollered from across the produce section.

Hayley kept typing as fast as she could: Have to cancel dinner tonight. Will call later to explain.

"Hayley!" Garth was red-faced and now screeching.

He didn't like to be kept waiting.

Hayley hit send.

She prayed Aaron would understand.

And later she would give him fifteen hundred reasons why he should forgive her.

Hell, forget cooking him dinner.

She would treat him to a fancy meal at a five-star restaurant after this unexpected payday.

Chapter 10

The following morning as Hayley sat at her desk, she was downing coffee and slapping herself a couple of times to keep from nodding off to sleep. She was up cooking for Garth until four in the morning and only had managed to get three hours of sleep before her alarm clock buzzed and she was forced out of bed to get ready for work. She was operating on fumes after slaving over a hot stove for the Christmas party and Midnight Madness. But finally there was a light at the end of the tunnel. All she had to do was deliver her food to Garth's warehouse after work and then go home and collapse into a coma.

It had been a particularly rough night and not just because she was chained to the kitchen whipping up dishes for Garth. She was feeling blue over a return text from Aaron acknowledging her canceling their dinner.

Okay.

Simple.

To the point.

No fuss.

No mess.

Still, it bugged her. It would've been easier if he wrote back an angry message: how he was pissed that she promised to cook dinner for him and then wound up disappointing him; how this was not the end of it and they were going to sit down and discuss why she canceled at the last minute, and why Missy Anne Higgins saw her smooching Lex Bansfield in his hospital room.

She desperately wanted a long, impassioned text from Aaron.

She wanted him to be infuriated.

Enraged.

That would mean on some level he wasn't giving up on her.

But all she got was *Okay*.

And that frightened her. Because she didn't want to lose him.

Hayley also had to deal with her drama queen daughter, Gemma, who was home rehearsing the role of the Virgin Mary for Reverend Staples's Nativity pageant. Gemma made the mistake of asking her brother, Dustin, to run lines with her and he proceeded to make fun of her stiff acting; then all hell broke loose. Gemma was already nervous over the prospect of playing a leading role, and her brother's teasing was only fueling her insecurities. So while rolling her walnut-size bourbon balls in coconut, Hayley also had to play referee with her kids.

Christmas was always one of Hayley's favorite holidays, but this year she just wanted to hide under her bedcovers and wake up after New Year's.

Hayley stood up and crossed to the coffeepot and poured herself another cup. She added a little sugar and milk and was stirring it with a spoon when the door to the office blew open and Bruce Linney charged inside. He shook off his coat, stomped the snow off his boots, and tossed the coat on the rack.

He never once glanced at Hayley.

"Good morning, Bruce," Hayley chirped. "Feeling better?"

Bruce grunted a reply and headed to the back bull pen.

As he passed Hayley, she said, "Don't you think it might be a good idea to talk about it?"

Bruce stopped, looking straight ahead. "Talk about what?"

"What happened at the Christmas party. I was going to bring it up yesterday, but I took a personal day."

"I was out sick, so I wasn't here anyway. But I have no idea what you're babbling about."

Hayley suspected as much.

He didn't remember a thing.

"So you have no memory of being drunk and groping me in the copy room and trying to kiss me while you were wearing that ridiculous mistle-toe hat?"

Bruce's whole body tensed. "No."

Hayley shrugged. "Okay."

She was about to let the whole thing go and let him off the hook.

But then Bruce had to go and open his mouth.

And when Bruce opened his mouth, he was always his own worst enemy.

"I don't know what you *think* happened in that copy room, Hayley, but you and I both know you're awfully fond of your cocktails too, and maybe you're just remembering what you *want* to remember."

Hayley stepped back, aghast. "Are you suggest-ing I'm making this up?"

"No. Maybe I got a little too friendly. It was a party. Everybody was drinking. I'm merely suggest-ing you may be embellishing the story just a tiny bit given how you feel about me."

"How I *feel* about you?"

"Come on, Hayley, everybody knows you have a crush on me. Ever since we were in high school."

"No, Bruce. Nobody knows that, because I *don't* have a crush on you. I have the furthest thing from a crush on you. I have an anti-crush! I am repelled by you. And you do not get to tell me I'm embellishing what happened, because I'm not. I didn't have a drop of punch the other night. I was stone-cold sober. Actually, I wish I had been drinking, so I wouldn't have such a crystal clear memory of your sweaty hands on my ass and your puckered lips attacking my face!"

"Prove it," Bruce spit out.

"She doesn't have to," Sal said, storming out of his office. "I can."

Sal's sudden presence surprised both of them.

Bruce suddenly clammed up as Sal held his iPhone in front of Bruce's face.

There was a video of the party playing on the screen: reporters laughing and conversing; somebody's kid sneaking some spiked punch.

"I thought it might be fun to record some of the party," Sal said.

The video swung around toward the copy room, where there was a clear view of Bruce pinning Hayley up against the copier.

Bruce's face blanched. It was all there for him to watch in horror:

Hayley ducking his kiss.

Bruce's lips landing on the Xerox machine.

Hayley pressing the copy button to blind him so she could get away.

Hayley stopping at the door as Sal lowered the phone.

The camera aimed at the floor as Sal asked her, "Everything okay in there?"

Hayley lying, telling him, "Yes, everything's great."

The video stopped and Sal pocketed the phone. "Satisfied, Bruce?"

Bruce nodded. He glanced furtively to Hayley and then back to Sal. "I'm not feeling very good, Sal. I may be having a relapse."

He grabbed his stomach as a wave of nausea apparently swept over him.

"Well, you best be getting home then, Bruce," Sal said flatly.

Bruce, humiliated, turned and hightailed it out the door after grabbing his coat off the rack.

Sal turned to Hayley. "It's okay if you want to make an issue out of this."

"He was plowed, Sal. It was a Christmas party. These things happen."

Sal nodded. "Good. Let's get back to work."

The phone rang as Sal pivoted and returned to his office.

Hayley sat down behind her desk and scooped up the receiver. "*Island Times*. This is Hayley speaking."

"Hey, sis. You will never guess what Sergio got me for Christmas!"

It was Randy, Hayley's younger brother.

"I hate playing this guessing game with my kids. Just tell me, please," Hayley said, rubbing her eyes.

"I was snooping around the attic, you know, peeking around to see what I could find—"

"You're worse than Dustin," Hayley said, laughing.

"Anyway, I stumbled across this giant box wrapped in this fabulous paper with pictures of all these hot, bare-chested muscle dudes wearing Santa hats, and I thought it might be that fifty-two-inch flat-screen TV I've been begging for all year. But when I picked it up, it was really light. I mean, it felt like this huge box was just full of air. Well, needless to say, I was dying of curiosity—"

"Tell me you didn't open it."

"I did—but very carefully. I mean, peeling that Scotch tape off without tearing the paper was no small feat. It takes years of practice. I felt like I was performing surgery."

"Randy!"

"I know, I know. It's wrong, and I am going to hell, but I just couldn't help myself. Inside was an envelope. And opening that was even harder than the box. I had to be really careful with the letter opener, but I managed to leave enough of that sticky stuff to seal it up again so he'd never know."

"I'm at work, Randy. I need you to get to the point before Christmas Eve."

"Tickets for a gay cruise! Through the Mediterranean next June! Spain, Italy, and France! Can you believe it?"

"Omigod, Randy, that's fantastic!"

"Did you know about this?"

"No. You know Sergio doesn't trust me. I tell you everything. Listen, put everything back the way you found it. Sergio is a cop. He's an expert at examining the evidence. If he suspects you tampered with that gift, he might not give it to you."

"That's the same threat you use on your kids."

"Yes, but Sergio's not the pushover I am. He could actually mean it!"

"You're right. I better go. Oh, one more thing. Can I tag along with you and your gal pals tonight for Midnight Madness? I'm closing the bar early and Sergio's hosting an open house at the police station, so I'm on my own."

"I'm skipping Midnight Madness this year, but I'm sure Mona and Liddy would love having you join them. If I don't get some sleep soon, I'm going to drop dead."

In hindsight Hayley would soon realize "drop dead" was a severely unfortunate choice of words.

Chapter 11

Hayley left the office at the end of the day and rushed home to heat up the dishes she had prepared for Garth. Just before 6:00 P.M., she received a text from him instructing her to bring everything over to the warehouse promptly at 7:00 P.M. to set up. He asked if she could stay and help, since he was busy cooking a Dijon pork roast with cranberries for a party he was catering on Sunday.

Hayley instantly texted him back, telling him not to worry. She would be there on time with the dishes he requested. Hayley had made an additional garlic ham for the kids to have for dinner; that was the last thing she put in the oven to heat up. Gemma was still at the church rehearsing the Nativity play, and Dustin was with his math tutor.

Once the food was boxed and loaded into her car, she drove over to the warehouse.

As she parked the car in front of the building and got out, Hayley decided to let Garth know she was there so he could help her carry the boxes inside. She cautiously walked up to the entrance to the warehouse and knocked on the door to Garth's kitchen.

She could hear music playing next door.

Classic rock.

Aerosmith or ZZ Top.

Obviously, Nick the foreman's choice.

It was more from his generation.

She assumed Lex's construction crew was having a few beers and kicking back after a long day sawing plywood and pounding nails.

The music wasn't too loud, so Garth would have no reason to complain.

What was she thinking?

Garth would always find a reason to complain.

No one came to the door.

She knocked again. Louder.

Then tried the handle.

It was locked.

Hayley waited a few more moments and then plucked her phone from her coat pocket and texted him: **Garth, I'm outside. Need help with the food.**

She waited five more minutes, blowing into her winter gloves because the cold winds were gusting and the temperature outside was dropping.

She heard laughing coming from Lex's office.

The crew was probably on their third or fourth six-pack.

Hayley checked her watch.

It was going on ten past seven.

They really needed to set up before people began showing up looking to get fed by the Great Chef of Bar Harbor.

Hayley crinkled her nose. There was a smell in the air. A burning smell.

Then she heard a dog barking. It was coming from inside the warehouse. Behind the door. It was Bagel, Garth's devoted bloodhound.

Something was wrong.

Seriously wrong.

Hayley raised her phone and punched in three numbers.

"911, what's your emergency?"

"I'm at Garth Rawlings's kitchen warehouse at the corner of Center Street and Main. I think the building may be on fire!" Hayley yelled. "Please hurry!"

The burning smell was getting stronger.

She noticed small puffs of smoke coming through the bottom of the locked warehouse door.

More barking. This time more frantic.

Hayley tried the door handle again, knowing it was locked, but feeling as if she had to do something.

A siren blared in the distance, getting closer by the second.

Hayley shoved herself hard against the door, trying desperately to bust it open, but only succeeding in almost dislocating her shoulder.

A fire truck pulled up to the warehouse and two

firemen jumped down and raced over to join Hayley. Another one was uncoiling the hose as two more were turning on the water pump.

"Please step aside, Hayley," one deep-voiced fireman said, gently taking her by the arm and moving her to his right.

He was so young. Hayley thought she might have babysat him when she was a teenager, but she couldn't quite place the name.

After he assessed the situation, Fire Captain Dean Kendrick ordered his men to unlatch a long battering ram. Within thirty seconds four of the firemen were charging the door.

It took two tries, but the door finally gave. As it collapsed inside the warehouse, smoke poured out.

Three of the firemen raced inside, armed with fire extinguishers. The other two remained outside, ready with the hose.

Hayley hugged herself, praying Garth and Bagel would be rescued unharmed.

One of the firemen, the deep-voiced one, emerged, carrying Bagel in his arms. The poor dog looked shell-shocked but otherwise fine.

After what felt like an eternity, Captain Kendrick and one other fireman walked out. The captain was on his cell phone.

"Building's okay—just some burning food in the oven. Fire's already out. But you better get down here, Chief, because we found a body."

Hayley's heart skipped a beat.

"There wasn't enough smoke for him to die of

inhalation. I'm guessing he was dead before the food started burning. Heart attack, maybe? Who knows? I'll let you do your job and decide what happened to him."

Hayley knew the answer, but she had to ask anyway. "Is it Garth Rawlings?"

"He was facedown when we found him, so I can't be sure," Captain Kendrick said. "All I can tell you is he was wearing a white apron and a chef's hat."

Island Food & Spirits
by
Hayley Powell

Every year around the holidays I always wax nostalgic and recall memories of Christmas past. That was certainly the case the other night when I was turning off the lights on the Christmas tree. I thought about an incident that happened years ago when I was still married and my kids were very small. It was early December and my then-husband, Danny, announced that the family was going to drive to Gilley's Christmas Tree Farm, outside of town, to pick out our Christmas tree. The kids screamed with delight. I could only manage a low groan. It's not that I didn't want a tree. It was the agony of us having to choose one. Or should I say, *Danny* choosing one. He always insisted on having the perfect tree to show off to the neighbors, and every year it had to be bigger and better than the previous tree.

The prior year he had picked a tree that he swore would fit in our living room. However, after three tries of trying to shove it through the door, he was forced to trim half its branches and saw off the bottom four times in order to get it to fit into the tree stand and not hit the ceiling.

There was no getting out of Danny's tree trip. So the next morning, after filling my Crock-Pot with one of our favorite Christmas stews for our supper that night, we bundled up the excited kids and packed them into the car and embarked on the hour ride to Gilley's while singing Christmas carols at the top of our lungs.

Sounds like the idyllic beginning of a fun family road trip holiday adventure? Well, it was—for about the first five minutes. That's roughly the attention span my kids have singing Christmas carols. Especially since they didn't really know the words to any yet. The singing in the backseat quickly devolved into whining: "Are we there yet?" "I'm hungry!" Plus the perennial favorite, "I've got to pee!"

Danny started grumbling from the driver's seat that he had asked everyone to use the bathroom before leaving the house so he wouldn't have to stop until we arrived at our destination. The angry sound of their father's voice immediately caused the kids to cry, which just got Danny even more frustrated. He pulled into the Hulls Cove General Store and huffily unloaded the kids from the car so they could use the restroom and grab a snack. It's normal to make pit stops on any road trip, but the Hulls Cove General Store is only ten minutes from our house!

Finally, after returning the chocolate reindeer, which Dustin didn't seem to think he had to pay for, we were back on the road. Danny said if he heard any more complaining, he would turn the car around and we would go straight home with no Christmas tree.

Of course this was met with more tears and crying. I was silently praying he would make good on his threat so we could skip this grueling tradition of searching for the perfect tree in the woods on a farm in the bitter cold with whiny children. I yearned for the day when Danny would be too tired and we could just drive over to the True Value hardware store and purchase a tree right from the lot next door, run by the local Boy Scout troop. But as we crossed the Trenton Bridge, I knew that was just a dream. Danny was more determined than ever to see this "Christmas Tree Mission" through.

We finally arrived at the Christmas tree farm and piled out of the car while Danny collected an axe and a sled from Mr. Gilley, who, I swear, hadn't changed a bit since I was a kid. He looked eighty years old then. He looked eighty years old now. Must be the rough Maine winters.

I looked at what seemed like miles and miles of perfect-looking Christmas trees and could have picked one out right then and there. But that would be too easy. I knew in my heart we had a long day ahead of us.

I will not force you to endure the five-hour search for the perfect tree, but I will try and briefly sum it up for you!

> *On the twelfth day of Christmas, my family gave to me . . . twelve crying jags, eleven "stop that fighting"s, ten "Mommy, I'm starving"s, nine "Daddy, I'm tired"s, eight "Just pick a damn tree"s, seven "I can't feel my toes"s, six "I've got to pee now"s, five almost-perfect trees, four people shivering, three frozen noses, two broken saws, and one perfect Powell family Christmas tree!*

After paying for the tree, loading the kids into the car, and tying the tree on the roof, we began our journey home. We had barely pulled into the driveway when the kids began complaining that they were hungry. I silently congratulated myself for having the foresight to put our supper in the Crock-Pot before we left the house that morning. Soon we would be warming up with big bowls of my delectable Christmas stew. As we piled out of the car, I realized Danny wasn't following us. I turned to find him just staring at the car with a shocked expression on his face. It took a moment for it to sink in that there was no Christmas tree tied to the car roof!

Apparently, the rope Danny used to tie it down with had come loose. Somewhere between Gilly's Christmas Tree Farm and our house, there was a perfect Christmas tree lying in the middle of the dark road, waiting there for someone to rescue it and take it home.

Well, Merry Christmas to that lucky someone who was now in possession of that perfect tree! I was not about to turn around and go search for it, since it was pitch-black by 4:00 P.M. in December. I guess losing the tree was just too much for Danny that year. He said there would never be a perfect tree like that one ever again. I finally got my wish to pick out a tree right in town at the Boy Scout tree lot. And I've been doing that every year since.

When winter arrives, I always whip up my world-famous Powell family Christmas stew recipe. Well, "world-famous" might be an overstatement. Mostly, I make it for friends and family. There is nothing more comforting, especially in December, than filling our bowls with this scrumptious beef stew and filling our mugs with hot apple cider. (The adults get an added bonus of a shot of rum!) Try these holiday recipes and you too will be giving thanks!

Powell Family Hot Apple Cider and Rum

Ingredients

1 apple
2 teaspoons whole cloves
1 orange, thinly sliced with peel
2 quarts your favorite apple cider
½ cup light brown sugar
1 teaspoon allspice
Pinch of grated nutmeg or half teaspoon ground nutmeg
1 cup of your favorite dark rum or more, if you prefer
Cinnamon sticks for garnishing

Poke your whole cloves into the apple. In a saucepan combine the apple with the cloves and all of your ingredients, except the rum. Slowly bring to a simmer over low heat. Simmer for 10 minutes. Remove from the heat and add your favorite rum. Discard the apple. Ladle the mixture into mugs and garnish each one with a cinnamon stick. Serve immediately for the full and tasty results!

Powell Family Crock-Pot Christmas Stew

<u>Ingredients</u>

2½ pounds beef stew meat, cut into 1-inch pieces
1 28-ounce can stewed tomatoes with the juice
1 cup chopped celery
4 sliced carrots, cubed potatoes
3 onions, chopped
3½ tablespoons cornstarch
2 beef bouillon cubes
½ teaspoon dried rosemary
½ teaspoon dried thyme
½ teaspoon dried marjoram
¼ favorite red wine
½ cup flour
2 tablespoon oil
1 teaspoon each salt and pepper

In a Ziploc bag combine your flour and salt and pepper, add the meat, and shake until all of the meat is coated. In a large frying pan add the 2 tablespoons oil and bring up to medium-high heat. Add your floured beef to the pan and sear on all sides by stirring until all of the meat is browned and then add to the Crock-Pot.

Add your cornstarch to the wine and whisk and add to the pot. Then add all the rest of your ingredients, give a quick stir to combine, and turn the Crock-Pot on low and leave alone for 8 to 10 hours until the meat is tender and you're ready to eat.

As always, feel free to add your own touches, such as a bag of frozen peas the last couple of hours of cooking.

Chapter 12

The police chief, Sergio Alvares, was on the scene in less than five minutes. He stepped out of the squad car—looking tall and dreamy in his blue flak jacket, sporting a shoulder holster with a gun—and took full command. He was like a Brazilian version of Ryan Gosling playing a brooding detective in some indie feature. Sadly, for most of the women in town, Sergio was also gay.

He consulted with fire Captain Kendrick outside the warehouse before heading inside to take a look at the corpse. There were no other officers on the scene yet, so nobody was holding back the small crowd of onlookers, which had undoubtedly heard about the fire on their home police scanners.

Hayley casually followed Sergio inside. Even though he was her brother-in-law, she guessed he still might object to a civilian sticking close to him while he investigated the scene. But Hayley had gained a reputation in town as an amateur crime-solver, so perhaps she might get lucky and be allowed to watch. Sergio was distracted and it would be difficult to ask for his permission while he was working, so she decided just to take matters into her own hands and sneak inside, undetected, to steal a glimpse of what was happening.

Hayley crept closer to the kitchen, poking her head in to hear Sergio conversing with Captain Kendrick.

"Looks like he was in the middle of cooking when he died. Maybe a heart attack. Could have killed him instantly. Food was still in the oven and started burning, which caused the fire," Sergio said.

It made perfect sense. Garth had told her he was busy preparing some dishes for a couple of weekend parties he was catering.

Sergio continued, scanning the scene. "No signs of a break-in."

"Door was locked, presumably from the inside," said the dashing captain, who removed his hard hat to scratch an itch on the top of his head. "Took all four of my men to bust it down with a battering ram."

Sergio nodded and knelt down next to the body.

Hayley knew it was definitely Garth. She could see his face, cold and still. His eyes were closed.

Sergio noticed a pipe still lodged between

Garth's fingers. He withdrew a white rag from his back pants pocket and used it to pick up the pipe and examine it. "A few of the tobacco embers are still burning. He was obviously smoking when he died."

He then searched Garth's pocket and found his wallet. He opened it and looked inside. It was filled with bills. He pulled them out and fanned through them. "Must be close to nine hundred bucks here. I think it's safe to say someone didn't barge in here and rob him. Especially since the door was locked when you guys got here."

Sergio took another look around. "So all we've got is a barking dog and some burning food in the oven."

"Excuse me, Hayley," a voice said from behind her.

It was loud enough to alert both Sergio and Captain Kendrick, who spun around to catch Hayley eavesdropping on their conversation.

The voice belonged to Rusty Wyatt, a young, energetic, and adorable paramedic in his twenties, with tousled blond hair and cheeks you just wanted to squeeze like an overenthusiastic grandmother. Rusty also had a killer smile and was flashing his pearly whites at a chastised Hayley, who kept glancing back at the stern expression on Sergio's face.

"You get prettier every time I see you," Rusty said, giving her a subtle wink.

"Thank you, Rusty," Hayley said, surprised this kid was shamelessly flirting with her under such serious circumstances.

"You mind if we slip past you with this gurney, honey?" Rusty said, still with the killer smile.

"Oh . . . no! Excuse me! I'm sorry . . . ," Hayley said, stepping aside as Rusty and another paramedic, whom she didn't know, passed her with the gurney and lugged it over to Sergio, fire Captain Kendrick, and Garth's body.

"You can take him straight to the morgue, boys. County coroner can decide whether or not to do an autopsy," Sergio said.

Rusty was staring back at Hayley. He had a lascivious look on his face, as if imagining the two of them skinny-dipping together on some tropical island in the South Pacific. Like Brooke Shields and that long-forgotten curly-haired blond boy in *Blue Lagoon,* a movie Hayley loved as a child.

She was now officially dying of embarrassment.

"Rusty, did you hear what I said?" Sergio asked.

"Yes, sir! We'll take care of it right away."

They lifted the body up off the floor and set him down on the gurney and went about strapping him in.

Sergio walked toward Hayley, mumbling to her as he passed. "You can go home, Hayley. This isn't a crime scene."

Hayley nodded and followed him out.

Outside the warehouse there was now a larger crowd, which was being kept at bay by Sergio's two junior officers, Donnie and Earl, or as Hayley preferred calling them, "Officers Dumb and Dumber." She knew the reference dated her, but it was too perfect not to use. Sergio was stopped by Lex's foreman, Nick Ward, the handyman Billy Parsons, and the quiet, withdrawn young man who always seemed to be tagging alongside them. Nick wanted to know what was going on and Sergio filled him in. The three men seemed genuinely rattled by the news that Garth Rawlings was dead.

"Did you guys see or hear anything?" Sergio asked.

"No, Chief," Nick said, holding a can of beer. "We were inside having our own little holiday party. The kid here, Hugo, thought he smelled something funny, a burning smell, but we didn't think too much about it until we heard the sirens and saw the trucks pull up."

"So you had no interaction with Mr. Rawlings at any time tonight? Did he complain about the music you guys were playing next door?"

"No, sir," Nick said, shaking his head.

Nick glanced over and spotted Hayley, who was watching him closely. She had been there two days before to witness the argument the three men had with Garth over the noise from their machinery.

And he knew it.

"We did have a minor altercation with him just the other day. Some of our equipment caused one of his soufflés to collapse and he was not too happy about it. But we smoothed things over, and Billy here even knocked on his door to invite him over to have a beer with us earlier."

"What time was that?"

"Around five. I knocked a few times, but he didn't answer," Billy said. "I thought maybe he didn't hear me, so I tried the door, but it was locked."

Nick lowered his head and asked quietly, "Does Tiffany know yet?"

Sergio shook his head. "I'm heading over there in a few minutes to break the news before she reads about it on Facebook."

Hayley noticed all three men appeared visibly saddened by the circumstances, especially Hugo, who looked as if he was about to cry.

"Okay," Sergio said. "I may have some more questions for you later, so I'd appreciate it if you could make yourselves available."

"Absolutely, Chief," Nick said. "Whatever we can do to help."

Sergio turned and walked to his squad car.

Hayley ran to catch up to him.

"What are you thinking?" Hayley asked.

"No pills or drugs were found at the scene. Doesn't appear to be any kind of overdose. I'm inclined to believe Garth Rawlings died of natural causes."

"Natural causes? Sergio, Garth was only in his midforties."

"We know he smoked a pipe and we all know the dangers of smoking. We also know he's high-strung and prone to tantrums, which can lead to high blood pressure. Maybe his habits and behaviors finally caught up with him."

Something inside Hayley told her that pipe smoking and a boorish personality were not what killed Garth Rawlings.

Chapter 13

By Saturday, the town of Bar Harbor was buzzing with gossip and speculation surrounding the details of Garth Rawlings's untimely and downright-shocking death. Bruce was able to suppress his embarrassment over what had happened at the *Island Times* Christmas party and focus on digging up details that might shed more light on what caused Garth to die so suddenly and unexpectedly. But mostly everyone was waiting for Sabrina Merryweather, the county coroner, to finish her autopsy on the body.

Hayley wouldn't have hesitated in the past to pick up the phone and call Sabrina, with whom she went to high school. Sabrina was one of those mean girls who joyfully tortured Hayley when they were teenagers, but Sabrina had mostly forgotten about her past behavior and in the ensuing years had considered themselves to be the best of friends. But after Hayley began investigating a few local homicides on her own and managed to step on Sabrina's toes, their friendship had cooled somewhat.

So it was surprising when earlier in the day, Sabrina called Hayley out of the blue and asked her to join her for a drink at Randy's bar, Drinks Like A Fish, the popular local watering hole. Hayley usually would pop by for a cocktail and quality time with her two BFFs, Mona and Liddy, after work; but this weekend Liddy was away in New York for one of her bimonthly shopping sprees and Mona was stuck at home nursing three of her kids who were down with the flu. Aaron finally called her on Friday evening after his ominous text to apologize for not being available for the next few days, as he had a full patient load of family pets and was planning on working the entire weekend. Hayley knew he wasn't making it up, because Gemma was also working at his office that weekend while rehearsing her lines for the Christmas pageant.

Still, Hayley sensed Aaron was being distant on the phone.

And she knew it had to do with Lex.

As for Lex, Hayley continued to deliver home-cooked meals to him while he was on the mend, dropping them off at his apartment above the drugstore on Main Street. Lex had been discharged from the hospital and was told to finish recuperating at home. Hayley made sure just to set the food down on his dining-room table and beat a hasty exit to ensure no one got the wrong idea. She just didn't want Lex chowing down on Milky Way bars and drinking Budweiser while he was unable to shop for any food of nutritional value.

When Hayley arrived at Drinks Like A Fish, Randy was tending bar and chatting with Sabrina, who was propped up on Liddy's usual stool and sipping a dirty martini. Hayley walked over and sat down on the stool next to her. She immediately spotted some smeared mascara on her face and knew Sabrina had been crying.

Randy looked at his sister solemnly. "The usual Jack and Coke, sis?"

Hayley nodded and Randy left them to go make her drink.

"Sabrina, what is it? What's wrong?"

Sabrina pulled a tissue out of her purse and dabbed her eyes. "It's just been a little tough for me lately. A lot of pressure at work and . . ." Her voice trailed off.

"I know things haven't been so great between us these past few months, Sabrina, but you can tell me what's bothering you. Maybe I can help."

"I never like to talk about my personal life and my marriage to Jerry. . . ."

Ever since they had reconnected, all Sabrina did was talk about her personal life and her complaints about her marriage to her artist husband, Jerry.

But now was not the time to remind her of that.

"He says I nag him all the time about not having

a real job. How can he say that? I am fully supportive of those ridiculously expensive artist retreats he goes on, and I barely say a word when I'm out the door at seven A.M. and he sleeps until noon and then quote-unquote paints all day—even though when I get home, the canvas looks exactly the same as when I left it that morning."

Hayley found it hard to believe that Sabrina said barely a word to her layabout husband. However, she just nodded and gently patted Sabrina on the back. "When one spouse is the sole breadwinner, it's bound to cause some friction."

"It's not just that. We've grown apart. I worked until midnight last night, conducting an autopsy, and when I got home, Jerry didn't even bother waiting up for me or leaving me any dinner. I had to microwave a Lean Cuisine. And this morning he went skiing with his buddies, without even saying a word."

The autopsy.

Garth Rawlings.

Hayley couldn't ask about it.

That's not why Sabrina invited her here.

But she was dying to know.

"Somehow it was okay when I was enjoying my job, but lately I've been feeling unfulfilled and underappreciated and part of me just wants to open my own private practice and forget about working for the county. I'll make more money. I'll have more freedom."

"You have to do what makes you happy, Sabrina. Life's too short," Hayley said.

Randy delivered Hayley's drink, and sensing the private moment between them, scooted to the other end of the bar to pour some tap beers for a couple of fishermen.

"But the idea of leaving Jerry and suddenly being alone, and also overhauling my entire career at the same time, would be just too daunting."

"That's why they call it a 'fresh start.'"

"Do you think I should leave Jerry? This would be my second failed marriage."

"Matt cheated on you. How is that *your* fault?"

"Matt said I was too career driven and I wasn't home enough, so he found comfort in the arms of his yoga instructor."

"And his sales rep. And his chiropractor."

"And Jerry doesn't seem to want me around at all. He says I disrupt the flow of his creativity."

"Maybe the problem is your choices in men. You jumped from Matt to Jerry in a matter of months. Maybe you need to take some time alone to figure out what kind of relationship you really want."

Sabrina turned to face Hayley.

Hayley feared she had insulted Sabrina and braced for a lecture about her blatant insensitivity. But instead Sabrina simply raised her martini glass and clinked Hayley's glass with the Jack and Coke.

"You're right. It's them, not me."

Not quite what she meant.

But why not go with it to keep the peace?

"Thanks for listening, Hayley."

"That's what friends are for."

Normally, Hayley would choke on those words. She had a hard time letting go of Sabrina's treatment of her in the past. Plus she was never really a big Dionne Warwick fan. But right now, in this moment, she felt sorry for Sabrina and what she was going through.

"Now I suppose you want to hear about the autopsy?" Sabrina said, signaling Randy at the other end of the bar for another round.

"Sabrina, that is not why I came here tonight. I know your work is confidential and you can't talk about it."

"*Please*. Those bastards I work for leak details to the press all the time. Why shouldn't I be loose-lipped, especially when the details are so tantalizing?"

"They are?" Hayley asked casually, pretending not to be on the edge of her seat, but salivating with curiosity.

Randy set another dirty martini down in front of Sabrina, which thrilled Hayley, because she knew the more the county coroner drank, the more likely it was that she would eventually spill all of the juicy details.

Fortunately, she didn't have to wait too long.

One sip and Sabrina was off and running. "I noticed severe trauma and bruising on Garth Rawlings's body. Something hit him really, really hard.

His internal injuries were so bad, they were more in line with a car crash victim or someone found under a heavy fallen object."

"That's surprising. There was nothing around the kitchen that suggested he was hit or anything fell on him."

"Well, he had a broken rib and a hole in the left atrium of his heart. Oh, not to mention a blow to the chest that was so severe he would have bled out in about thirty seconds."

Hayley gulped her drink down. This was not just surprising. It was shocking. Especially since she initially agreed with Sergio.

Natural causes.

Garth just had a heart attack.

"What does all this mean, Sabrina?"

"It means I'm ruling his death a homicide."

Chapter 14

After Hayley said good night to Sabrina, she ran to her car and called Sergio on her cell phone to tell him the news, but he had already read Sabrina's official autopsy report.

"It doesn't make sense," Sergio said. "The physical evidence just doesn't add up."

"Unless Garth was beaten to death somewhere else and the killer returned to the warehouse with the body and carefully placed it on the floor," Hayley offered, trying to be helpful.

"But the door was locked. He had food cooking in the oven. His dog was there. Everything points to him being in the warehouse alone at the moment he died."

"Someone might have had a key and let himself or herself inside and then killed him. But if some sort of violent struggle took place in the warehouse kitchen, why would he be dead on the floor with a lit pipe in his hand? And wouldn't Lex's crew next door have heard the commotion?"

"Maybe. Maybe not. They were drinking beers and listening to music at the time, which might have drowned out the sounds of a fight. They all stated that they didn't hear anything until the fire trucks arrived."

"So, where do we go from here?"

"First thing I need to do is find out who else had access to the warehouse, which means talking to Rawlings's widow."

Tiffany Rawlings.

"Sergio, Tiffany Rawlings and I have done a few bake sales and bike rides to raise money for breast cancer awareness. We have a pretty good relationship, so I thought maybe . . ."

"Yes, Hayley. If you really think she will be more comfortable answering my questions with you there, then by all means come with me."

Actually, Hayley wasn't 100 percent certain Tiffany would feel more comfortable. But at the very least she could offer her condolences and be there if she needed a shoulder to cry on, since Sergio had a tendency to ignore the feelings of a victim's loved ones and focus entirely on the interrogation at hand.

Sergio picked Hayley up at her house late Sunday morning and they drove over to the Rawlings residence, just outside of town in Otter Creek, a large two story frame house located a few hundred feet off the main road in a woodsy area.

Tiffany had made it clear she would not miss church services and would only accept visitors after the noon hour. When she greeted Hayley and Sergio at the door, she was dressed in a black dress, with white pearls hanging around her neck. She wore her normally wavy long brown hair in a severe tight bun. She was clearly in mourning, as this was not the Tiffany whom Hayley knew from the bake sales and bike rides. She was usually much more provocatively dressed and a free spirit.

Hayley instantly felt pity for the grieving widow.

Tiffany led them into her living room, where she had set out some tea and freshly baked scones.

"Thank you for seeing us, Tiffany. I know this is an extremely difficult time," Hayley said.

Tiffany nodded and motioned for them to take a seat on the couch. She sat down opposite them in a floral-print upholstered chair.

"I just have a few questions I would like to ask," Sergio said, barreling ahead in his "bull in a china shop" kind of way.

Hayley kicked his foot with her own and he slightly winced.

Tiffany didn't notice. She was staring at the mantel above the fireplace, gazing at a framed wedding photo of her and Garth on a beach in Hawaii. "I can't believe we were married fifteen years. It seems like yesterday when we took the plunge in Maui. We still had so many plans. . . ."

Hayley sensed Sergio was about to speak, so she kicked his foot again. Sergio turned to Hayley, who glared at him, silently ordering him to give the poor widow a few moments to remember her husband before so callously diving in with his questions.

"We were going to expand the business. Maybe open a restaurant next summer. We were drawing up plans to build a new house in Seal Harbor. And, of course, we wanted to travel more and see the world. Just last month Garth received an invitation to teach a course at Le Cordon Bleu in Paris. Can you believe that? I've never been to France."

"That's such an honor," Hayley said. "You must have been so proud of him."

"I begged him to take better care of himself— to give up tobacco, exercise more—but he was so stubborn. I go to the gym five times a week. Him? Never. I always feared his smoking and those rich, heart-clogging sauces would finally catch up to him."

Tiffany lifted the silver teapot to pour them some tea.

Hayley and Sergio exchanged a quick look.

Sergio cleared his throat. "Mrs. Rawlings, I'm afraid your husband did not die of a heart attack, as we originally believed. His death has been ruled a homicide."

Tiffany dropped the teapot and it crashed into the half-full teacup, knocking it over and spilling tea all over the service tray. "What?"

"We just received the coroner's report last night."

"It can't be," Tiffany said, eyes welling up with tears. "Who would want to hurt Garth? He was a loving husband. A decent man. He had no enemies, to speak of. The coroner is wrong. That's the only thing that makes sense. We all know she's been wrong before."

"I read the report," Sergio said. "Based on her findings, the evidence unequally suggests—"

"'Unequivocally,'" Hayley said.

"*Unequivocally* suggests someone killed him," Sergio said, rolling his eyes at Hayley. "And at this point, I'm inclined to believe her. We're just having a hard time figuring out how it happened."

"But everybody in town loved Garth!" Tiffany wailed.

That was a tough sell. Anyone with a passing familiarity with Garth Rawlings's personality would wholeheartedly disagree with his distraught widow.

"There must have been someone, Tiffany, maybe from Garth's past who might not have believed he was a swell guy at some point," Hayley said.

"Well, yes, of course. I mean, when you're as successful as Garth, you don't get there without stepping on a few toes. But that's all in the past now. All was forgiven."

"Who are we talking about?" Sergio asked, leaning forward.

"Ken Massey."

A local businessman. Very successful. Owns a

few restaurants and t-shirt shops frequented by the summer tourists.

"Garth and Ken had a falling-out?"

"When Garth was starting out, he didn't have the capital to get the business going, so he brought in Ken as a silent partner. Ken paid the initial investment. When the catering business started making money, Ken tried to take control and dictate everything, and it got ugly for a while. Garth felt like Ken was keeping him in a straightjacket, but that was years ago. Ken went on to start a number of other successful businesses, and he finally agreed to let Garth buy him out."

"Was there any bad blood between them after the buyout?" Sergio asked.

"No, not at all. They have long buried the hatchet, and Garth and I had dinner with Ken at the Town Hill Bistro just a few months ago, before they closed for the season."

"One more question, Mrs. Rawlings, and then I promise we will stop bothering you. Were your husband and Ken still partners when he rented the warehouse space?"

"No. Why?"

"So he wouldn't have had a key to get inside?"

"No, absolutely not. My husband had a few faults and one of them was paranoia. He was always terrified that someone would steal his recipes and his trade secrets, so he never gave anyone a key to that warehouse. He kept the master key in a safe here at home. I don't even know the combination. Trust me, it could not have been Ken."

Ken Massey didn't have the best reputation in town. He'd been called a "snake," a "cheat," and much worse by the people he plowed over to make his fortune.

Sergio didn't look as convinced as Tiffany Rawlings that Ken was a completely innocent party.

And, frankly, Hayley wasn't inclined to believe it either.

Ken was a smart, driven, can-do guy.

If he wanted to gain access to Garth Rawlings's warehouse kitchen, he would most likely have found a way.

Chapter 15

After they left Tiffany's house, Hayley drove over to the local True Value hardware store, where a Christmas tree farm had been set up behind the building by a local Boy Scout troop for locals to shop for the perfect tree to take home and decorate for the holidays. They also sold homemade ornaments, festive colored lights, wreaths, swag, and garland. It was like one-stop shopping.

Hayley was in need of a new Christmas tree skirt. While she had been making eggnog in the kitchen, Blueberry had eaten some strands of tinsel and had thrown up all over her old skirt. The stain came out easily enough, but Hayley didn't want to have to think about placing her wrapped presents on top of something that used to smell of kitty vomit.

She parked her car across the street and headed over to the lot, where about a half-dozen people were perusing the various trees in all shapes and sizes. Paul Applewood, the rosy-cheeked, pudgy, balding manager of the hardware store, greeted Hayley with a smile. "I thought I already sold you a tree this year, Hayley. Something wrong with it?"

"Oh, no, Paul, I just need a new skirt for the base. You have any nice ones left?"

"Got a real pretty one with a reindeer print the wife just finished last night. It's around back, underneath the big pine tree next to my truck."

"Thanks, Paul," Hayley said, smiling, before walking through the tree nursery to the back of the hardware store.

She heard a man's frantic, hushed voice as she rounded the corner.

"I don't know what the police chief wants, but he called my cell and left a voice mail asking me to come by the station to talk to him!" the man said.

Hayley recognized the deep, scratchy, manly-man voice immediately.

It was Ken Massey, Garth's former business partner.

"I heard on the car radio this morning that the coroner ruled Garth's death a homicide! What the hell am I going to do if Chief Alvares thinks I had something to do with it? He'll never leave me alone!"

Hayley followed the sound of his voice through a thicket of trees. She finally spotted Ken—a tall, distinguished-looking man, with graying temples, in a black waffle-knit ski jacket. He paced back and forth, with his Android phone jammed to his ear.

Hayley sidled up next to a very thick spruce tree, which hid her from his view. She crouched down and continued to eavesdrop on his conversation.

"You're my lawyer! I was hoping *you'd tell me* what to do!" Ken wailed before catching himself and lowering his voice. "We both know I can't be implicated in this. It would ruin me!"

Hayley leaned forward into the spruce tree, moving some branches aside to get a closer look at Ken on the other side. He was rubbing his eyes and shaking his head.

"This is bad, Ted. Really, really bad," Ken moaned.

"Hayley, did you hear a word I said? The Christmas skirts are all the way around back. You're not even warm over here."

The voice startled Hayley and she lost her balance, falling into the tree, which tipped over and crashed to the ground just inches from Ken Massey, who spun around, alarmed.

"What the hell!" Ken cried.

The sight of Hayley lying in front of him on top of a fallen spruce tree suddenly clicked in Ken's mind and his face soured. "Ted, I'm going to have to call you back. Bar Harbor's very own 'Miss Marbles' just showed up on the scene."

Ken stuffed his phone in his coat pocket as Paul

Applewood helped Hayley to her feet, brushing branches and twigs off her.

"'Miss Marple,'" Hayley said quietly, turning to face Ken.

"What?" Ken asked, annoyed.

"It's 'Miss Marple.' You said 'Marbles.'"

"I don't give a damn, Hayley! And I don't appreciate you spying on me."

"Oh, she wasn't spying on you, Ken," Paul Applewood said, trying to be helpful. "She was just looking for a Christmas tree skirt and got turned around. With all of these trees, it's like a forest here—"

"Stay out of this, Paul!" Ken screamed.

Paul Applewood reared back, stunned. He nodded and quickly shuffled off, mumbling, "I think I see some customers ready to pay for their tree."

Ken stepped forward, with his dark eyes fixed on Hayley. "Now you listen to me. I've heard all of the stories about you—how you poke your nose where it doesn't belong, how you chase after people asking questions and pointing fingers. Well, I won't allow you to do that to me. You can tell that police chief brother-in-law of yours that I have nothing to say about Garth Rawlings's death because I don't know anything about it. I'm as innocent as they come—and if he thinks differently, he can talk to Rusty Wyatt."

"Rusty Wyatt? The paramedic?"

"Yes. Rusty's a good buddy of mine. We met up

at the gym last Thursday around four P.M. and worked out for about three hours. Crunch training, cardio, and weight lifting. We were on a roll. But then, Rusty had to take off because he was on call. Got word there was a dead body found at the scene of a fire. If your own paper is to be believed, Garth Rawlings died between five and seven."

"That sounds about right."

"Well, then. I was with Rusty right up to the moment he left the gym to meet his fellow paramedic at the scene with the ambulance. And he will be more than happy to back me up. And that, my dear, is what you call an airtight alibi."

Hayley was inclined to believe him.

Except for the fact he was fidgety and flustered and his eyes shifted back and forth and the finger he was waving in her face was shaking slightly.

Ken Massey was nervous and upset.

And Hayley's experience told her that a nervous and upset suspect was more often than not guilty of something.

Chapter 16

Hayley made sure she was at the office extra early on Monday morning in order to catch up on all of the work she had ignored because of the dramatic events the previous week. Sal wasn't expected in today; he had driven to Augusta, the state capital, to do a story on a local congressman from the district. It was just Hayley and a handful of reporters holding down the fort.

And then, of course, there was Bruce Linney.

He blew through the door, eyes downcast, biting his lip, as he shook off his jacket and hung it on the rack. He wore a plaid green shirt and red sweater.

"Good morning, Bruce. You're looking festive today," Hayley said. "Someone's getting into the holiday spirit."

Bruce refused to make eye contact.

He just grunted a reply.

Hayley tried again. "Did you have a nice weekend?"

Bruce shrugged, crossed to the coffeepot, stopping just for a second before thinking better of it, and decided to keep going to his office in the back.

"Bruce, wait," Hayley said.

Bruce froze in the doorway, so close to an escape.

"I think we need to talk," Hayley said quietly, making sure that there were no other *Island Times* employees within earshot.

Bruce slowly turned toward Hayley. His face was flushed. The poor guy was dying inside.

"I don't want there to be any weirdness between us," Hayley said. "I want us to go back to picking at each other and getting on each other's nerves and complaining about the other to anyone who will listen. Just like old times."

"Me too," Bruce said, eyes fixed on the floor.

"So, why don't we just forget what happened at the—"

"It's forgotten. And I'd appreciate us never speaking of it again."

"Okay, that's good. Me too."

Neither knew what to say next.

There was an awkward pause.

Bruce finally couldn't take the silence anymore and blurted out, "So, what does Sergio have to say about the Garth Rawlings murder?"

The murder case. Safe ground.

"I'm not sure. I guess he's still going over the evidence."

"Come on, Hayley. He's your brother's husband. You're around him all the time. You must have heard something."

"Bruce, just because Chief Alvares is family doesn't mean he shares anything pertaining to his open investigations with me. I'm just his kooky, young sister-in-law, who writes recipes in the local paper."

"Young?"

"I was hoping that would go by without being commented on," Hayley said.

"I'm just having a hard time believing, given your nosy nature, that you don't ask him for details on occasion. Or, at the very least, get your brother to divulge any pillow talk that might clue you in to what's going on."

"Sergio is a professional. His reputation is above reproach. And he would never, ever display any favoritism simply because we're related by marriage. He gives me absolutely no extra consideration."

Hayley's cell phone buzzed on her desk. She casually flipped it over to read the text on her screen. It was from Sergio: **Going to warehouse to brush the place one more time for clues. Care to join me?**

Comb.

Comb the place.

Hayley was proud of herself. She was getting

exceptionally good at deciphering her brother-in-law's malapropisms.

Hayley quickly turned the phone over face-down again so Bruce wouldn't catch a glimpse of the text.

Okay, so maybe family did have its privileges.

But why tell Bruce and have to endure that infuriating smug look on his face, or worse, a lecture about professional ethics?

Hayley grabbed her bag from underneath her desk and threw on her coat.

"Where are you going?"

"We're low on office supplies, and you know how Sal hates it when we run out of his favorite Pilot Razor Point pens. I'll be back in a little while."

Hayley scooted out the door, not looking back, knowing Bruce probably had a suspicious look on his face.

After driving to the warehouse and parking her car behind Sergio's police cruiser, Hayley crossed the street to the front door. She noticed Lex's workshop was closed and there were no signs of his construction crew. Maybe they were meeting at Lex's apartment while he was laid up.

Inside the kitchen Hayley found Sergio sitting at Garth's desk, poring over stacks of paperwork and contracts.

"Find anything interesting?" she asked.

Sergio shook his head. "No, everything seems to be in order. This man kept metaphysical paperwork."

Meticulous.

Meticulous paperwork.

"I came across the contract agreement between Garth Rawlings and Ken Massey," Sergio said. "It all seems to be on the up and down."

Up and up.

"Garth paid him off with a tidy sum, so it's hard to picture Ken having any animosity toward him," Sergio said, rubbing his eyes, tired from reading through the stack of papers.

He handed Hayley the contract and she read the terms.

It *was* a very generous buyout.

Nearly a hundred thousand dollars for Ken just to walk away.

Maybe Ken Massey was telling the truth, but why was he so frantic when he was on the phone with his lawyer? What was he worried about?

Hayley and Sergio spent the next twenty minutes sifting through the file folders in Garth's office cabinet. They were nearly through all of it when Hayley stumbled across a white envelope stuffed with receipts from the current month of December. She spread them out on the desk and began reading through them. One of them caught her eye.

She picked it up and handed it to Sergio. "Take a look at this."

"Who is Sammy Kettner?"

"Locksmith. He has a little shop next to Sherman's Bookstore."

Sergio studied the piece of paper. "Looks like Garth had a key made recently."

"Right. And look at the notation near the bottom. 'Warehouse.' Tiffany said Garth was paranoid about the local competition stealing his recipe files so he kept only one key to this place."

"Maybe he just lost his key and had it replaced."

"He would need the original key to make a copy. You went over all of his personal belongings. Were there any keys found on him?"

"Yes—a key to his car, one to his house, and one presumably to here."

"Well, did the key to the warehouse look shiny and brand-new like it was a fresh copy?"

"No, as I recall, it was all scratched up and the copper was fading."

"Then maybe Garth had a key made for someone else. And that person would have had access to the warehouse, and could have locked it when he or she left, leaving behind a dead body and food burning in the oven. . . ."

Chapter 17

Hayley and Sergio entered the small locksmith shop and the bell above the door chimed. A wiry kid, with stringy brown hair down to his shoulders and thick black reading glasses, sat behind the counter, flipping through a comic book. He didn't even bother to look up. He kept his nose buried in the latest issue of *Aquaman*. The kid wore a sleeveless black t-shirt with a retro picture of the Justice League of America members. It was obviously a superhero lineup from the late 1970s. Hayley knew most of the characters because her son, Dustin, was a DC Comics fanatic.

Superman, Batman, Wonder Woman, Hawkman. The six-inch guy, Atom. The stretchy one. Not Plastic Man. No, he wore dark glasses. This one was . . . Elongated Man. And the blonde in the fishnet stockings? The one who could take out bad guys with her sonic cry.

Oh, yes. Black Canary. Hayley was quite proud of herself for identifying everyone on the t-shirt.

Sergio was at the counter, hovering over the kid, and clearing his throat before the eighteen or nineteen-year-old even bothered to tear himself away from his comic to see who had come into the shop.

"Can I help you?" he said in a flat voice.

He couldn't possibly have been less interested in helping anyone.

"We are looking for the owner," Sergio said. "Mr. Kettner."

"He's not here," the kid mumbled before returning to Aquaman's exciting underwater adventures.

Sergio snatched the comic out of the kid's hand, finally getting his attention. "Well, I would really like to talk to him."

Sergio slapped the comic facedown on the counter, but he kept an index finger on it to keep the kid from taking it back.

The kid eyed Sergio, annoyed, apparently unconcerned he was ticking off the town's chief of police. "He went Christmas shopping up in Bangor, so he put me in charge."

The kid stood up. He was well over six feet and towered over Sergio.

It suddenly dawned on Hayley that this was Sammy Kettner's son, Connor.

The last time she saw him he was around eight years old.

Now he looked like the center for the Boston Celtics.

"Yeah, I'm filling in until he gets back," Connor said, casually reaching for his comic book.

Sergio kept his finger pressed down on it.

Connor tugged on it a couple of times before giving up.

He scowled at Sergio.

"Maybe *you* can answer a couple of questions for me," Sergio said, pulling the receipt out of his jacket pocket. "Do you recognize this receipt?"

Connor eyeballed it for a second and turned to glare at Sergio. "Yeah, it's one of our receipts."

"Take a look at the date and time. Were you here working that day?"

"Yeah. Probably. But it was a Friday, so I don't usually get here until—close to three-thirty."

"Well, the time stamp on the receipt is four-ten P.M. So, do you remember seeing Mr. Rawlings come into the shop that day?"

"Nope. Sorry."

Sergio lifted his finger from the comic book and Connor seized the opportunity to grab it back. He put it under the counter, out of Sergio's reach.

Something on his computer screen caught Connor's attention. His eyes widened with concern and he plopped back down in the chair and began furiously typing on the keyboard. "Hold on a minute."

Sergio glanced back at Hayley and shrugged.

"No, no, no, no, no, no, no!" Connor wailed, slapping the side of the computer monitor in frustration.

The business phone on the counter rang and Connor scooped up the receiver. "Quick Time Locksmith. This is Connor speaking. Nathan! I didn't get it, bro! I've been bidding on it for two weeks and it got down to the wire and some lame dude from Oregon beat me by a couple of bucks! This is so wrong, dude! When are we going to find *The Joker* number six on eBay ever again? I'm never going to complete my series collection!"

The Joker.

Batman's archnemesis.

Number six.

Remarkably, Hayley knew exactly what Connor was talking about.

DC Comics published a comic-book series featuring the villainous Joker in 1975. There were only nine issues. Very rare. The only reason she knew about it was because Dustin spent the entire year when he was ten tracking it down for his own collection. He located the complete series in a comic-book shop down in Melbourne, Florida, and begged his grandmother Sylvia, who lived in nearby Vero Beach, to drive to the store and buy it for him as an early birthday present. And then, less than a year later, as he was helping his uncle Randy clean out an old storage space, which Randy had kept since college, Dustin found another lot of the complete *Joker* series. Randy was an avid comic-book fan, too, when he was Dustin's age. Now the kid had two sets: one to be preserved in plastic wrappers and the other one to be left in his room and read from time to time.

"Man, this blows!" Connor whined, slamming the phone down.

Sergio was seriously losing patience.

Hayley walked over to the counter and gently stepped in front of Sergio. "Connor, I don't know if you know me, but I'm Hayley Powell."

"Dustin Powell's mom. Yeah, I know. I run into him at the comic book store in Ellsworth sometimes," Connor said, near tears. He crossed his arms on the counter and rested his head.

"So I'm sure you know Dustin is a big comic-book collector too, and it just so happens he has not one but two number six issues from *The Joker* 1975 series."

Connor looked up, eyes suddenly full of hope. "Two? How did he get two?"

"It doesn't really matter. What matters is, I'm sure Dustin would be happy to give you one of them so you can complete your collection."

"Really? For free?"

"Yes. Consider it my Christmas present to you."

"Thank you, Mrs. Powell! That would be so sweet! Man, Nathan's never going to believe this!" Connor said, grabbing the phone receiver again and punching in his buddy's number.

Hayley plucked the phone out of Connor's

grasp and hung it up. "You can call Nathan with the good news later. First I need to teach you a little life lesson, okay? Here it comes. Nothing in life ever really comes for free."

"Bah, humbug, Scrooge. How much do I have to come up with?" Connor sighed.

"Oh, I'm not talking about money. I'm talking about information."

Connor stared at Hayley for a brief moment and then glanced at Sergio. He then slowly picked up the receipt again and stared at it.

"I really don't remember this Rawlings guy coming in here. My dad must have handled the order, but let me think. Four-ten. That's usually around the time I take my smoke break," Connor said before catching himself and turning to Sergio. "Just don't tell my dad I smoke. Cigarettes, I mean. Not weed, which I know is illegal."

Based on Connor's half-open eyelids and slow, hazy demeanor, Hayley was not inclined to believe him.

"Where do you take your smoke break?" Sergio asked, trying hard not to lunge across the counter and slap the kid silly.

"In the alley between our shop and Sherman's Bookstore," Connor said. "Hey, this Rawlings dude is a chef, right?"

"Yes," Sergio said. "Why? Do you remember something?"

"I think I remember seeing a green van parked in front of our shop with the guy's name written on the side. 'Garth Rawlings Catering' or something like that."

The pothead's memory was finally coming into focus . . . at last.

"So Garth used his own key to have the copy made and paid cash, according to the receipt," Hayley said to Sergio, her mind racing. "But if he was so paranoid about a break-in, why did he have a second key made? Who was it for?"

"Maybe for the chick who was with him," Connor said, pulling his *Aquaman* comic book out from underneath the counter and flipping it open to the page where he left off reading.

"He was with somebody?" Sergio asked, leaning forward.

"Uh-huh," Connor said, gazing at the artwork in the comic. "This underwater stuff is a freakin' trip."

Sergio snatched the comic out of Connor's hand and waved it in front of him.

"Focus, Connor. Work with me! You saw him go into your dad's shop with a woman?"

"No. I didn't see him at all. I must have gone for a pack of cigarettes when he pulled up. But I remember the green van and the woman who was sitting on the passenger side while it was parked there. She was hot. A total babe."

"Can you describe her?" Sergio asked.

"Yeah, she was a few years older than me. She was wearing a bright green coat. Kind of matched the color of the van."

"What else?"

"She had red hair. I'm talking bright red. I smiled at her and she smiled back, which totally got me excited, because you know what they say about girls with red hair."

"What do they say?" Sergio asked.

"Freaky in bed."

Hayley suddenly had an image of the young woman.

She knew who it was.

"Did she show her dimples when she smiled?"

"Oh, yeah. She had the cutest dimples. And a nice rack too. Just thinking about her now makes me want to—"

Sergio stuffed the *Aquaman* comic in Connor's mouth. "I don't want to hear it."

Early twenties.

Bright red hair.

Dimples.

Green parka.

It had to be the same woman Hayley saw at the warehouse when she first hired Garth for the *Island Times* Christmas party.

Connie Sparks.

And she was lying about why she was there that day.

She wasn't a potential client for Garth.

She was his mistress.

Chapter 18

"Would you be interested in purchasing a set of our snowcapped, cone-shaped pines for your Christmas village, Mrs. Powell?" Connie Sparks asked, desperately trying to change the subject.

Hayley had only moments before asked Connie if she would confirm that she was having an affair with the late Garth Rawlings.

Connie's face turned red with embarrassment and her skin matched most of the decor in Mrs. Claus's Christmas Village Shop, where she worked as a seasonal employee during the holidays.

Hayley knew the owner of the shop, Cindy Callahan, a former Delta Airlines flight attendant who retired to Bar Harbor and bought the Starfish Diner. Cindy's impressive business know-how had turned the failing coffee shop around, and it was now a must stop for the locals, who flocked to the diner for a plate of the famous blueberry pancakes and a cup of fresh coffee. Not one just to sit around and savor her success, Cindy rented some space next door and opened a holiday shop that specialized in Christmas decorations. Cindy loved Christmas villages and so she made sure to stock the place with sets that included such village staples as Santa's workshop, the Holiday Bed-and-Breakfast, churches, bridges, and a bakery. There was also a handcrafted limited-edition electric train for sale, which circled around the store over a bridge and through a tunnel and back around again.

"Did you hear what I said, Connie?" Hayley asked, folding her arms.

Connie nodded and then reached down and picked up a porcelain figurine. "We have Rudolph for sale. And if you buy all of the other reindeer, we can give you a ten percent discount."

"Connie—"

"Please, Mrs. Powell, don't ask me that again!"

There was a brief silence, interrupted only by the train whistling as it passed by them.

"If you don't talk to me, you're going to have to talk to Chief Alvares."

"What?" Connie gasped. Her hands were shaking so badly that she dropped the poor Rudolph figurine and it smashed into pieces on the floor.

"I asked him to let me come speak with you first because I know how traumatic it might be for you if Chief Alvares hauled you into the police station for questioning. Someone could spot you in the back of the squad car or see you being led into the station, and then you would have to endure all that speculation as to why you were arrested."

"*Arrested?* I'm going to be arrested?"

"Oh, no, of course not. But you know how gossip flies around in this town."

"I know what I did wasn't right, but I didn't break the law," Connie said, nervously twisting her bright red curly hair around her finger.

"So you admit you were having an affair with Garth Rawlings?"

Another long silence.

And then more whistling as the train passed by again.

Connie finally nodded.

"And he had a key to the warehouse made for you so you two could rendezvous there. You just pretended to be a catering client so as not to arouse suspicion."

Connie nodded again.

She pulled a wadded-up tissue out of the side pocket of the Christmas wreath holiday sweater she was wearing and wiped away the tears streaming down her cheeks before blowing her nose with a loud honk.

"He didn't want anyone finding out about us. He was worried about his image because he was trying to market himself as the 'Family Man Chef.' He had the whole thing planned out—TV show, cookbooks, a kitchenware line with Macy's. It would be inconvenient if people found out he was cheating on his wife and sleeping with a girl half his age."

"That must have been very difficult for you."

Connie shook her head and wiped her nose. "I didn't mind. I loved him. I know he had a temper and could rub people the wrong way, but he was very kind to me and made me feel special."

"Did you see him on the night he died?"

"No. He told me he had too much to do preparing for his weekend parties and opening up the warehouse to the public for Midnight Madness. I knew he had hired you to help him, so I made sure to steer clear."

"So you were nowhere near the warehouse that night? You never used your key to let yourself inside at any point?"

"No. I was at home with my roommate. She'll vouch for me. We decorated our little tree and then made sugar cookies and watched some old cheesy Christmas movie rerun on Hallmark or Lifetime with Tori Spelling."

"Did you lend anyone your key?"

"No. I had it on me the whole time."

Hayley's cell phone chirped.

She checked the caller ID.

It was Sergio.

"Excuse me, Connie, I need to take this."

Hayley walked a few feet away, trying to get out of Connie's earshot.

She answered the call and talked in a hushed tone. "Hey, Sergio. I'm with Connie Sparks now.

She says she was home with her roommate the night of Garth's murder. So, if you want me to follow up and talk to the roommate—"

"You don't have to. She's telling you the truth."

"How do you know?"

"I'm at the Grand Hotel, which has security cameras set up outside. The warehouse is directly across the street, so the cameras pick up everyone coming and going. I just finished looking at all of the footage. Connie Sparks was never there that night."

"What about Lex's crew next door? Did they ever come outside for any reason?"

"No. They were inside their own office the whole time and never had any interaction with Garth."

"So they're telling the truth too. They were playing music and drinking and didn't hear a thing."

"The only two people the camera picks up outside the warehouse is Garth letting himself in, around eleven in the morning, and then you showing up around seven that evening when Garth Rawlings was already dead. No one else ever entered or exited Garth's kitchen space the whole day."

"Then who could have killed him? The Ghost of Christmas Past?"

"Who's that? Do you have any contact information for that person?"

How do you say in Portuguese that it's A Christmas Carol *reference?*

"Never mind. I'll see you later for dinner."

Hayley ended the call and turned back to Connie, who was pretending not to listen while she rearranged some figurines of children skating on an ice rink in the village set up as a window display.

"You're in the clear, Connie. The chief is not going to need to question you."

"Thank you, Hayley."

Hayley smiled at her. "Merry Christmas."

She was halfway to the door when Connie spoke up. "I could never do anything to hurt Garth. He seemed so strong on the outside, but inside he was very sensitive."

Hayley found that hard to believe, but why argue? "I'm sure he was."

"I loved him. I wanted to protect him. He had been hurt enough already."

That stopped Hayley.

She spun around.

"What do you mean by that? Who hurt him?"

"That awful wife of his," Connie spat out.

"Tiffany?"

"Yes. That coldhearted bitch broke his heart. Garth and I were just friends at first, but then he confided in me what he was going through, and I helped him through the pain of his wife's betrayal. It was only later that we developed romantic feelings for each other—when Garth knew his marriage was basically over."

"You're telling me Tiffany cheated on him *first*?"

Connie's eyes narrowed as she vigorously nodded her head.

"With whom? Can you tell me a name?"

"No. Garth never mentioned a name."

Hayley sighed. "Okay."

"Just that they were former business partners."

Business partners? Ken Massey.

The grieving widow was sleeping with the ex-business partner with a grudge.

The whole case was starting to come into focus in a big way.

But the million-dollar question remained.

If Ken and Tiffany did conspire to kill Garth for his budding cooking empire, how on earth did they do it?

Island Food & Spirits
by
Hayley Powell

I have this habit of marking every
occasion by what entrees and goodies
were consumed. Last year's Fourth of
July party in my brother Randy's backyard? A German potato salad recipe
from Mona's aunt. September's Labor
Day potluck fund-raiser for the
church? A creamy spinach dip from
Reverend Staples's wife, Edie. Mona's
annual holiday party in early December? Chocolate rum balls. I swear,
George Clooney could crash Mona's
party and all I would remember were
the nine chocolate rum balls I ate that
were brought by Mona's cousin
Tammy down visiting from Pittsfield.

Last year's holiday party I made my
delectable onion Brie palmiers. Actually, last year I remember more than

just what food I brought—no matter how hard I have tried to forget. You see, Liddy had returned recently from a trip to China. Actually, to clarify, Liddy had recently returned from a trip to Chinatown in New York, but she thought telling everybody she had been to China sounded far more exotic and glamorous. She brought with her a box of large Chinese lanterns. Her plan was to light all of the small discs inside, which would heat and inflate the lanterns; then we could watch in awe as they lit up and floated up into the night sky. It was Liddy's attempt to give Mona's soiree an international flavor.

Not to be outdone by that show-off Liddy, Mona trekked to the new fireworks store in Bangor and purchased a load of firecrackers to add her own special touch to what was fast becoming a Chinese-themed holiday party. Fireworks were finally legal in Maine, but, unfortunately, the Bar Harbor City Council had recently voted not to allow them to be lit off in the town. Mona was either unaware of this new law or chose to ignore it. She arrived home with a box full of them.

Well, the party was in full swing. The Christmas punch was flowing freely as the adults laughed and competed to tell the best stories (the same ones they told every year). The food table looked like a war zone as the kids fought for every last scrap. It was safe to say a good time was being had by all!

It was a beautiful, cold, cloudless night, with the stars shining bright, and Liddy ordered us to venture outside to light up our large globelike Chinese lanterns. After a few false starts with a faulty lighter, we finally got them glowing. They slowly floated up into the sky, which was followed by lots of "oohing and aahing" from both the children and the adults. Well, Mona decided the time was right to follow this up with her fireworks. She and her husband grabbed fistfuls from the box and started setting them off up into the night sky. The kids howled with delight at the loud booms and flashes of light. It was just like Disney World!

That's right about the time all hell broke loose. As I've mentioned on many occasions, almost everyone who lives in Bar Harbor has a police scanner. And when residents began spotting these giant glowing orbs in the sky, a few people—okay, to be more accurate, hundreds of people—immediately assumed our quaint little town was under attack by aliens. To make matters worse, everybody thought the booming noises from the fire-crackers were the aliens destroying the island. It was a full-on invasion! People feared that the Town Hall had been blown up like the White House in that movie *Independence Day*! Except Will Smith was not here to save us by infecting the aliens' ship with a simple computer virus, which was always hard to swallow, if you ask me.

My brother, Randy, and his partner, Sergio, who is the chief of police, had to leave the party because the dispatcher at the station was overwhelmed by the huge volume of 911 emergency calls. We continued on with our merriment, blissfully unaware of what was hap-pening.

Another thing about our little town: Whenever anything slightly dramatic happens, half the town jumps in their cars and races to the scene. Well, it didn't take long for them to pinpoint the center of the alien invasion, and soon Eagle Lake Road, where Mona's house was situated, was clogged with traffic as people drove slowly past the house, hanging out the windows, craning their necks to get a good look at the alien ships hovering above and apparently firing upon Acadia National Park.

Mona's guests still did not have a clear picture of the drama unfolding outside until we heard the sound of the sirens approaching. Mona, Liddy, and I exchanged nervous glances, hoping the squad cars would pass right by the house. By the grace of God, we got our Christmas miracle. The cruisers zipped past us and the sirens faded into the night. But our elation was cut short when Sergio returned and informed us of the commotion our Chinese lanterns and fireworks had caused. Mona hid in the bathroom, fearing an arrest was imminent, but Sergio just shook his head and suggested we just call it a night. (Insert a big sigh of relief.)

It was hard keeping quiet about

how we had nearly caused a riot, especially when the front-page story in the paper two days later reported possible UFO sightings and strange lights and sounds above Acadia National Park. People talked about it for months before the hoopla finally died down around Memorial Day. So now I'm fessing up to my role in the Bar Harbor UFO story that blew up one Christmas Eve, not so long ago.

I remember that night as if it were yesterday. And, of course, I remember what dishes I made, which I will share with you here. But first let's get the holiday party started with a Christmas punch that will knock your reindeer socks off!

Christmas Eve Punch

<u>Ingredients</u>

2 cups water

¾ cup sugar

½ teaspoon ground cinnamon

4 cups chilled cranberry/apple juice

1 46-ounce can chilled pineapple juice

1 liter chilled ginger ale

In a large saucepan bring your water, sugar, and cinnamon to a boil, stirring to dissolve the sugar. Chill. Before you serve, add the sugar water mixture, chilled juices, and ginger ale to a large punch bowl. Serve in party glasses over ice.

Hayley's Onion Brie Palmier

Ingredients

2 medium onions, thinly sliced
3 tablespoons butter
2 tablespoons brown sugar
½ teaspoon white wine vinegar
1 sheet puff pastry, room temperature
4 ounces of your favorite Brie cheese, softened (remove rind)
2 teaspoons caraway seeds
1 egg
2 teaspoons water

In a large skillet cook your onions in the butter, brown sugar, and vinegar over medium low heat until the onions are golden brown, stirring frequently. Remove the onions with a slotted spoon; cool to room temperature.

On a lightly floured surface, roll your puff pastry into an 11-inch x 8-inch rectangle. Spread the softened Brie cheese over the pastry. Cover the cheese with the onions; sprinkle with the caraway seeds.

Roll up one long side to the middle, and the other side to the middle, so you have two rolls. Using a serrated knife, cut the rolls into ½-inch slices. Place them on a parchment-paper-lined baking sheet and flatten to about a ¼-inch thickness. Put in the refrigerator for about 15 minutes.

Preheat your oven to 375 degrees. In a small bowl beat an egg and some water; remove your onion Brie palmiers from the refrigerator and brush the egg mixture over the tops. Bake for 12 to 14 minutes until puffed and golden brown. Serve warm and enjoy!

Chapter 19

As she slurped her energy drink behind the reception desk at the Bar Harbor Gym, Kiki Richards stared at Hayley. "I'm sorry, Hayley. I must not have heard you correctly. What did you say?"

"I'm serious, Kiki. I'm here to work out."

Kiki abruptly giggled, spitting up a little of the fizzy concoction she was guzzling. She set the can down and typed a few keys on her computer. "I'm sorry. It's just that you haven't been here in so long. When was the last time you were here?"

"I don't remember," Hayley said quietly.

"I think it was last January. Am I right? You always come in right after New Year's because you weigh yourself on the first and can't believe how many pounds you packed on during the holidays. Then you sign up for a few boot camp classes, show up to the first one, and then we don't see you again until after the following new year."

"Well, I must say I'm impressed with how familiar you are with my behavior patterns, Kiki. Now, if you don't mind buzzing me in, I'd like to do some time on the treadmill."

"I can't. Your membership has expired."

"When?"

"Last June. We sent you a letter and left a message on your home voice mail, but you never got back to us."

"It's been a very busy year," Hayley said. "I'm just now catching up with my to-do list. Number eight, get in shape. So here I am, ready to renew my membership."

"Why are you really here, Hayley? There has to be some other reason besides wanting to work out."

It wasn't that the toned, blond, annoyingly pretty Kiki was a smart, intuitive person. In fact, she only got through high school because some of her male teachers were more understanding than her less forgiving female teachers. But Kiki didn't have to be a brain trust to know Hayley had ulterior motives showing up at the gym today. Everyone in town knew she hated working out. A short run with Leroy on the park trails a few times a year basically summed up her workout routine.

"Okay, fine, Kiki. I was hoping to find Tiffany Rawlings here."

"She showed up about twenty minutes ago. Today is her cross-training day," Kiki said, nodding, her blond ponytail bouncing from side to side.

After leaving Connie Sparks, Hayley had called the office to see if Sal was back from Augusta. She didn't want him noticing she had been gone most of the day. Bruce informed her that Sal would not be coming back to the office and was heading straight home because he had the sniffles. Hayley seized upon that opportunity to drive back over to Tiffany's house to prod her gently about the rumored affair with Ken Massey. The house was locked up tight and Tiffany's car was gone, so Hayley pulled out her phone and checked Tiffany's Facebook page. She had checked in at the local gym. Hayley loved Facebook. In the past a detective would have to tail a subject day and night to keep tabs on him or her. Now, thanks to Facebook, most of the time the subject of your surveillance did all of the work for you.

"Okay, how much to renew my membership?" Hayley asked, pulling her wallet out of her bag.

"Why not make this easier on yourself and just purchase a day pass? It's only ten dollars. That way you won't feel the pressure of coming back again because you bought a full year membership."

It disturbed Hayley how well Kiki knew her. She opened her wallet and pulled out a ten-dollar bill and slapped it down on the reception desk.

Kiki smiled and slid the bill in a drawer and pressed a button to buzz Hayley through the glass door separating the lobby from the gym area.

After changing in the women's locker room into some black spandex pants and a pink top, which seemed to take a perverse joy in highlighting her love handles, Hayley wandered around the gym, hoping to spot Tiffany.

"Sweet mother of Christ! What are you doing here?"

It was Mona.

She was dressed in faded-gray sweats and Reeboks, huffing and puffing on a StairMaster, her face red and splotchy from the exertion.

"Me? What are *you* doing here?"

"Losing my baby weight."

"Mona, you popped out your last kid almost two years ago."

"You know me. I don't like to rush things," Mona said, gasping. She was almost out of breath; her arms and legs were moving in tandem with the machine. "This is like a friggin' torture wheel! Wanna bag this place and go get a drink at Randy's place?"

"In a few minutes. I need to find Tiffany Rawlings. Have you seen her?"

"Yeah, over there on one of the spinning bikes," Mona panted.

Hayley glanced over to see Tiffany, who wore a tight green top that accentuated her curvaceous figure and very short yellow shorts. Her bum was in the air, and she was cycling as fast as she could. Sweat poured down her face, and she had a look of fierce determination in her eye that just made Hayley feel tired.

Mona hit a button on the StairMaster console and climbed down. "I'm done."

Hayley looked at the digital timer on the machine. "Six minutes. Not bad."

"I'm up two. Yesterday I stopped at four. I don't know why I'm even trying to lose this baby weight. Both you and I know I'm just going to get knocked up again anyway. It's the only thing my husband's good at. I'm going to hit the showers. I'll meet you in the lobby in twenty minutes."

Mona plodded away toward the women's locker room, and Hayley veered off in the opposite direction toward Tiffany, when suddenly she felt a hand cupping her butt. She spun around to see the handsome curly-haired blond paramedic Rusty Wyatt in a ratty, ripped white tank top, which fell over his muscular, smooth chest.

If only Hayley were ten years younger.

Hell, she'd still be too old for him.

"I sent Santa my wish list and here you are," Rusty said, trying hard to be cool and relaxed.

"Nice to see you again, Rusty," Hayley said, uncomfortable with him ogling her breasts.

"You looking for a partner?" Rusty asked, grinning from ear to ear.

"I've been seeing someone, Rusty. Someone age appropriate."

"I mean a workout partner. I was going to find you one. I'm here with my workout buddy, Ken," Rusty said, gesturing across the gym to Ken Massey. He was only a few feet away from Tiffany, who was now cooling down on her cycle. Ken huffed and puffed as he lifted some very heavy-looking weights.

They were both clearly going out of their way pretending not to notice the other so people wouldn't get the wrong idea.

"So you and Ken work out here together all the time?" Hayley asked, removing Rusty's hand from her butt.

"Every day. Right up until closing."

"Unless you're on call and someone needs an ambulance, and then you're on duty. Like the day Garth Rawlings died."

"Yup. We were doing reps over there when I got the call and had to take off early. But I made up for it the next day with some extra crunches. It takes a lot of hours to get a body like this, Hayley," Rusty said, flexing his pecs, which were so heavy with muscle you could almost feel them slamming against his body as he bounced them. "Sometimes I ask myself, I say, 'Rusty, what are you doing all this for? Your health?' Maybe. But then I think, 'I'm young. I've got years of good health ahead of me. No, Rusty. You're staying in tip-top shape for that one special woman who is going to swoop in and change your life. Really rock your world. You probably haven't even met her yet.' Or maybe I have."

His hand found Hayley's butt again.

Hayley brushed it away again. "Well, I'll be sure to keep my eye out for her."

She left Rusty flexing his pecs and turned toward Tiffany, who was off the cycle now and toweling the sweat off her face.

Kiki passed in front of Hayley with an armful of freshly laundered towels.

Hayley stopped her. "Kiki, are you here every week night until closing?"

"Two to eight, five days a week."

"And you see Ken Massey and Rusty Wyatt working out together every day?"

"Like clockwork. Those two are obsessive, which is why they're both so incredibly hot," Kiki said, practically drooling. "I tell the bosses we should photograph them for an ad promoting the gym."

"So you were here working on the night Garth Rawlings was found dead in his warehouse kitchen and they were both here the entire time?"

"Yes. Like I said, every night. Oh, wait a minute. Didn't they find him on the day of Midnight Madness?"

"That's right. The coroner said he died sometime between five and seven in the evening. Why?"

"Well, we closed early that day because the owners needed to set up. They decided to give out free energy drinks and protein shakes and pamphlets to the gym to any locals who dropped by during the business crawl."

"How early did you close?"

"Five o'clock. We had to shoo everybody out, and, believe me, they were not happy about it."

"So Ken and Rusty both left the gym at five o'clock?"

"Actually, I don't remember seeing Ken. Or Rusty, come to think of it. Neither of them worked out that day, which I found odd, because they're *always* here."

Ken Massey was lying. He wasn't working out at the gym during the time of the murder. And Ken's airtight alibi, Rusty Wyatt, was lying too.

But why?

Ken Massey certainly had a motive to kill Garth. But what did Rusty Wyatt have against the victim?

And just because they were both lying about their whereabouts still didn't answer the question as to how they got inside a locked warehouse and fatally beat a man to death.

But given their muscles, they were certainly capable of it.

Kiki sauntered off with her towels as Hayley turned around, suddenly finding herself face-to-face with Ken Massey. He had been standing only a few feet behind her during her conversation with Kiki and must have overheard everything.

His tight blue t-shirt was drenched with sweat stains and his gray shorts were borderline obscene as they showed off his manly bulge.

"You need a spotter while you lift weights, Hayley?"

"No, thanks, Ken," Hayley said, trying to pass him.

He reached out and grabbed her wrist, squeezing it hard. "I think I could seriously help you stay healthy. We can start by dropping this whole Garth Rawlings business."

"Let go of me," Hayley said through gritted teeth.

Ken gripped her wrist tighter. "I had nothing to do with it."

"Then why did you lie about being here? Where were you? With your girlfriend?"

Hayley pointed to Tiffany, who could no longer pretend to be ignoring Ken. She was staring at the two of them, mouth agape, clearly rattled by their tense conversation.

"How d-did you . . . ," Ken stammered, the blood draining from his face.

He instantly let go of Hayley.

She rubbed her wrist and marched off to the women's locker room.

Hayley had barely made it to her locker and was just starting to spin the padlock to the right combination numbers, when someone came up fast behind her and yanked her back by the hair. Hayley tumbled over the long wooden bench dividing the rows of lockers and nearly cracked her head on the hard tile-floor surface.

Tiffany Rawlings hovered over her, hands on hips, eyes blazing.

"I think it's time you stopped spreading false rumors about me," Tiffany sneered. "Or we're going to have a major problem."

"I have no interest in rumors," Hayley said,

using the bench to lift herself back up. "I only care about the facts. And we both know the facts now, don't we, Tiffany?"

Tiffany stepped forward. She was lean but strong, and almost a foot taller than Hayley. She pressed a finger hard against Hayley's chest. "Stop snooping into my private affairs, precious. Because I can get mean if I have to."

"It's amazing how fast you've gone from tearful, fragile widow to tough-talking ballbuster," Hayley said, her defiance pissing off Tiffany even more.

Tiffany lashed out, grabbing Hayley by the throat, choking her.

Hayley gasped and clawed at Tiffany's hands, unable to break her iron grip.

"You have no idea what you're talking about!" Tiffany growled.

Hayley couldn't breathe.

Tiffany's clutch was crushing her windpipe.

There was no one around to help her.

But then the running water in the shower stopped and Mona emerged in a white towel, shaking water out of her hair. She stopped suddenly at the sight of her drinking buddy being strangled by some statuesque she-beast.

"What the hell is going on here?"

Hayley couldn't speak because the she-beast had her by the throat.

Tiffany glanced over at Mona, unconcerned. "It's none of your business!"

Mona adjusted her towel and strutted over to Tiffany. "This *is* my business because that's my best friend and you seem to be choking her. Why don't you pick on somebody your own size?"

Tiffany may have been tough, but good ole Mona was a Mack truck. She grabbed Tiffany's hand that was holding Hayley and stepped between them and then twisted it around until Tiffany finally let go of Hayley, who sank to the floor, gasping for air.

Tiffany assumed it was over and turned to leave, but Mona wasn't finished.

There was a little something called defending her friend's honor.

Mona spun Tiffany back around, gave her a hard shove, and sent her reeling to the floor.

Tiffany raised herself up again, brushed herself off, and then glared at Mona before charging toward her, swinging at her with a roundhouse punch. Mona anticipated the move and ducked in time for it to miss her jaw with a *whoosh*.

Hayley watched from the floor in awe as Mona then seized Tiffany's right arm and yanked it behind her, wrenching it up high enough for Tiffany to yelp in pain.

Mona forcefully led her into the shower room.

Hayley heard the water gushing and Tiffany screaming.

She could only imagine Mona holding her

opponent's head under the freezing water so she would literally cool off.

God love Mona.

If she could stop getting pregnant, she would definitely have a future with the Gorgeous Ladies of Wrestling!

Chapter 20

"It is crazy to me that I am supposed to investigate these suspects when I still have no idea how the murder was committed," Sergio said, shoveling a spoonful of mashed potatoes out of a ceramic yellow bowl and slapping it down on the plate in front of him. "Just crazy."

"Well, as long as Sabrina has classified Garth's death a homicide, then you really don't have a choice," Hayley said, snatching the bowl away from him and handing it to Dustin, sitting next to her, who started loading his plate.

"How did I get it so wrong?"

"That's the million-dollar question. You examined the crime scene thoroughly. There were no signs of a struggle, and yet the evidence Sabrina wrote in her report proves otherwise," Hayley said, jabbing a few carrots with her fork and eating them.

Randy sighed and picked up a bread basket. "Another roll, Gemma?"

"No, thanks, Uncle Randy. I am on a strict diet. The Virgin Mary was poor and in need of shelter, so I can't eat carbs until after the Nativity pageant."

Randy had invited Hayley and the kids over to dinner that evening at their sprawling, rickety, two-story, old New England house, near the town's shore path, which sported an impressive ocean view.

"How did the killer even get inside the warehouse? I searched that place high and low, and there are no windows or secret entrances. The only way inside Garth's kitchen was through the front door, which was locked. It just does not make any sense." Sergio sighed, then gulped down a glass of wine before pouring himself another.

Randy suddenly slammed down his fork. "Okay. That's enough. No more shop talk. I went to a lot of trouble making this meal and I don't want it ruined by all this chatter of murder and mayhem. So . . . let's focus on something else. Dustin, how was school today?"

"Nothing special," Dustin said, pouring gravy on his potatoes from a ceramic boat that matched the yellow bowl of potatoes.

"Okay, well, what did you do after school?" Randy asked, trying to coax a conversation out of him and failing miserably.

"Cleaned my room," Dustin said, mixing the gravy with the potatoes and then taking a small bite. "Mom said if I didn't, she was going to cancel Christmas and take all of the cool gifts she bought me back to the store."

"You told him that?" Randy asked, turning to Hayley, an incredulous look on his face.

"It's called 'tough love,'" Hayley said. "And it worked, didn't it?"

"These potatoes need salt," Dustin said, crinkling his nose.

"I'm sorry I'm not the gourmet chef your mother is," Randy huffed, nearly hurling the salt-shaker at Dustin. "What about you, Gemma?"

"Reverend Staples cast the role of Joseph today and he is a total stud! I snuck a photo of him at rehearsal today and posted it on Instagram. All of my friends are totally jealous. Want to see?" Gemma said, pulling out her phone.

"Yes!" Randy exclaimed, a bit too enthusiastically before catching himself. "I mean, if you really want me to."

Gemma handed him the phone.

"Nice-looking boy, but you can barely make him out. It's so dark."

"The tech guys were doing a lighting check and it was between cues. Trust me, he's, like, nineteen or twenty and hot. I knew you'd like him, because I got my taste in men from you, Uncle Randy. I invited him over to the house to run lines before our dress rehearsal."

Hayley swiped the phone from Randy and studied the photo. "Let me see this older boy you invited over to the house without telling me."

"I just did, Mom."

The boy was in the shadows and it was hard to see him, but Hayley could tell he was definitely a looker. There was also something strangely familiar about him, like she had seen him somewhere before.

Sergio clapped his hands together, startling everyone. "Hayley, would you mind helping me clear the plates and serve dessert?"

Randy set his napkin down on the table and started to stand up. "No, that's all right. I can do it."

Sergio placed a firm hand on his shoulder and pushed him back down. "No, babe. You went to the trouble of making this delicious meal. Let Hayley and me clean up."

Hayley waited for Dustin to scoop up the last of his third helping of mashed potatoes and shove it in his mouth before stacking the kids' plates on top of her own and following Sergio out of the dining room.

"I'm not stupid! I know this is a ploy so you two can discuss the case in the kitchen," Randy yelled.

Once they were in the kitchen, Sergio opened the fridge and pulled out a pecan pie and a bowl of freshly made whipped cream, with Saran wrap covering it. Hayley placed the dirty dishes in the sink and reached into the cupboard for some dessert plates.

"So you think Ken Massey and Garth's wife, Tiffany, were secretly seeing each other behind Garth's back and plotted to get rid of him?" Sergio asked as he cut the pie into slices with a knife.

"Yes. They both got very nervous, not to mention physically abusive, when they suspected I was onto them. Garth's catering business was far more successful this year than it was when Ken walked away from it. It was probably killing him that Garth was thriving without his business acumen. Not only did he want to get his hands on Garth's business, he also wanted to get them up Tiffany's skirt. But if Garth found out Tiffany was two-timing him with an old enemy, there would be hell to pay. So maybe Ken got rid of him so he could wind up with both Garth's business *and* his wife? They could wait a few months for all of the hoopla over poor Garth's death to die down, and then, very slowly, they could roll out the next phase. Be spotted having dinner together. Just old friends bonding over their shared loss. Then a few more very public dinners. Maybe show up together at a couple of town events. Six months down the road the town gossips start speculating. No one is surprised. It's natural that their mutual mourning would lead to romantic feelings. How can those poor soul mates be expected to fight their intense attraction? The town will be rooting for them. And they will have gotten away with murder."

"Boy, you really thought this out, didn't you?"

"I read a lot of trashy novels."

"It sounds like a popular theory."

"No, I just thought of it. Nobody else knows about it," Hayley said, and then realized what he meant. "Oh, you mean *plausible*. It sounds like a *plausible* theory."

"Yes, Hayley. That's what I said."

No, he didn't.

But why argue?

"But we are going to need hard evidence if we ever hope to make an arrest, especially since we are still stumped as to how they did it."

Hayley was certain of one thing.

After getting manhandled by Ken and nearly choked by Tiffany, she was more determined than ever to bring this small-town Bonnie and Clyde to justice.

Chapter 21

When Hayley and the kids got home from dinner at Randy and Sergio's, Hayley quickly checked to make sure they did their homework and rushed them off to their rooms. She then cleaned up the kitchen, inspected the dog and kitty bowls to make sure there was enough dry food to satisfy them until the morning, and dragged herself upstairs to her bedroom, where she disrobed, pulled on some sweats and a t-shirt, and climbed on top of her comforter, cradling her laptop to begin making a few notes on her next column, which was due by the following midday.

Leroy padded into the room. After a few attempts to jump up on a bed that was way too high for him to reach, Hayley leaned over the side and scooped him up, his tail wagging excitedly. He settled down next to her and closed his eyes. Blueberry sauntered into the room only a few seconds later. His own tail was swishing, but not out of excitement. It was more out of contempt. He obviously didn't want to be alone downstairs, but he certainly was not going to give Hayley or Leroy the satisfaction of knowing he wanted to be in their company. He plopped down on a woven area rug by the foot of the bed and licked himself clean.

Hayley was trying to come up with the perfect holiday recipe when her phone rang. She hoped that it might be Aaron calling to wish her a good night and say he missed her.

No such luck.

It was Liddy.

Hayley pressed the talk button. "Hey, how was the party?"

"I rocked it!" Liddy gushed, shouting so loud that Hayley had to pull the phone away from her ear. "When I swept into the Northeast Harbor Club on Sonny's arm, wearing my Dolce and Gabbana sleeveless full-skirt lace combo in bright red for the holidays, jaws dropped! It was everything the woman at Bergdorf Goodman said it would be!"

Liddy had just returned from one of her famous shopping trips in New York City the weekend before.

"I'm sure you looked smashing!" Hayley said,

a little envious that Liddy had such a sizable clothing budget due to her real estate successes. Hayley's biggest wardrobe splurge this month was a discounted Liz Claiborne faux-wrap sweater dress at JCPenney and she found a tear in the fabric after she wore it just once.

"I know some of the small-minded people in this town have been judging my relationship with Sonny because I'm a few years older than he is!" Liddy screamed.

Sonny was twelve years younger than Liddy.

"So it was my mission to look fabulous and just blow people's minds and put to rest this ridiculous obsession they have with our age difference!"

"Liddy, why are you yelling?"

"Sorry! I am in bed with Sonny and he's snoring so loud right now I can't hear myself think!"

Oh, dear God.

"Hold on, Hayley! I'm going to try to get him to stop!"

She heard a loud honking sound and heavy breathing on the other end of the phone. It cut off for a few seconds and was followed by short, loud gasps. Suddenly she heard Liddy howl, as if in pain.

"Liddy! Liddy! Are you there? What's wrong?"

"Damn it! I pinched his nose closed to get him to stop snoring and he took a swing at me in his sleep! His hand hit the side of my nose! My cute pert nose is one of my best features!"

"Can we please resume this conversation in the morning? I really don't want to picture you in bed with Sonny."

"No! I didn't just call you to let you know how jealous those spiteful, judgmental bitches at the party were of me tonight, I have actual, useful information."

"About what?"

"What?" Liddy screeched.

"I said, 'About what'!"

"Sonny! Sonny! Wake up! I can't hear what Hayley's saying! Sonny!"

She was obviously trying to shake him awake, but to no avail.

The snoring and wheezing and heavy breathing were deafening.

"This is what happens when he drinks too much! I had to drive home because he spent too much time at the punch bowl bragging to his golfing buddies about all of the big cases he's working on."

Sonny was a fresh-faced young attorney in town who recently set up his own practice right out of law school. He had been successfully poaching some high-profile clients from the shingle of Ted Rivers, Bar Harbor's longtime premier lawyer.

"Liddy, I have to work tomorrow! I can't be up all night! What kind of information do you have for me?"

"It's about the Garth Rawlings murder!"

Hayley sat up in bed with a start. Her laptop fell off to one side, smacking into an irked Leroy, who had to adjust his sleeping position.

"What, Liddy? What did you find out?"

"Well, you know how Sonny is—young and idealistic. He's always going on and on about his professional ethics until I want to put a gun to my head. He takes all that attorney-client-privilege crap way too seriously."

"That kind of goes with the territory."

"*Please!* I'm his girlfriend. He should be able to tell me anything. Anyway, I heard a couple of gossipy hens by the dessert table talking about Garth Rawlings and how rumor was he was planning to divorce his wife because she was cheating on him."

So word was getting out.

"I already know that, Liddy. She's been sleeping with Ken Massey."

"Okay, fine! Way to steal my thunder! But did you know there was an ironclad prenup?"

"*What?*"

"Well, I guess you haven't uncovered every clue, now have you?"

"How did those women know about the prenup?"

"They didn't!" Liddy screamed over Sonny's earsplitting snores. "Just a minute, Hayley! I'm going into the bathroom."

After a few seconds of sighing and shuffling and a door slamming, Liddy was back on the line.

"After I heard them talking, I got to thinking. With all of Garth's business holdings, if he was going to file for divorce, then he would most certainly have to hire a crackerjack lawyer. Garth would never go to Ted Rivers because Ted hated him."

"He did?"

"Yes. Don't you remember? Ted's wife, Sissy, hired Garth to cater a cocktail party at their house last year and Garth had put peanut oil into one of his dipping sauces. Ted has a peanut allergy and blew up like a blowfish and was hospitalized for two days."

"I don't know how I missed that one."

"Anyway, there is only one other lawyer in town with the killer reputation of a barracuda, and that's my Sonny."

"This is all starting to come together now. We both know how loose-lipped Sonny can get when he's been drinking."

"That's right. I made sure his plastic cup was full of spiked punch all night long. Then, when the party was winding down, I confiscated his car keys and got him singing like a bird all the way home. According to the prenup, Tiffany was going to get nothing if they divorced due to infidelity. Just a small monthly stipend for living expenses. All of the stocks, bonds, and the entire business would remain his."

"Let me guess. But if Garth died when they were still married, she would get it all."

"Every penny. But there's one thing that doesn't make sense. Garth was the face of the catering business. He was the one with the talent. Tiffany may be a smart, conniving black widow, but can she even boil water?"

"She wouldn't have to. The public would be rooting for her. Picking up the pieces after the devastating loss of her husband, trying to carry on. She would have access to all of his secret recipes. She could hire a couple of culinary-school grads to re-create Garth's most sought-after dishes. After a few successful parties and events, she could then confess she has no head for numbers and decide to bring in her husband's former partner to help run the business side of things. Publicly beg him. 'Do it for Garth,' she would say. Ken would then ride in like a knight in shining armor to the rescue. It's the perfect arrangement. Together they can take the business to the next level as a tribute to Tiffany's beloved late husband. Before you know it, she's Maine's answer to Rachael Ray, paving the way for cookbooks, a kitchenware line, maybe a cable-TV show. Everything Garth dreamed of for himself."

"And no one would have any idea they had planned the whole thing from the beginning," Liddy said. "That's cold."

"Having seen the nasty side of both Ken and Tiffany, it's very easy for me to believe."

Yes. It was a solid theory.

But the nagging question still remained.

How? How did they do it?

Chapter 22

Hayley spent the following day catching up on her office workload, avoiding Bruce who still found it impossible to be in the same room with her, and coddling Sal, who managed to blow up a minor case of the sniffles into a full-on flu attack. The only bright spot in her day was a text from Aaron asking her to join him that evening for the Christmas tree lighting ceremony in the village green.

She rushed home after work to change into a nice red cashmere sweater her mother had given her last Christmas and some dark slacks she had bought with the Macy's gift card that the kids bought her for Mother's Day. There wasn't much she could do with her frizzy hair, because it would take too long to heat up her curling iron, so she tied as much of it back in a ponytail as she could and put on a sporty gray Stetson cashmere beanie hat, which Liddy had received from her mother last Christmas. Liddy wore it once and decided she hated it, so she regifted it to Hayley for her birthday. Thank God for holidays and birthdays—otherwise, Hayley would be going out naked.

Hayley desperately wanted to put her best foot forward with Aaron. Really make an effort. Because she hadn't been the most available girlfriend lately, and she wanted to make sure he knew that she was still committed to the relationship.

She left the house in plenty of time to walk to the village green and meet Aaron at the appointed time of six o'clock, and she even arrived a few minutes early. The town band, made up of ten local musicians, played Christmas carols in the village green gazebo. Children ran around, chasing each other and making angels in the snow that had fallen the night before. A large crowd was gathering around the massive ten-foot-thick pine tree beautifully decorated by local volunteers with handmade ornaments.

Hayley checked her watch: 6:03 P.M.

"Hey, cut me some slack for being a few minutes late," Aaron said. "I had to deal with a sick schnauzer who ate an entire chocolate Santa. It's an epidemic this time of year."

Hayley looked up to see Aaron, who looked dapper in a burgundy wool sweater and an open L.L.Bean navy warm-up jacket, standing in front of her.

He leaned in and kissed her . . . on the cheek.

That didn't seem like a particularly good sign.

"I've missed you," Hayley said.

"Well, we've both been busy."

Hayley nodded, not quite sure what to say.

There was a pregnant pause in the air that felt like it lasted a full five minutes, but more than likely was just a few seconds.

"How's Lex?" Aaron asked, clearing his throat.

"Bansfield?"

Of course he means Lex Bansfield. How many men named Lex live in Bar Harbor?

She had to deal with this now, before it drove a further wedge between them. It was time to address the uninvited kiss at the hospital and the rampant town gossip that quickly followed.

"He's on the mend. Resting at home. Aaron—"

"I've been debating with myself on how to bring this up, and I wasn't sure when or if I was going to do it tonight, but my gut is telling me just to come right out with it. So here goes. Do you still have feelings for him?"

The question startled Hayley.

Not that she was at a loss for an answer.

She was just surprised he beat her to it.

"Okay, I was hoping you might answer a little quicker than that," Aaron said, frowning.

"No, Aaron. I don't. Lex and I are just friends now. What we had is over," Hayley said, staring straight into his eyes.

Owning it.

Meaning it.

Believing it.

"And I'm very happy being with you."

Aaron studied Hayley's face and body language, trying to size up her sincerity.

"Okay," Aaron said, putting his arms around her and hugging her.

She rested her head against his broad chest.

But then he let go and took a step back.

It felt too soon—almost as if he was eager to distance himself.

He still wasn't 100 percent convinced.

And that bothered her because she knew she was speaking from the heart. And she didn't know how else to convey her true feelings.

Suddenly the sounds of children screaming jarred her out of her own thoughts. All of the little kids in the park raced toward the gazebo, where Santa Claus was arriving on the scene. Two horses—both wearing colorful red-and-white fleeces, sashes made of wreaths, and hoods with reindeer antlers—pulled a red buggy decorated with garland. Santa Claus and Mrs. Claus, gussied up in their traditional costumes, waved to the crowd while an elf on the carriage top held the reins. A giant sack of presents donated by the townspeople was stuffed in the back. The excited children surrounded the buggy as Mr. and Mrs. Claus tossed small plastic-wrapped candy canes to them, causing a near riot as the children fought to scoop them up off the ground.

Hayley recognized Santa as the esteemed judge

Ronald Carter, and Mrs. Claus was Mayor Eliza Richards. In real life the two despised each other, but they chose to bury the hatchet at least temporarily to portray the North Pole's royal couple for the sake of the local rug rats. It took a little more time to recognize the elf driving Santa's sleigh. But since she had just seen him at the gym the day before, it quickly came to her.

Rusty Wyatt.

His taut muscles from working out every day were camouflaged by an oversize red-and-green felt tunic. You could still admire his defined calf muscles because of the matching tights—one leg red, one leg green. A plush red-and-green hat that had giant ears on the sides covered his curly blond hair, and pointy shoes with bells on the tip were on his feet.

Judging by the hangdog look on his face, Hayley guessed Rusty was not too happy in his subservient role to jolly ole Saint Nick. Hayley surmised that poor Rusty was strong-armed into participating in the Christmas tree lighting. Judge Carter probably excused some unpaid parking tickets or disorderly conduct on the condition Rusty play ball and was undoubtedly backed up by the mayor.

Rusty jumped down from the carriage top and angrily shooed the kids away as he held out a hand to help Mrs. Claus out of the carriage first. As she stepped down, she gave him a dead stare, adjusting her tiny reading glasses. Rusty quickly forced a smile on his face.

Santa was next, waving to the kids with one white-gloved hand while rubbing his belly with the other. Hayley knew there was no pillow underneath the red coat. Judge Carter was naturally hefty, given his penchant for huge prime rib dinners and rich, decadent desserts.

As Santa and Mrs. Claus greeted the children, Rusty stormed off toward a beverage stand that offered hot drinks, on the far side of the park, away from all the commotion. The stand was run by Mr. Streinz, a local accountant, whose family had emigrated from Germany when he was a child. Mr. Streinz loved to re-create the authentic feel of a German Christmas market, which he so enjoyed as a little boy. His biggest seller this time of year was *Feuerzangenbowle,* a traditional German alcoholic drink. It featured a sugar cube flambéed with rum, then dripped into mulled wine. Hayley watched as Rusty slapped a few dollar bills down on the counter and barked something to Mr. Streinz, who went about fixing him his signature hot beverage.

Hayley turned to Aaron. "We still have a few more minutes before the lighting. Why don't I go get us something to drink?"

"Make it strong. It's been a long day."

"Mr. Streinz has just what you need," Hayley said, smiling.

By the time she weaved through the crowd and

made her way over to Mr. Streinz, there was no sign of Rusty.

"*Gute Nacht,* Hayley!"

"*Gute Nacht.* I would like two of your *fergie . . . zebra . . . bowels. . . .*"

"*Feuerzangenbowle,*" he said.

"Yes. That. Two of those."

"*Zwei!* Coming right up!"

She reached for her wallet in her bag, when she heard bells ringing. They were coming from behind a large oak tree a few feet away. She walked over and could hear a man talking. She peered around the tree to see Rusty pacing back and forth; the tiny bells on the tips of his pointy felt shoes were tinkling. His cell phone was clamped to his ear as he raged to someone on the other end of the phone through clenched teeth. He wasn't concerned with being overheard because most of the crowd was on the other side of the park.

"Don't you dare threaten me, Ken! We both know the damage I can do if you don't do exactly what I want!"

Ken Massey.

Obviously, the two chummy, muscle-bound workout buddies with the "airtight alibis" were now on the outs.

"You know what I want! I want you to stop seeing Tiffany. Don't call her. Don't text her. Don't e-mail her. Just stay the hell away from her! Or else I drop by the *Island Times* and sit down with Bruce Linney and spill everything! That's right. Just try maintaining your six percent body fat in a friggin' jail cell!"

"Hayley! Hayley!"

Hayley spun her head around to see Mr. Streinz holding up two plastic tumblers of his famous *Feuerzangenbowle* and searching for Hayley, who was suddenly AWOL.

She frantically waved at him to be quiet, but he didn't see her mashed up against the tree like a mosquito on flypaper.

Rusty Wyatt stared at her in shock.

Hayley stepped out of hiding and slowly approached him.

He just stood there, speechless—his mind obviously racing—worried about how much she heard.

"Rusty, can I talk to you for a second?"

"I need to get back. I'm supposed to hand out the presents to the kids after the tree ceremony."

"Rusty, why did you lie about working out with Ken on the night of Garth Rawlings's murder? The gym closed early that day because of Midnight Madness. There was no way you and Ken were there. What are you two hiding?"

Rusty stared at her for a few moments and then suddenly bolted away as fast as his cute tiny felt elf shoes could carry him.

"Rusty, wait!" Hayley yelled, chasing after him past Mr. Streinz, who just held out the two plastic tumblers, a perplexed look on his face.

Rusty was in shape and could easily outrun Hayley, but he was in a panicked state and wasn't thinking clearly. Instead of trying to lose Hayley on foot, his frantic mind decided the best course of action was to hijack Santa's sleigh.

Hayley dashed across the village green, leaping over children, hurtling herself toward the horse-drawn buggy, which Rusty was now trying to climb into. The bells on his pointy shoes were still ringing.

The festive crowd hardly noticed the hubbub of the chase as they circled around the tree, anxiously awaiting the lighting ceremony hosted by Santa and Mrs. Claus, who now used microphones to address the crowd. Santa encouraged everyone to join him in a chorus of "Rudolph the Red-Nosed Reindeer."

Rusty finally made it onto the seat of the carriage top and tried untying the reins as fast as he could, but he made the knot too tight and it was a bit of a struggle, which allowed Hayley enough time to make up a few precious seconds. However, it wasn't enough. Rusty managed to loosen the knot and unfurl the reins, snapping them hard against the horses' holiday fleeces. They jumped with a start, whinnying and shaking their manes, before setting off. Their hooves clomped as they galloped away from the village green, pulling the buggy behind them.

Wheezing, leg muscles burning, only inches from the back of the buggy, her arms outstretched,

Hayley grabbed the back of the carriage just as it soared away. She lifted herself up, swinging one leg onto the trunk area, which held the enormous gunnysack filled with presents.

She wished Rusty had tried to escape in the much slower tractor trailer that pulled a makeshift train behind it for the kids to ride in, which was the special surprise from last year's tree lighting instead of the horse-drawn Santa sleigh.

As Hayley mounted the bag of presents, praying she wasn't crushing a fragile doll that some poor little girl would unwrap later to a flood of tears, she saw Aaron watching her ride away. He had a stupefied look on his face.

She would have to explain later.

That is, if he was still speaking to her.

Hayley tried balancing herself. The cold winter winds blew the sporty hat she was wearing right off her head. "Rusty, please! Stop this thing!"

The sound of her voice spooked Rusty and he jerked his head around to see Hayley on top of the Christmas presents. His mouth dropped open; without thinking, he let go of the reins.

At that moment something snapped.

The horses kept galloping forward at full speed, but the carriage disengaged. It rolled down the street, out of control.

Hayley watched in horror as everything happened in slow motion.

The buggy sideswiped a parked car.

Rusty jerked his head around, his mouth open in a silent scream.

A police cruiser rounded the corner from Cottage Street onto Main Street.

Hayley was able to make out Sergio behind the wheel. His eyes almost popped out of his head at the sight of the unhitched carriage barreling toward him.

The cruiser and the buggy were about to crash in a head-on collision.

The cruiser stopped.

The buggy didn't.

Hayley leapt out of the buggy, landing on the hard pavement, bashing her knee against the cement sidewalk.

She couldn't look.

She just heard the sickening crash, followed by a few seconds of silence.

Then Sergio, hollering all sorts of Brazilian swear words, snapped handcuffs on Rusty Wyatt and read him his rights.

In English.

Chapter 23

Hayley finally forced herself to watch as another cruiser arrived on the scene and Sergio ordered Officers Donnie and Earl to haul Rusty Wyatt down to the station and book him on suspicion of drunk driving.

Okay, it was a horse and buggy.

But it was still driving under the influence.

Hayley was about to intervene and explain the facts of what really happened, but she stopped herself.

Even though she knew for a fact that Rusty was stone-cold sober, the threat of jail time and a heavy fine might get him talking to Sergio.

Perhaps he even might offer the information Hayley wanted to get out of him in order to secure his release and make sure he was home in time for *Jimmy Kimmel Live!*

Besides, she would rather not be the one to highlight her own role in the fender bender that was going to cost the department some serious cash to repair the front grill of the police chief's cruiser.

Officer Donnie put a hand on top of Rusty's curly blond head, his elf hat blown clear across town by now, and guided him into the backseat of the car. Officer Earl was already in the driver's seat starting the engine while Sergio talked on his cell phone, presumably to someone with a tow truck.

Hayley limped back to the village green, her right knee throbbing.

She saw in the distance the lights on the giant pine tree flick on to wild applause.

The town band started up again, playing "O Christmas Tree," as the red and green lights blinked on and off, almost in time with the music.

When Hayley arrived at the park, she made a beeline for Mr. Streinz and quickly paid for the plastic tumblers of *Feuerzangenbowle;* then she carried them over to the now-thinning crowd, where Aaron waited patiently for her.

She handed him a tumbler.

"That didn't take long at all," Aaron said with a smirk.

"I suppose I should explain—"

"That's all right. You don't have to."

"No, I really should."

"It's fine. I know what's really going on here."

"You do? What?"

She really wanted to know.

"You have an elf fetish."

Hayley nearly spit out her *Feuerzangenbowle*.

"Aaron—"

"No, I get it. You've got this thing for guys with pointy ears who like to wear tights. You go wild when one's around, and you lose yourself, and you get so excited you wind up chasing him around, trying to play with him, like an overexcited kitty with catnip."

He was a vet, so he could be forgiven the metaphor.

"No, really—"

"Seriously, Hayley, let me *believe* you have an elf fetish. Otherwise, I'm going to have to know the truth of why you just did what you did, and, frankly, I'm not sure I'm emotionally ready to handle that."

"Okay."

"You want to grab some dinner? The tree lighting is pretty much over. FYI. You missed it."

"I know. I'm sorry. Dinner sounds great."

They walked down Main Street to Geddy's, one of the few local establishments open during the winter months, passing a tow truck driver using a dolly to slot the damaged cruiser's two front tires in order to drive it up onto the trailer hitch of the truck.

Aaron shot Hayley a look.

He instinctively knew she had something to do with this.

Hayley kept her eyes straight ahead, feigning innocence.

A couple of beers, a plate of nachos, and some fried shrimp later, Hayley and Aaron were laughing over some silly joke, holding hands across the table, both remembering what had attracted them to each other in the first place.

It was so easy with Aaron.

And those eyes.

And that smile.

Hayley took a deep breath. She had to control herself. They were in a public place.

Her cell phone in her back pants pocket buzzed. She chose to ignore it.

Their date was finally back on track and she was not going to jeopardize it again by becoming distracted. The buzzing finally stopped.

Hayley flagged down the waitress and asked her for a dessert menu. She knew Aaron had an insatiable sweet tooth.

Plus she wanted to prolong their date—she was having such a nice time and didn't want it to end.

Her butt began buzzing again.

She shifted in her seat.

No. She was not going to answer it.

More buzzing.

This time it was coming from across the table.

Aaron reached into his own pants pocket, pulled out his phone, and checked the screen. "I have to take this. It's Mrs. Delaney calling me. I have to break the news that her collie has parvo. It's always a tougher call when it's this time of year. I'll be right back. Order whatever you want."

Aaron grabbed his coat and headed out the door to talk to his patient's owner. Hayley immediately reached into her own back pocket and retrieved her cell.

It was Sergio. She hurriedly answered.

"Sergio? Did you question Rusty Wyatt? What did he say?"

"Good evening to you too."

"I only have a few minutes to talk, so make it fast."

"You know when I talk fast, I slip into Portuguese."

"I'm on a date, Sergio!"

"I cut a deal with Rusty. I told him if he paid for the damage to my cruiser *and* came clean about why he lied for Ken Massey, I would drop all charges. So he sang like a caterpillar."

Canary.

Not caterpillar.

Canary, Sergio.

But they were short on time, so she was not going to bother correcting him.

"It turns out the grieving widow, Tiffany Rawlings, was not only cheating on her husband, Garth, with Ken Massey, she was also sleeping on the side with Rusty Wyatt."

Hayley gasped. "Are you kidding me? My God, the woman gets around!"

"Rusty admitted he was with Tiffany at her house

at the time of Garth's death. He went so far as to tell me they were in her bed, cuddling, when he got the call that there was a body at the warehouse and they needed a paramedic at the scene."

"Why did he agree to lie for Ken?"

"Because Ken came to him in a panic. He didn't have an alibi on the night of the murder and he knew suspicion would fall on him, given his rocky past with Garth. Also, if it came out that he was having an affair with the victim's wife, the public would bury him. But he didn't tell Rusty that part. He didn't want anyone to know. He just convinced his good buddy to help him out so he wouldn't be arrested for a crime he didn't commit."

"So Rusty must have found out the truth about Tiffany and Ken, became enraged with jealousy, and threatened to go to the cops with the truth if he didn't end his affair with Tiffany. That's what they were arguing about on the phone when I approached him at the village green."

"So, if Rusty is telling the truth and he was with Tiffany the whole time, then Ken is the only one left standing without an alibi."

"Which means he could more than likely be the killer," Hayley said as she spotted Aaron coming in from outside and pocketing his phone. "Got to go, Sergio. Talk to you later."

Hayley hid her phone underneath a napkin as

Aaron returned and took his seat across from her. "Sorry about that. I know it's rude."

"You're forgiven this time," Hayley said, winking.

Ken Massey.

She was sure it was Ken Massey.

But unless he was a master magician, Bar Harbor's very own David Blaine, how did he get in and out of a locked warehouse without a key?

Chapter 24

Hayley and Aaron sat in his Ford Explorer in the driveway outside of her house. Their arms were wrapped around each other; their warm bodies were pressed together; their lips were locked. Hayley's knee still throbbed in pain from the tumble off Santa's sleigh, so she focused on the tingling sensation that swept through the rest of her body.

She felt like she was in high school all over again—the good part of high school, like when she made out with the tight end from the football team in his father's Chrysler LeBaron after the victorious homecoming game senior year. Not the bad part, when her face broke out with acne three days before junior prom and her date dumped her in favor of her archrival Sabrina Merryweather, with the model-worthy complexion.

Aaron moaned softly as he devoured Hayley.

It felt so satisfying to be back in his arms.

She opened her eyes to look at his face.

His eyes were closed.

His hair was slightly mussed from their intense groping.

But there was no denying just how good-looking he was.

She couldn't believe this incredibly sweet and handsome man had come so unexpectedly into her life.

She could go on like this all night.

However, whenever a thought like that crossed her mind, there was always something that interrupted the game plan.

And something moving outside, dashing past the car's headlights, was tonight's hitch. Hayley pulled away from Aaron and stared into the darkness of the driveway, past the reach of the lights.

"What is it? What's wrong?"

"I thought I saw something."

Aaron reached for the door. "Want me to check it out?"

"No, it's probably nothing. We get deer foraging around the neighborhood all the time. Last week I had to honk my horn to shoo one away, just so I could back out of my garage. Forget I said anything."

She leaned in to start kissing again, but she wasn't fast enough.

Aaron checked his watch.

"It's getting late. My first appointment is at seven tomorrow morning."

See? The best-laid plans!

He brushed his lips across hers and whispered, "I had a really nice time tonight."

"Me too."

Then he gently placed the palm of his hand on the back of her neck and pulled her closer for one last intoxicating kiss.

"Let me walk you to the door."

"No, you go home and get some sleep. I still have to write my column and walk Leroy. Good night, Aaron," Hayley said, opening the passenger-side door and nearly floating out. She was so high from the evening.

"Good night, Hayley," he said, smiling.

She shut the door. Aaron waited for her to reach the back door to her kitchen safely before he waved, backed his Explorer out of the driveway, and sped off. Hayley was delighted with how the evening had gone. After a few missteps maybe this relationship—for lack of a better word—was now on track to developing into something more serious.

Hayley was halfway inside the house when she heard a noise coming from behind her detached garage.

Is that another deer? A raccoon? Maybe a neighbor's dog?

She flipped on the porch floodlight, illuminating most of the backyard, but she saw nothing. She walked over to the side of the garage, checking to see if she could see anything.

Just darkness.

The only movements she could make out were some trees swaying with the night breeze.

She pivoted to head back to the house, when suddenly a hand clamped tightly over her mouth and an arm, which felt as if it were made of steel, wrapped around her waist. She struggled mightily, reaching back with her hand to claw at her assailant's face, but he was sturdy and strong as he flung around and backed her up against the sidewall of the garage so she was facing him.

Hayley screamed through his meaty palm as she recognized her attacker.

It was Ken Massey.

"Shhh, Hayley, please, I didn't come here to hurt you. I just want to talk to you. Please be quiet."

Hayley was having none of it. She already felt discomforted by him after their run-in at the gym. Plus she was reasonably confident he had something to do with Garth Rawlings's death, given his debunked alibi. She struggled in his grip, but Ken was sinewy and big. He had more muscles than Stallone in his prime.

He kept his hand pressed over her mouth as he pinned her to the wall with his thick free arm, holding her in place. "Listen to me. I just heard Rusty's been talking to the cops. I know he's blowing my alibi to bits because he's jealous I was having a relationship with Tiffany Rawlings, just like he was. So you were right about me not being at the gym the night Garth died. I was home. Watching TV. Alone. Not a soul can back me up. When I heard the coroner ruled Garth's death a homicide, I got scared, because I was afraid I would fall under suspicion. I've seen enough crime shows to know if I didn't have a solid alibi, everybody in town would automatically assume I did it. So I begged Rusty—my friend, my buddy, my confidant—to back me up and say we were working out together. Which he did do, until he found out I was also seeing Tiffany. Hayley, you have to believe me. I'm innocent. I didn't kill anybody!"

Hayley stopped struggling in his grip.

Ken relaxed slightly. "If I take my hand away, will you promise not to scream?"

Hayley nodded.

Ken waited a few more seconds to be sure and then slowly withdrew his hand.

Hayley screamed bloody murder.

She didn't believe this man for a second.

Ken tried covering her mouth again, but then he gave up. He bolted away, passing by the house as Gemma raced out onto the porch.

"Mom, where are you? Are you okay?"

Hayley stumbled out onto the lit driveway, limping, favoring her good knee and joined her daughter on the porch.

"What happened? Did you fall? Was that Mr. Massey running away just now?"

She didn't want to alarm her daughter, but she

wasn't going to lie either. "Yes. We were having a discussion, and it got a little heated."

Gemma put her arm around her mother and helped her inside.

Hayley sat down on one of the kitchen table chairs to catch her breath.

"What were you two talking about?" Gemma wanted to know.

"The Garth Rawlings murder."

"You think he had something to do with it?"

Hayley nodded. "I'm still trying to piece it together, but I'm fairly certain he was involved."

"Really?" a voice asked from behind her.

It was a boy.

But it wasn't Dustin.

Hayley whirled around.

"Mom, this is Hugo. He's playing Joseph in the Nativity play. We've been rehearsing."

It all clicked into place.

She had seen this kid before, and not just from the dark photo Gemma surreptitiously took of him at the church after he was cast.

She had seen him at the warehouse crime scene.

This was the quiet, withdrawn kid on Lex's crew.

He was the young intern who was partying with the foreman, Nick Ward, and Billy Parsons.

"Nice to meet you, Mrs. Powell," he said, looking down shyly.

"We've met before, Hugo. Don't you remember? At the warehouse the night Garth Rawlings was murdered. I know there was a lot going on."

"Oh, yeah," Hugo said, although the memory only vaguely registered.

Or he wanted it to appear that way.

Hayley studied him, which made him supremely uncomfortable.

He cleared his throat.

Looked at his feet.

"So . . . you think Mr. Massey broke into the warehouse and killed Mr. Rawlings?"

"I don't have a clue how he did it, Hugo. So far, the facts are not lining up with the condition of the body. But I have a strong feeling he's responsible in some way."

Hugo shoved his hands in his pants pocket. "I need to go home soon, so we should finish rehearsing our scenes, Gemma."

"Okay," Gemma said. "Want some more soda?"

"No, I'm good."

Gemma led Hugo back to the living room. As he turned to follow her, he mumbled, "Maybe you shouldn't focus so much on Mr. Massey."

Hayley's ears perked up. "I'm sorry, Hugo. I missed that. What did you say?"

"Nothing," he said, thinking better of it.

"No, what did you say about Mr. Massey?"

"I just think maybe he didn't do it, and people should just leave him alone."

"And by people you mean *me?*"

Hugo sighed. "I don't know. All I'm saying is, if everybody starts to think Mr. Massey did it and they arrest him and convict him and send him off to prison, it would be a shame if he was actually innocent."

"I agree. A man is innocent until proven guilty. But what piques my curiosity, Hugo, is why do you think that? Why do you think Mr. Massey didn't do it?"

Hayley noticed a slight look of panic in Hugo's eyes.

"I didn't say I know for a fact he's innocent. I didn't say that at all. I don't know if he is or isn't. I don't know anything!"

The kid was losing it.

Gemma stepped forward and put a hand on his arm. "It's fine. We don't have to talk about it anymore. Let's just go run lines."

"No, I have to go home now. We can rehearse at the church tomorrow," Hugo said, hightailing it out the back door.

Hayley turned to Gemma. "Is he normally this jumpy?"

"No. I've never seen him like this."

Something strange was going on inside that kid's head.

And Hayley was suddenly determined to find out what.

Chapter 25

When Hayley took Leroy on his nightly walk around the neighborhood, she couldn't shake the feeling that Hugo knew more about what had happened that night at the warehouse than he was letting on. What if Lex's crew, which was supposedly partying next door and didn't hear a thing, was lying? What if their drinking and carousing led to Garth flying off the handle again? It could have spiraled out of control, and one of the construction guys—Nick Ward or Billy Parsons—flew into a drunken rage and beat Garth to death? The only problem with that theory was there were no obvious signs of a fight or struggle either outside the warehouse or inside, where the body was found, or even in Lex's shop, where the three men were at the time of the murder. Sergio had searched the place thoroughly during his initial investigation. Also none of the men appeared particularly drunk when questioned by Sergio that night. There was also the nagging detail of the locked door and security footage. How did they get in or out? How did anybody get in or out unless there was another key, besides the one Connie Sparks had? A key that everyone who knew Garth said didn't exist—unless they were all lying. But why?

Still, the look on Hugo's face when he realized he had probably said too much was very revealing. In Hayley's mind, in order to take the suspicion off Ken Massey, the hapless Hugo only had managed to direct it toward himself.

Leroy stopped by a fire hydrant and lifted his leg as Hayley admired a neighbor's "Candy Cane Lane" Christmas display. Rows of giant illuminated candy canes led to a giant tethered balloon of Frosty the Snowman. Ridiculous. Garish. Over the top. Hayley absolutely loved it! It was much more impressive than the simple Christmas wreath hanging on her front door, with a red envelope taped to it containing a holiday bonus for the postman.

Leroy was just about finished, and ready to resume the sprint back to the house, when Hayley noticed someone following her.

Walking toward her.

His face in the shadows.

Picking up speed.

Closing in.

Has Ken Massey come back to finish the job?

She cursed herself for not calling Sergio and

reporting him right away for pouncing on her on her own property.

Hayley yanked Leroy's leash and the poor little guy dropped his leg and yelped as she dragged him into the neighbor's yard, where she hid with him behind one of the biggest plastic candy canes on the snow-covered lawn. She poked her head around to see if the man was still there, lurking, but he was gone. She waited a few moments, just to be safe, and was about to come out of hiding, when she heard a crunching sound. Like the heel of a boot grinding into the hardpacked snow. Hayley grabbed the first weapon she could find: a plastic red candle with white wax and a yellow flame. It was the size of a baseball bat. It would have to do.

Just as the man came around the candy cane and on top of Hayley, she reared back with the candle and let him have it. She pounded him mercilessly. The man ducked and covered his head.

"Stop it! Stop it, Hayley!" he begged. "It's me! Bruce Linney!"

"Bruce! What the hell are you doing skulking around my neighborhood and scaring me half to death?"

"'Skulking around'? I don't *skulk*, Hayley! I came over to your house to talk to you! I saw you walking Leroy, so I was just trying to catch up to you."

"Whatever it is you need to say, couldn't it have waited until the morning?"

"No. It's impossible to talk discreetly in that office. The place is filled with reporters with big ears and even bigger mouths!"

"What, Bruce? What's so important that you had to stalk me and nearly stop my heart from fright?"

"I'm worried Sal is going to fire me!"

"Fire you? For what?"

"Sexually harassing you at the Christmas party!"

Hayley burst out laughing.

"I fail to see what's so funny!"

"Bruce, I'm reasonably confident your job isn't in jeopardy. You just had a little too much to drink. We all do things we regret when we're under the influence."

More than she was willing to spill to Bruce, that's for sure.

"In two weeks' time, nobody is going to even remember your grossly inappropriate behavior," Hayley said.

"Are you calling me 'gross'? I mean, wow, Hayley, I may not be your type, but do you have to be so mean?"

"I'm not calling *you* 'gross,' Bruce! I'm saying *your behavior* was *gross*. There's a difference. Seriously, just forget it."

"But Sal has the evidence recorded on his phone to use against me. I've been worried sick about it. I need this job, Hayley."

"Do you want me to talk to him?"

"You would do that for me?"

"Yes. If you were to get fired, it would be weird not having you around irritating me. I'll go to Sal tomorrow and tell him we sorted it all out and it's over and done with. Maybe I'll even get him to delete the recording."

"Thank you, Hayley, thank you! If there is ever anything you need from me—"

"Good night, Bruce," Hayley said, smiling and shaking her head, tugging on the brown leather strap leash to get Leroy, who was sitting on the pavement staring up at them, back up on his feet to make the short journey home.

She stopped suddenly. "Wait. There is one thing."

"Anything, Hayley. Just name it."

"You can share your notes on the Garth Rawlings case."

Bruce flinched slightly. He was hypercompetitive and loathed sharing any kind of information he was gathering for one of his columns. However, he knew he owed Hayley big-time, and he had just made a big show of doing her any favor.

"Just this one time?"

"Of course, Bruce. Once the recording on Sal's phone is sent to the trash bin, it's your word against mine and you can go back to shutting me out so I don't horn in on your glory as Bar Harbor's top—and might I add 'only'—crime reporter."

"Okay," Bruce sighed, resigned to discuss his current working theory. "Chief Alvares let me take a look at the security camera footage at the convenience store across the street from the warehouse, and he was right that no one was seen coming or going that night. So I have been focusing on the people in nearest proximity to Garth right before he died."

"Lex Bansfield's contracting crew."

"Yes. Nick Ward. Billy Parsons. And the kid, Hugo something."

"I've gone down this road already, Bruce. There are no secret doors or hidden tunnels from their shop into Garth's kitchen. The only way in there was through the front door and it was locked. There was no way for them even to get to him."

"I know. Nothing makes sense. But I've been hammering away at Nick Ward and Billy Parsons, trying to get a complete picture of what happened that night. Nick was very straightforward with his story, never wavered. He repeated the same details over and over. They were just hanging out and drinking beer the whole time. Never left the office until they heard the sirens outside. I interviewed Billy separately, and he basically told the same story. Backed up everything Nick said. He was adamant that they never argued with Garth that night or even saw him. Maybe it was his body language, I don't know, but my gut told me he was not telling me everything. So I pressed him, not knowing where it might lead, and Billy suddenly got very nervous. Then he just said he had to get back to work and asked me to leave. I have a hunch he's hiding something, Hayley. I showed up at his apartment this morning to let him know I had a few follow-up questions and his truck was gone. Landlord said she saw Billy toss a suitcase in the back of his truck at dawn this morning and drive off like he was in a real hurry."

"He blew town?"

"Looks like it."

Maybe Gemma's soft-spoken pageant costar wasn't so off the mark.

Ken Massey had motive and opportunity, and he clearly was unhinged at the terrifying thought of being arrested, which was why he jumped Hayley and begged her to believe he was innocent. But motive and opportunity did not add up to hard evidence.

And now, thanks to Bruce sucking down too much rum-spiked punch and losing all sense of propriety in the copy room, Hayley had a fresh lead to follow.

Hugo was trying to dissuade Hayley from assuming Ken Massey's guilt because he knew the real story of what happened that night.

Hugo knew the identity of the real killer.

And perhaps the real killer, fearing intrepid crime reporter Bruce Linney might eventually coerce the truth out of the two men he was with that night, decided to flee the scene of the crime.

Billy Parsons was on the run.

Island Food & Spirits
by
Hayley Powell

I make the same Christmas stuffing every year. It's a holiday dish that's been in my family for generations. And every year I lose the recipe. I'm not proud to admit that I am not very organized. I would like nothing more than for you to think that all of my favorite recipes are neatly organized and alphabetized in binders and lined up on lovely bookshelves in my kitchen. But, unfortunately, that is only a fantasy. I usually stuff them all in drawers in my kitchen after I'm through with them, which means, of course, I'm constantly pulling out stacks of every size of paper and notecards, searching through them, and tossing them aside until my kitchen looks like a paper factory exploded. Remarkably, I always eventually seem to find what I'm looking for, which is exactly what I was doing last night as I tried to find my stuffing recipe to share with you.

There was only one Christmas I didn't prepare this mouthwatering dish for my friends and family. A few years ago, for the first time, Liddy insisted on throwing her own holiday party, which meant she would hire a housekeeper to sweep her floors and dust her furniture and rely on all of her close friends and intimates to bring all of the food. Liddy, however, did have a fully stocked bar, so that counted for something—especially with our crowd.

A few days before, I was having "Christmas Spirit" cocktails with Liddy and Mona at Drinks Like A Fish, which is a soothing cocktail special that Randy happened to be serving in his bar that evening. We were planning our menu for Liddy's party—and as usual were feeling no pain—and Mona made a crack about how Liddy never had to do any of the hard work. I must have laughed a little too much, because at that point Liddy stood up from her bar stool without warning and declared that she would be preparing all of the dishes for the entire dinner all by herself with absolutely no help from us. All we had to do was get ourselves there by 6:00 P.M.

It was as if the world had stopped. You could have heard a pin drop in the bar. Even the jukebox playing a holiday song by Nat King Cole went silent. My brother, Randy, froze in midshake behind the bar as he prepared a vodka martini. We all just stared at Liddy in complete and utter shock.

We all love and adore Liddy, but the poor woman is no chef. I won't even go into the 2002 microwave oven dinner fire incident. We immediately tried to talk some sense into her, without hurting her feelings. But in the end, as we called a cab to drive us home because of the three rounds of Randy's potent "Christmas Spirit" cocktails, we agreed to let Liddy do the dinner her way. We would just show up at the appointed time.

The night of the holiday party arrived, right along with one of the worst Maine blizzards of the year. But we being true "Mainiacs" and positive thinkers, we considered ourselves to be just like the United Postal Service carriers: *Neither snow nor rain nor heat nor gloom of night stays these couriers from the swift completion of their appointed rounds.* Or something like that! In any event we all headed onward to Liddy's house for an evening of Christmas cheer!

We all arrived around the same time. Mona and her husband and their whole rowdy brood, Randy and Sergio, me and my kids, plus a few other stray friends with nowhere else to go. It was now snowing so hard that we decided to pull into Liddy's un-plowed driveway, just off the main road, and walk the rest of the way to her house to make it easier for every-one to get out later. We piled into Liddy's house, covered in snow, laugh-ing and yelling, "Merry Christmas!" She wasn't there to greet us. I should have suspected something was up. Usually when you arrive at someone's house for a holiday party, you smell a turkey roasting in the oven or a pie baking. Something. Anything.

We trudged into Liddy's spacious

kitchen. No pots on the stove. No pies cooling on the counter. Not even a green bean casserole covered in cellophane ready to be heated up. There was just poor Liddy sitting on a stool at her kitchen island. She had her head in her hands and her usually perfect hairdo sticking completely straight up and all over the place. She was wearing old torn sweats and an oversize men's white t-shirt with makeup stains all over it. She had obviously been using it like a tissue and wiping her face. Her eyes were puffy from crying.

We all stood there in silence. Even Mona's kids. That's right. *Even Mona's kids!* Liddy took one look at us and burst into tears again as Mona and I rushed to console her and find out what was wrong. Finally, after Randy had the foresight to find the biggest wineglass in Liddy's cupboard, pour it to the rim with a Merlot that didn't even have time to breathe, and hand it to her, Liddy was calm enough to speak.

After setting out to prove she could prepare a holiday feast for her loved ones, Liddy quickly realized the next day that her impressive confidence and bravado was surely enhanced by the "Christmas Spirit" cocktails at Drinks Like A Fish. However, she was too stubborn to admit her mistake, so she did a little online research and found a talented, award-winning catering firm out of Bangor with an impressive list of clients and booked them to prepare and serve our meal. She didn't want to use a local because she didn't want anyone to get wind of what she was doing. (Especially since she was ready to claim that the catering staff was just serving the food that she had so lovingly prepared herself!)

Unfortunately, the unexpected blizzard had waylaid the entire catering team, and they canceled because it was too dangerous to drive to Bar Harbor. Liddy offered to double their fee, but they were more concerned with their personal safety. This threw Liddy into a tizzy. She frantically called the only two restaurants open that night, only to discover they were both closing early because of the storm and could not even deliver an order of chicken wings.

Liddy was so embarrassed and humiliated, she promptly collapsed again on her kitchen island in another fresh flood of tears. That's when Sergio took matters into his own hands and promptly directed Randy to start mixing us all some much needed cocktails. He instructed the children to go into the living room and put on a Christmas movie, and he ordered Mona and me to start going through the cupboards and pull some kind of dinner together. Then he guided Liddy and her glass of wine toward her bedroom to freshen up a bit for the evening so she wouldn't scare the kids anymore with her frazzled and wild-eyed appearance.

Well, I'm happy to say that in the end it was a raucous and memorable party, with lots of laughs, as we chowed down on peanut butter and jelly sandwiches, crackers, canned sardines, microwave popcorn, and a jar of caviar. I would be lying if I didn't admit the fully stocked bar helped us get through it admirably as well. We left Liddy's cupboards and fridge bare when we were finished, except for a couple of eggs. We decided to let her have them the next morning for breakfast—if she could figure out how to crack them open.

Well, since I am fairly certain most of you know how to make a peanut butter and jelly sandwich, let me share my promised Christmas stuffing recipe, which, I hope, will become one of your own holiday family traditions. But first don't forget to liven up your own holiday party with Randy's "Christmas Spirit" cocktails, sure to be a hit with all of your drunk relatives!

Randy's "Christmas Spirit" Cocktail

<u>Ingredients</u>

2 ounces Midori Melon Liqueur
½ ounce lemon juice
1 teaspoon simple syrup
Maraschino cherry for garnish

Pour all of your ingredients into a cocktail shaker filled with ice and shake well. Strain into a chilled cocktail glass and add a maraschino cherry for garnish. This will start your night out the right way.

Christmas Stuffing

<u>Ingredients</u>

½ pound Italian bulk sausage
4 cups of your favorite cubed sea-
   soned stuffing
1½ cups crushed corn bread stuffing
   mix
½ cup toasted pecans
½ cup minced fresh parsley
1 tablespoon fresh sage, minced
1½ cups slice baby portabella mushrooms
1 cup sliced button mushrooms (feel
   free to use your favorite)
1 large onion, chopped
1 cup chopped apples
1 celery rib, chopped
4 tablespoons butter
2 cups of your favorite chicken broth
Salt and pepper to taste

In a large skillet cook and crumble
your sausage until no longer pink;
drain. Transfer to a large bowl. Stir in
the stuffing cubes, corn bread stuffing, pecans, parsley, sage; salt and
pepper to taste.

In your skillet sauté mushrooms,
onion, apple, and celery in butter until
tender. Stir into the stuffing mixture.

Add enough of the broth to your desired moistness. Transfer to a 4-quart Crock-Pot. Cover and cook on low for 3 hours, stirring once.

As always, feel free to add your own touches to the stuffing and serve it with your favorite holiday meal.

Chapter 26

Hayley was up early the next morning to whip up a batch of her spicy gingerbread cookies, which she planned to deliver to the nurses at the Bar Harbor Hospital during her lunch break. She wasn't overcome all of a sudden by the holiday spirit. No, it was a far more calculated act of generosity. The rumor around town was that Nurse Tilly McVety, who just happened to work the day shift, had been in recent months casually dating local handyman Billy Parsons. Therefore, this would be the perfect opportunity for Hayley to pump Tilly for information.

Hayley downed three cups of coffee upon her arrival at the office and tore through her in-box at record speed to get her work done so there would be no reason for her to have to work through lunch. She hid the plate of cookies underneath her desk, tucking them away from those untrustworthy reporters, whose stomachs always began grumbling before noon, which inevitably led to them scavenging for any snacks lying around. Hayley was determined they would not get their grubby hands on her cookies.

When the fire department blew the noon whistle, Hayley gathered up her tote bag and plate of cookies and called back to Sal, alerting him that she was taking an early lunch. She then drove straight to the hospital.

When she arrived at the nurses' station, she was surprised to find the hospital staff and a few elderly patients, who had been wheeled out of their rooms, drinking a candy cane punch and gorging on an assortment of Christmas-tree-decorated cupcakes, white-chocolate star-shaped pretzels, and powdered doughnut snowman treats. Hayley's spicy gingerbread cookies didn't seem quite so special anymore.

Nurse Tilly McVety was manning the punch bowl and ladling the creamy pink punch into plastic cups and handing them out to everyone. Out of the corner of her eye, she spotted Hayley approaching. "You've got to try some, Hayley. I made it myself from a recipe I found online. It's so delicious. The only ingredient I left out was the rum because we're on duty. Although I suspect Mr. Pinkett over there has a flask tucked in the pocket of his bathrobe—he's almost mowed down three orderlies with his wheelchair already!"

Hayley spied Mr. Pinkett, an apple-cheeked, glassy-eyed, merry-looking eighty-year-old with a skeletal frame and wisps of white hair sticking up from his head, leering at the backside of a nurse passing by and then rolling his wheelchair after her.

"No, thanks, Tilly. I just came by to bring . . ."

Too late. Tilly had already poured her a cup.

Resigned, Hayley took a sip.

Tilly wasn't lying. It was so yummy that Hayley resisted the urge just to pick up the punch bowl and drink directly from it. Instead she set her plate of cookies down next to the other Christmas treats.

"That's so sweet of you, Hayley. How did you know we were having a little Christmas party on the ward today for the patients?"

"Actually, I didn't. I wanted to bring you something as a token of my appreciation for how well you treated Lex when he was here, because I know he was a handful—"

"You didn't have to do that, Hayley."

"Oh, it's no trouble—"

"No, really, Lex already brought flowers and chocolates and balloons this morning and made a big heartfelt speech apologizing for any anxiety his behavior may have caused the nursing staff. He's right over there."

Hayley twisted around to see Lex, hobbling around on crutches, popping a white-chocolate pretzel into his mouth as he chatted with a few of the younger, fawning nurses, who were beaming and giggling and hanging on his every word.

Hayley had blown right past without even noticing him when she had gotten off the elevator. He had definitely seen her. He nodded and winked at her as she stared at him and then went back to his conversation.

Hayley swung around again as Tilly handed another cup of punch to Mr. Pinkett , who blew her a kiss before wheeling away to a corner and reaching into the pocket of his ratty blue bathrobe for his secret stash.

"Any big plans for the holidays, Tilly?"

"Working a double shift on Christmas Eve," Tilly said with a sigh. "And Christmas Day I will probably spend fighting with my mother, who will have too much to drink and say something to make my sister cry, and then I'll come to my sister's defense and she'll start yelling at me, too, and then my brother will have to intervene and my mother will make a point of announcing he was always her favorite. Happens every family holiday. Good times."

"Well, look on the bright side. At least you have a special guy to ring in New Year's with," Hayley said.

"My, word does get around. Somebody told you about me and Billy?" Tilly cooed, eyelashes flapping, swooning to the point where she almost tipped over.

"My brother owns a bar. I hear everything. Billy's a real catch," Hayley said. "I'm so happy for you."

"Well, it's only been a few months and I don't want to jinx it by talking about it too much, but so far it's been heavenly. Billy is sweet and kind, and he treats me like the Duchess of Cambridge, who is my personal hero, by the way."

"Because of her charity work?"

"No. Her fashion sense."

Hayley chose to let that one go.

The phone in the nurses' station rang and Tilly scooped up the receiver. "Ward three. Nurse McVety speaking."

She hoisted her index finger up to indicate to Hayley she would just be a second.

"Yes?" Tilly asked, her face darkening as the person on the other end of the line spoke.

"How dare you call me at work and say such things! Yes, there is a logical explanation, but I am not about to waste my breath explaining it to you!" Tilly seethed, slamming down the phone. "Good Lord, Hayley, how do you put up with that muckraking bastard on a daily basis?"

Bruce. It had to be Bruce. Calling to get Tilly's comment on Billy's mysterious disappearance.

Hayley knew Tilly would never tell anything to a surly, self-important, aggressively confrontational crime reporter.

But a friendly gal pal who just happened to drop by with spicy gingerbread cookies? Hayley was counting on it.

"Really, Hayley, he is so smug and off-putting!"

"You don't have to tell me, Tilly," Hayley said.

"He implied that Billy ran away scared because he had something to do with the Garth Rawlings murder. That is ludicrous! Billy is the kind of guy who uses a newspaper to pick up a spider and take it outside instead of stomping on it—which is what I would do, because they give me the willies."

"Oh, I didn't know Billy left town," Hayley said, trying hard to be convincing.

"Yes. This morning. I probably should have told Bruce the truth, but he just made me so mad! Now he's going to write whatever he damn well pleases and make it seem like Billy was somehow involved."

"Where is Billy?" Hayley asked nonchalantly, just a casual question from a curious friend.

"He drove to Newburyport."

"Massachusetts?"

"Uh-huh. He got a temporary job on a shrimping boat, just for a few days. He told me he wanted to earn some extra money so he could buy his special girl something nice for Christmas. Isn't that adorable? I told him I didn't need anything, but he wouldn't listen."

"So he'll be back in time for Christmas?"

"Of course."

Billy could have lied to her and just come up with the Massachusetts job as an excuse so Tilly wouldn't suspect he was actually escaping from the authorities before they closed in on him and secured the evidence needed to arrest and indict him.

Hayley knew it would be pointless to run Tilly's explanation by Bruce Linney. He would just automatically assume the worst and discard her story as pure fiction. A simple lie told by a duplicitous boyfriend who needed to get out of town. She knew once Bruce locked on a suspect he would relentlessly pound the facts to fit his theory. The actual truth became secondary.

Tilly stood up and pulled an iPhone out of the pocket of the white knit sweater she was wearing over her nurse's uniform. "I almost forgot. I promised to take pictures for the hospital's Facebook page." Tilly scooted out from behind the nurses' station and snapped away.

Hayley decided to peruse the sweets selection before heading back to the office. As she zeroed in on one of the cupcakes, Lex teetered over to her, still trying to get used to his crutches.

"I thought I spied your famous spicy gingerbread cookies. You know I can't resist them."

Hayley smiled, picked up the plate, and held it out for him to take one.

She watched as he bit into the cookie, closing his eyes and savoring the taste.

Suddenly Mr. Pinkett whizzed by in his wheelchair, now drunk and out of control, the side knocking into one of Lex's crutches, which caused Lex to lose his balance. He was about to take a nosedive, but Hayley jumped in under his arm to steady him.

Hayley noticed Tilly capturing the moment with her iPhone.

"You okay?" Hayley asked Lex.

Lex nodded. "Fine. Frustrated. I don't like being laid up like this. I need to get back to work."

"Count your blessings. After the nasty fall you took, it could have been a whole lot worse."

Lex's arm was still around Hayley's neck.

She remembered those romantic winter nights when they were dating, evenings spent at the care-taker's house that he lived in on the Hollingsworth estate: the bottle of wine, crackling fire, curling up together on the couch, watching the flames dance. His arm would be around her, just as it was now. Lex had his faults, but so did everybody. No man had ever made her feel so safe and protected. She lost herself for a brief moment, immersing herself in memories of their time to-gether; but then the reality of the situation finally took hold and she called for an orderly to pick up Lex's crutch from the floor and hand it to him. Once he was back holding both crutches, Hayley swiftly slipped out from underneath his arm and backed away, keeping her distance.

It was over.

She was never going back there.

She was with Aaron now.

Aaron.

Not Lex.

Tilly wandered back over to the nurses' station. She was glued to her phone.

Hayley suddenly remembered the photo Tilly took.

"Tilly, do me a favor. Don't post that photo of me and Lex on Facebook, okay?"

"I'm sorry, Hayley. I already posted it. And I tagged you."

That meant all of Hayley's friends would see it in their newsfeed.

Aaron included.

"It already has twenty-seven likes."

Tilly handed the phone to Hayley.

She looked at all the people who gave the thumbs-up to the photo.

Her heart sank.

Right near the top was Aaron Palmer.

It wasn't as if he actually liked the photo.

He was sending a message that he had seen it.

Chapter 27

The night of the Congregational Church's Nativity pageant finally arrived. By the time Hayley made it home to shower and change, Gemma had already left for a late-afternoon tech rehearsal. Dustin was attending the show with a group of friends and was having a quick bite beforehand at Pat's Pizza. The temperature outside had dropped to the low thirties, so Hayley slipped a heavy draped violet cardigan over her white blouse after blow-drying her hair. She heard loud honking in her driveway and dashed down the stairs and outside, waving at Liddy, who was perched in the driver's seat of her Mercedes and impatiently checking her watch.

They had arranged to meet Mona at the church, and found her already standing on the steps waiting for them as they pulled into the church parking lot. Of course Mona was on time. She was probably a half hour early—any excuse to take a break from her high-energy kids, who demanded her constant attention. That's why Mona loved her job so much. The grueling work of hauling lobster traps on the high seas was like a vacation compared to what awaited her at home.

"Randy and Sergio are saving us seats in a pew down front," Mona said as Hayley and Liddy scurried toward her from the parking lot.

"I want to go backstage first and wish Gemma luck," Hayley said making a beeline for the side door, which led to the church's parlor, where tea and coffee were served after services. Tonight it was being used as the backstage area for the cast and choir.

"Well, I'm going to go make sure I'm not stuck sitting behind Doris Sanborn, who is so fond of those ridiculously big, floppy, floral hats," Liddy scoffed. "Last fall she came into the Criterion Theatre and sat directly in front of me during that Ben Affleck *Gone Girl* movie and I couldn't see a damn thing happening on the screen!"

"Well, I'm going with Hayley," Mona said. "The last thing I want to do is spend the next ten minutes before the curtain goes up listening to you squawk about everything that annoys you."

"God will get you for that, Mona," Liddy said, turning on her heel and marching up the steps, where a young teenage usher then handed her a program. Liddy glanced at the cover and howled. "'*The Birth of Jesus*, Written by Edie Staples'? Are you kidding me? Does she actually believe she came up with the plot and dialogue? She doesn't even give the Bible a coauthor credit!"

Liddy snickered to the stone-faced kid cradling an armful of paper programs, but his lack of reaction just exasperated her and she brushed past him and went inside.

Hayley and Mona entered the parlor to find complete pandemonium. Ten first graders were running around in little sheep costumes. Hayley noticed one rebel kid refused to be a sheep and was dressed as a Teenage Mutant Ninja Turtle instead, complete with a blue eye mask. Reverend Staples, decked out in the Deluxe Shepherd Costume, which consisted of a full-length blue-gray-and-black-striped robe worn over a white tunic tied with a thin rope belt, complemented by a color-coordinated head garment, tried corralling the rambunctious kids with his tall wooden shepherd's crook. His wife, Edie, the auteur and author, who was apparently unfamiliar with the word "adaptation," hovered over Gemma's costar Hugo, who was slumped down in a chair in front of a table and mirror. He wore an off-white robe and brown sandals; most of his face was hidden by a shaggy, long beard and wig, which nailed Joseph's signature look. What Hayley could see of his face Edie was busy dabbing with a powder from her makeup kit. Hayley could certainly see Hugo's eyes, however, and they were wide with terror. The poor kid was stricken with a crippling case of stage fright.

"Any sign of Gemma?" Hayley asked as she and Mona glanced around the room. The choir, in their matching maroon robes and yellow sashes, was warming up with "Do-Re-Mi" from *The Sound of Music*. The Three Wise Men, with sparkling gold headpieces and sashes in purple, blue, and green, respectively, were running their lines at the last minute. And local fireman Wilbur White, clad in a long white shirt, wide burlap pants, and sandals, stood at the refreshment table and poured himself a plastic cup of red wine. Then he gulped it down and poured another.

"Who are you supposed to be, Wilbur?" Hayley asked as she and Mona crossed over to him.

"The crusty innkeeper who refuses to give Joseph and Mary a room. It's just one line, but I kept flubbing it in rehearsal. I'm scared of doing it during the performance."

"You'll be fine. Just save some of the Jesus juice for Sunday's Communion," Mona said, shaking her head.

"Mom!"

Gemma scooted over to them in full Virgin Mary mode, a baby blue robe flowing behind her as she moved, showing enough leg for them to admire her fetching Adult Goddess sandals. The Deluxe Mocha Brown Divine Wig, which Hayley found at Target, completed the startling transformation. Cradled in her arm was a Baby Jesus plush doll.

"Gemma, honey, you look fantastic!"

"Lot of good that's going to do me if I have no one to act with!" she wailed.

"What do you mean?"

"Hugo poked his head out to see if his cousin Dana made it down from Brunswick. He took one look at the packed house and has been in a catatonic state ever since!"

"I'm sure once he's out on stage, he'll be fine."

"He threw up on a kid in a camel costume. We had to cut the part from the play because we couldn't get it dry-cleaned in time."

They all glanced over at Hugo, who was still slouched in the chair, silent and motionless as Edie babbled on in his ear about something.

"Oh, this is going to be a disaster," Mona said.

Gemma's face fell.

"Mona, you're not helping!" Hayley said before grabbing Gemma by the shoulders. "He likes you, Gemma. You need to keep him calm and tell him everything's going to be all right, and that you two are in this together. If he forgets a line, you'll step in and help him."

Gemma nodded. "You're right."

They wandered over to the makeup table and Gemma knelt down, took his hand, and whispered words of encouragement to Hugo. His face relaxed slightly at her mere presence.

"Hayley, Mona, I'm so glad you both could make it to my little production," Edie said, grinning from ear to ear, before realizing what she had said. "Our production. I mean *our little production*. Opening night! Isn't it exciting?"

"I thought this was a onetime performance," Hayley said.

"Oh, it is," Edie said, adjusting the wig on Hugo's head as he squeezed Gemma's hand for support.

"Well, you know what they say about shows that open and close on the same night," Mona said, chortling.

Edie Staples gave them both a withering stare.

Hayley dug her heel into Mona's shoe as a warning to clam up.

"I'm going to go get Wilbur to share some of his Jesus juice," Mona said, wandering away to the refreshment table.

"It's Pinot Noir, Mona!" Edie said sharply before turning back to Hayley. "Hayley, knowing you, I'm sure you're right on top of this whole sad Garth Rawlings business."

Hayley eyed Hugo, who visibly tensed. "It's just one big, puzzling mystery."

"I should say so!" Edie exclaimed. "I read that the police are saying he was murdered, but they're stumped as to how it happened."

"That about sums it up."

"Well, if it *is* murder, I will bet our time-share in Boca Raton that it was that sleazy Ken Massey! Once when the Reverend and I stopped for clam rolls at the Trenton Bridge Lobster Pound, I saw him and Garth fighting like a couple of barnyard dogs."

Hayley glimpsed over to see Hugo watching her through the mirror in front of him. When they made eye contact, he immediately turned his attention back to Edie, who hadn't noticed he wasn't listening to her.

"Well, there's no denying Garth Rawlings and Ken Massey had a somewhat rocky past, and Ken does have a reputation for being a grade-A jerk," Hayley said. "But that doesn't necessarily mean he is a killer. Isn't that right, Hugo?"

Hugo let go of Gemma's hand and shifted in his chair uncomfortably.

"I don't know," he muttered.

"How could the poor boy know anything, Hayley?" Edie said, chuckling. "He barely knows where he is right now."

"Well, Hugo has made it clear to me that he believes Ken Massey is an innocent man and shouldn't be the subject of such wild accusations."

"I didn't say that. Like I said, I don't know anything."

"Mom . . . ," Gemma said, clenching her teeth, her eyes pleading with her mother to stop.

Hayley chose to bow to her daughter's wishes.

She could talk to Hugo after the show.

But Edie Staples was not so inclined.

She loved juicy gossip and dubious speculation.

Even moments before the curtains rose on her long-awaited Nativity play.

"Is that true, Hugo?" Edie asked, suddenly intrigued. "Do you think someone else killed Garth Rawlings?"

Hugo's eyes darted back and forth, searching for some escape from this distressing conversation. "Would you please just leave me out of this? How should I know who shot him?"

Shot him?

Hayley opened her mouth to speak, but Edie beat her to it.

"The coroner never said a word about Garth Rawlings being shot, Hugo. At least not in the papers. Where are you getting that information from?"

Hugo stood up, panicked. His hands were shaking.

"Places, everyone!" Reverend Staples bellowed as he finished gathering the adorable sheep in a flock around the shepherds and cued the choir. The choir members, their hymnals held up in front of them, filed out of the parlor, one by one, and into the church, singing.

"'O little town of Bethlehem, how still we see thee lie. . . .'"

Hayley and Edie kept their eyes glued on Hugo.

Gemma gently placed a hand on Hugo's arm. "Can we please discuss this after the show?"

And then Hugo had a full-on freak-out.

He shook off Gemma's hand and bolted out the parlor side door and into the night, leaving Reverend and Mrs. Staples without their leading man.

Joseph had left the building.

Chapter 28

The choir was on its last refrain of "O Little Town of Bethlehem." Once they took their seats, that would be the cue for Gemma and Hugo to take to the stage for the opening scene of the young couple in search of shelter for the night. Gemma had already stuffed a pillow up her robe to create the illusion of Mary's pregnancy.

Reverend Staples rushed up to his wife, Edie, and hissed, "Where in God's name is Hugo?"

"He left," Edie said, with a dazed look on her face.

"What? Why?"

"We were just talking . . . and . . . and . . ." The minister's wife's voice trailed off.

Out in the church they heard the choir finish singing, followed by feet clomping, indicating the choir members were now walking to their seats.

Edie clasped her hands together and closed her eyes.

"What are you doing?" Reverend Staples asked.

"Praying to the good Lord for a fast miracle."

"We don't have time for that! We need a Joseph right now!" Reverend Staples cried.

"I'll do it. I'll fill in for Hugo. I'll play Joseph," Hayley found herself saying, desperate to find a quick solution.

"That's preposterous," Reverend Staples said, scowling. "You look *nothing* like a boy!"

"Well, I'm the only one here not already cast in the play, so I don't see how much of a choice we have," Hayley said, picking up a bushy wig and beard attachment.

Mona ambled over from the refreshment table, feeling no pain after sharing the bottle of red wine with the fidgety and nervous Wilbur White, who was playing the innkeeper.

"What's the holdup? Let's get this show on the road!"

There was an awkward silence out in the church as the audience patiently waited for the play to start.

"Mona," Edie whispered. "Mona looks like a man."

"I beg your pardon," Mona said, a little too tipsy to be offended.

Hayley threw the wig on Mona and pasted the beard on her face.

"Gemma, go out there and stall for time until we find Mona a costume!" Edie said, pushing her out the parlor door into the main church, where

Gemma crossed in front of the first row of pews. Gingerly ascending the stairs, she tripped on the hem of her baby blue Virgin Mary robe, falling flat on her face. Just like Jennifer Lawrence at the Oscars.

The audience gasped.

Her uncle Randy bolted from his aisle seat and helped her stand back up.

Steadying herself, she made it up on the stage, which was decorated as a village and manger.

Polite applause met Gemma as she finally found the center-stage spotlight. Most people were just relieved the show was finally under way. Hayley could hear whoops and hollers from Gemma's wildly supportive uncles Randy and Sergio.

Reverend Staples shook his head until he was dizzy. "This is never going to work. This is never going to work."

"He's right," Mona said. "I don't know any of the lines. I don't even know what the play is about."

"It's the story of Christ's Birth," Hayley said.

"So who am I supposed to be? Moses?"

"Oh, dear God, we're doomed!" Edie wailed in despair.

"Look, I'm sorry. I just came here tonight to cheer Gemma on," Mona said. "I don't know anything about the Bible. The few times my parents made me go to church, I skipped Sunday school and went to the Rexall drugstore for a root beer float with some of the money the church gave us kids for staying quiet during the service."

"We don't pay children not to talk during church!" Reverend Staples said huffily.

"Well, my place of worship did. They had this big gold tin and it was overflowing with fives and twenties."

"That was the collection plate, Mona!" Hayley said. "You took the donations to the church!"

Hayley heard Gemma's voice calling from out on the stage. "Who will give my husband, Joseph, and me lodging in our time of need?"

Hayley snatched a white robe and hurled it at Mona. "I can tell she's dying out there! Here! Put this on and get out there and save my daughter from further humiliation."

"But I told you I have no idea what to say—"

"You can wing it! Just follow Gemma's lead," Hayley whispered frantically.

They could hear Gemma doing an admirable job keeping things moving until Joseph arrived. Feeling the baby kick. Pontificating on what name she would call her baby before finally settling on Jesus if it was a boy. And Caitlin if it was a girl. Wondering what could have happened to her husband.

Finally Mona trudged out the parlor door into the church, adjusting her beard. There were a few titters, but nobody recognized her right away.

Hayley closed the door just enough so she could still see what was happening on the stage.

"Joseph, I've been so worried. Where have you been?" Gemma improvised.

"Drinks Like A Fish," Mona said. "It was happy hour."

The audience roared with laughter.

At that point they all realized who was playing the part of Joseph and broke into more applause.

Mona, not a trained actress by any stretch of the imagination, turned and smiled and waved at the crowd.

A ham was born.

Gemma plowed on like a pro. "Why don't you knock on the door and see if the innkeeper has a room for us to stay tonight."

Mona looked around, dumbfounded. "What door? I don't see a door."

"Just pretend there's one there," Gemma whispered.

Mona then stomped her foot three times as she made a knocking motion with her hand.

"Damn! I forgot my cue!" Wilbur cried as he blew past Hayley, pushing her to the side, where she nearly bashed her head on the door frame.

Wilbur clomped up on stage. "Go away! I have no vacancies!"

"Of course you do! It's off-season!" Mona argued. "What do you think this is, Fourth of July weekend in Bar Harbor?"

More raucous laughter from the audience.

At the very least, Mona was personalizing the story for the locals.

Hayley wheeled around to see Revered Staples with a shell-shocked expression on his face and his wife, Edie, on the verge of tears as they watched the impromptu comedy act now unfolding on stage after weeks of hard work mounting their production.

Gemma and Mona muddled through the scene and then continued on in search of a manger to stay the night before it was mercifully time for the Three Wise Men to take to the stage to do a humorous bit about how two of them weren't so wise. It was a series of dumb jokes that couldn't be found in the Bible; it just afforded the auteur Edie the chance to add a little comic relief to her script, having no idea Mona would be providing most of the night's biggest laughs. The Three Wise Men weren't exactly the Three Amigos; most of their lines fell flat and even elicited a few groans. Edie Staples was no Tina Fey when it came to sharp and funny scriptwriting. It was obvious the audience was itching for Mona to come back.

Gemma charged into the parlor, where Hayley was waiting. "Mom, how could you do that? How could you scare Hugo off?"

"To be fair, I was willing to let it go, but it was Edie, who—"

"*You* started it!"

"You're absolutely right. I am so, so sorry. I never meant for this to happen."

"Come on! It was meant to be!" Mona said, proudly scratching her beard as she followed

Gemma into the parlor. "I'm a friggin' star! I'm killing it out there!"

Gemma was not amused.

"You don't believe me? Look!" Mona said, handing Gemma her phone. "Your own brother, Dustin, just tweeted this."

Gemma read it, sighed with an eye roll, and handed the phone to Hayley: **Mona steals show #laughingmyassoff**

"Not helping, Mona," Hayley said, tossing the phone back to her.

"Mom, why won't you leave Hugo alone?"

"Because I'm convinced he knows something he's not telling and it's eating him up inside and I know he would feel a lot better if he just told someone the truth."

"Then go talk to him after the show."

"I have no idea where to find him."

"Well, I do," Gemma said, bending over to stuff the pillow, which had made its way down to her ankles, back up her robe. "And I'll tell you if I don't die of embarrassment first from this train wreck of a pageant!"

With a deep breath Gemma marched back out on stage.

"What the hell is she talking about? We're a hit! We could take this show on the road!" Mona said, beaming, as she followed her out.

Chapter 29

Hayley used her iPhone as a flashlight as she approached the grand nineteenth-century weathered bay-front mansion, which was boarded up for the winter. The dirt road down to the main house was frozen solid, so she had to be careful not to slip and fall and crack her head wide open on the sheet of ice.

She heard a noise in the brush and stopped suddenly, aiming her illuminated phone to where the sound emerged. She spotted a wide-eyed coyote, who was just as surprised as she was, foraging for food there. They stared numbly at one another for a few seconds before the coyote thought it best to dash off into the woods to avoid any further contact.

Hayley continued toward the side porch, which wrapped around the mansion, and made her way up the creaky steps and to the screen door, which kept banging from the bitter-cold winter wind.

She swung it open and found the heavy back door behind it unlocked.

She heard someone coming up the steps behind her and spun around just as the light on her iPhone went out, plunging her into darkness. She could barely make out the shadowy figure advancing.

He looked as if he was wearing some kind of mask and was carrying something in his hands.

Was it a weapon?

An axe?

A baseball bat?

"Stay back!" Hayley yelled, pressing the button on the bottom of her phone so the light flashed back on.

The stranger froze just a few feet from her.

She pointed the phone at him.

Standing before her was Hugo.

He wasn't wearing a mask.

The hood of his heavy winter coat was just pulled up over his head to warm his ears.

And he wasn't gripping a weapon.

It was a pizza box.

He squinted his eyes in the harsh light.

"Mrs. Powell? What are you doing here? How did you find me?"

"Gemma said you might be here."

The mansion belonged to a filthy rich family from Chicago; they owned a company with a best-selling line of bacon products. The property was mostly frequented in the summer months by the founder's granddaughter, who was rather snooty. The locals referred to her behind her back as the "Pig Princess." Upon her departure in mid-September, she had hired Hugo's father to check up on the place occasionally during the winter months to make sure the pipes didn't freeze from the cold weather. It was a cushy gig for any local and Hugo's pop was paid hand-somely.

As they got to know one another, Hugo told Gemma that he would borrow his father's key from time to time and hang out at the mansion when he needed an escape from his life or a place to think. It was remote and quiet, and Gemma got the feeling that Hugo preferred spending time alone rather than socializing with other people. His worried mother had insisted he audition for the Nativity pageant because she wanted him to make more friends.

Hugo brushed past Hayley. "My pizza's getting cold."

"Hugo, I'm sorry. I didn't mean to upset you right before you went out on stage tonight," Hayley said, starting to follow him before he slammed the screen door in her face. "Please, can I just come in and talk to you for a minute?"

"How many times do I have to tell you? I don't know anything!"

"I want to believe you. I really do. But your face is telling me a different story."

"Why can't you just leave me alone?"

"Because a man has been killed. You may not have known him well. He may mean nothing to you. But he certainly meant something to a lot of people. His family. His neighbors. His clients. And if someone deliberately took his life, then he is owed some kind of justice, don't you agree?"

Hugo's bottom lip quivered.

He was trying not to cry.

Hayley slowly opened the screen door.

He didn't stop her.

She entered the kitchen.

Hugo still held the pizza box.

His hands were shaking.

"Hugo, you don't have to talk to me. I'm not a police officer or a detective. But it's very important you talk to Chief Alvares if you know something that can help with his investigation."

"I can't. . . ."

"Why not?"

"I just can't. . . ."

"Honey, if you willfully withhold key information that could lead to the arrest of the person responsible, then that's called 'obstruction of justice' and you could be arrested."

Hugo's eyes popped open and he dropped the pizza box to the floor.

"They could send me to jail?"

"Yes. That's why it's vitally important you tell the police anything you know."

Hugo gazed at the floor, his mind obviously racing.

Finally he glanced back up to Hayley. "Will you come with me?"

"Of course."

Hugo nodded and opened his mouth to speak, when all of a sudden they heard a loud thump.

Someone or something was lurking outside.

And whatever it was sounded much bigger than a coyote.

Chapter 30

The screen door squeaked as someone opened it and rattled the knob on the back door. It swung open fast. Hayley and Hugo jumped as Nick Ward, Lex's contracting foreman, entered the house and stepped into the light of the kitchen.

"Sorry, didn't mean to scare you," Nick said.

Hayley clutched her heart. "No, it's okay, Nick. I just didn't expect to see you here."

"That makes two of us," Nick said, smiling thinly.

"I just came by to have a little chat with Hugo," Hayley said, picking up the pizza box off the floor and setting it down on the counter.

"I see," Nick said, glancing at Hugo, who averted his eyes and stared at the scuffed brown snow boots he was wearing.

"I called Nick on my cell and told him I was coming here right before you showed up, Mrs. Powell," Hugo mumbled.

"He sounded upset and embarrassed about running out on the pageant the way he did. I wanted to swing by and make sure he got home safely. Maybe get him to share some of that pizza," Nick said, eyeing the pizza box from Little Anthony's.

"Well, help yourself," Hayley said. "And don't worry about driving Hugo home. I can do it. Where do you live, Hugo?"

"No bother at all. It will give Hugo and me a chance to talk over a few things. Work stuff. Lex is on the mend and planning to come back to the office tomorrow, so things have gotten much busier. You know how he likes to crack the whip."

"I sure do," Hayley said. "It's just that Hugo and I have an errand to run before I take him home."

"What kind of errand?" Nick asked, crossing to the counter and flipping open the pizza box.

There was no point in lying to him.

He would find out eventually.

"We're going to go to the police station and have a talk with Chief Alvares," Hayley said calmly, even though her stomach was doing flip-flops.

"Is that so?" Nick said, biting into a slice of pizza, the grease from the pepperoni dribbling down the side of his mouth.

Hugo shoved his hands in his pants pocket and kept his eyes glued to the floor.

Nick casually stepped closer to Hayley.

Not too close.

Just enough to make her nervous.

Hayley cleared her throat. "Hugo may have some information for him."

"About what?" Nick asked, picking a wad of cheese off the top of his pizza slice and dropping it into his mouth.

"Garth Rawlings's death," Hayley said, taking a small step back away from Nick.

"Such a tragedy," Nick said, shaking his head. "Someone so young and talented. *This* close to being famous. For his life to be snuffed out like that, just a real shame."

"Yes, it is. It's hard to imagine someone murdering him."

"Well, personally, I'm not so sure it *was* murder. The facts just don't add up from what I've been reading in Bruce Linney's column," Nick said, glaring at Hugo.

"The coroner's findings prove otherwise," Hayley said.

"You mean Sabrina Merryweather? I think Garth's wife should demand a second opinion, if you ask me."

"Are you questioning Sabrina's competence?"

"Why shouldn't I? You certainly have in the past, as I recall," he said, with a smug look on his face.

He was right.

Hayley had embarrassed Sabrina in a previous case.

And it nearly destroyed their friendship.

Or whatever word you would use to define their relationship.

"Friendship" might be a little too generous.

"You mind me asking what big revelation you're going to provide to the police now, Hugo?" Nick almost growled as he ripped off a thick piece of pizza crust with his teeth and began violently chewing it.

Hugo finally raised his eyes to meet Nick's, and Hayley saw the kid nearly shudder.

"That's between Hugo and Chief Alvares," Hayley said. "Let's go, Hugo."

She wanted to get them both out of there.

Nick Ward wasn't just making her nervous now. He was scaring her.

"Is that what you want, Hugo? You want to go with Hayley?" Nick said, locking eyes with the boy, stone-faced.

"No. I—I changed my mind," Hugo stammered.

"What?" Hayley asked, spinning around to him.

"I've got nothing to say. I don't know anything. The chief can arrest me all he wants for obstruction of whatever, but I can't tell him what I don't know."

"Let's talk about this in my car," Hayley said, putting a hand on his arm.

"No!" Hugo barked, jerking his arm away from her. "I want to go with Nick."

Nick Ward was now on his second slice of pizza and feeling empowered by his own impressive intimidation skills. "You heard the boy, Hayley.

But not to worry. I'll take good care of him and make sure he gets home safe and sound."

Nick put a thick, sinewy arm around Hugo's neck and drew him out the back door, determined to get the kid as far away from Hayley as possible.

Hayley could only watch them go and then kick herself for not getting Hugo out of there faster.

She was now certain of one thing: Hugo knew something that could incriminate Nick in the death of Garth Rawlings.

But Nick wasn't a ghost. He couldn't just pass through a wall into a locked warehouse and beat Garth to a pulp without leaving any marks or any signs of a struggle.

It was Nick. It has to be. She felt it in her gut. *But how did he do it?*

Chapter 31

"Oh, man, this is good," Aaron moaned as he slid the moist cake off his fork and into his mouth. "What is it?"

"Holiday spice cake with eggnog buttercream," Hayley said, sipping coffee from her Christmas Kermit and Miss Piggy coffee mug she had been given one year in an office Secret Santa exchange.

Aaron smiled, savoring every bite of the cake. When all that was left on his plate were a few scattered crumbs, Hayley cut him a second piece.

She had spent all Saturday afternoon baking the cake and roasting a turkey and whipping up all of Aaron's favorite side dishes. She knew Gemma would be out late at a wrap party for the Nativity pageant, and Dustin was spending the night at his buddy Spanky's house, so she seized upon the opportunity to serve Aaron a romantic dinner.

She had gone all out.

And he was basically surrendering to her efforts.

Which was made clear when he set his fork down and leaned in for a kiss.

His eyes closed. His lips pursed.

Looking dashing in a handsome red cashmere half-zip sweater.

The faint smell of a masculine aftershave wafting in the air.

Their lips touched and Aaron gently placed a hand on the back of Hayley's neck, drawing her closer until they were in a tight embrace.

They were picking up where they had left off that night they wrapped presents around the Christmas tree after the kids had gone to bed.

But there were no kids in the house this evening to make Hayley feel awkward and uncomfortable.

She had gone to great lengths to plan this date perfectly.

And to her relief and joy, it was working.

Until they heard loud banging at the front door.

"Who could that be? I'm not expecting anybody," Hayley said, almost to herself, as she pulled away from Aaron and stood up. "I'll be right back."

Aaron smiled ruefully, frustrated this long-awaited moment had been interrupted. He picked up his fork and began dabbing at the last bits of cake pieces on his dessert plate.

Hayley walked through the living room to the foyer and out onto the porch, where she unlocked the door and opened it to find Lex standing on the steps, still walking with crutches. His cheeks were rosy from the cold air, and he wore a plaid flannel shirt jacket and a gray earflap tracker hat.

He took the hat off at the sight of Hayley.

Always the gentleman.

Hayley gave him a puzzled look. "Lex, is anything wrong?"

"Yes, Hayley, there is. I'd like to come in and talk to you about it, if you don't mind."

"Well, actually, now is not a good time—"

"Why? Something up with the kids?"

"No, it's not that. The kids are fine. It's just . . ."

She glanced nervously back in the direction of the dining room.

Lex plowed ahead, not really listening to what she was saying. "I got a call from Hugo tonight. Poor kid was a basket case. He was worried the cops were going to show up at his house at any moment and arrest him right in front of his parents. He said it was you who told him he was going to go to jail."

"I was just trying to convince him that it would be in his best interest to talk to Sergio about the Garth Rawlings murder."

"What the hell does that poor kid know about the Garth Rawlings murder?"

"I don't know, but he knows something. My guess is he saw what happened and is covering for the murderer."

"Who?"

"Nick Ward."

"My foreman, Nick? Hayley, are you crazy? Nick has worked for me for years. I know the guy like he's my own brother. There's no way he's capable of violence."

"It was no secret he and Garth didn't like each other. Garth was always complaining about the noise coming from your workshop."

"Yeah, they butted heads a few times. Garth Rawlings was a highfalutin, self-obsessed, irritating jerk! I didn't think much of him either! That doesn't mean I'd do anything to harm him physically. My crew, Nick, Billy, Hugo, they're all decent, genuine, solid guys, Hayley. There's no way they had anything to do with this, so I want you to do me a favor and stop harassing them."

"I'm not *harassing* them, Lex."

"Seriously? You expect me to believe that? We were together almost two years, Hayley. I know how you get when you're focused on solving a mystery!"

"Yes! And the reason I can't let it go is because your intern, Hugo, is hiding something! I can feel it in my bones!"

"Fine! If he is, then let the cops bring him in for questioning! But guess what? If Sergio had anything, *anything*, tying one of my guys to the crime, he would've done that already! He's got nothing! And from what I've heard around town, he still doesn't even have a clue how it happened!"

"Everything all right out here?"

Hayley spun around to see Aaron staring down Lex.

She turned back around and gave Lex a weak smile. "No, everything's fine."

Lex gripped the steel rungs on his crutches. "Didn't realize you had company."

"Lex, you've met Aaron Palmer, right?"

Lex shook his head. "Nope."

"Really? I thought for sure you two would have met by now," Hayley said, her voice cracking, which it usually did when she was a bundle of nerves.

"Heard of him, though," Lex said, refusing to make eye contact with Aaron.

Aaron extended his hand. "Nice to meet you."

Lex eyed it warily before deciding it would be rude not to shake hands at least.

The two men gripped each other, the knuckles on both their hands turning white, each trying to demonstrate their manly strength. If they were sitting at a table opposite each other, it would undoubtedly turn into an impromptu arm-wrestling contest.

Lex let go first because he was about to lose one of the crutches helping to keep his balance.

Aaron smirked slightly, as if silently declaring himself the winner.

"How can we help you, Lex?" Aaron asked in a friendly tone, snaking an arm around Hayley and pulling her closer to him.

Lex did a slow burn.

He looked like he wanted to punch Aaron in the face.

And given his somewhat-checkered past, it was entirely possible he would go for it if Hayley didn't do something fast to intervene.

"Lex—"

"Hayley and I were having a private conversation," Lex said, cutting her off.

"Not too private. I could hear you shouting all the way back there in the dining room. I'm sure the neighbors probably heard you too."

"Well, if you head on back to where you came from and give us a little space, I promise to keep my voice down while I finish talking to Hayley. Is that okay with you?"

Hayley wriggled out from under Aaron's arm and stepped forward.

She had to put a stop to this before it escalated.

"Lex, why don't you go wait in the truck and I'll come out and we can finish discussing—"

"The thing is, Lex," Aaron interjected. "We were right in the middle of a nice dinner when you showed up unannounced, and I think the polite thing for you to do is let us get back to it. I'm sure whatever it is you need to resolve with Hayley can wait until tomorrow. Isn't that right, Hayley?"

Hayley had no idea what to do.

These two bulls were locking horns and she didn't have a red cape for distracting either of them.

Finally Lex slightly bowed his head. "I understand. We were just about done talking anyway. Good night, Hayley. Dr. Palmer. Oh, wait. You're a vet, right?"

"That's right."

"So can I call you 'Doctor' if you're not a *real* doctor?"

Aaron was about to leap at his throat.

Hayley quickly stepped in front of him. "Good night, Lex."

Lex turned to maneuver back down the front steps. One of his crutches hit a patch of ice and skidded out from under him. He was about to topple over before Hayley jumped down off the porch and grabbed him by the arm to steady him. They had twisted around so they were facing Aaron. Hayley was now underneath Lex's arm, the top of her head nestled just underneath his nose.

"Your hair smells good. Is that a new shampoo?"

Hayley muttered a reply.

Yes.

No.

She didn't even remember.

It was too awkward a moment and she just wanted to get past it.

Especially since she suspected Lex nearly falling was a calculated move; he knew she would immediately rush to his side.

If that was true, it was a genius move.

But she was angry that he would even try something so devious.

Aaron's hawkish expression never wavered.

He didn't flinch.

He was not going to give Lex the satisfaction of a jealous reaction and risk revealing his fear that the handsome, macho contractor was any kind of threat to him.

Aaron continued to stand his ground as Hayley extricated herself from Lex's grasp and hurried back up the steps as Lex used his crutches to limp toward his truck, which was parked next to the curb in front of Hayley's house.

Hayley didn't even wait for Lex to drive away before shutting the door and locking it. She turned to find Aaron standing there, arms folded, fuming.

"I'm sorry about that, Aaron."

"He still has deep feelings for you."

"That's silly. I told you, Aaron, it's over."

"Not in his mind. That man has not let you go. He's looking for a way to get you back. So the only hope of us ever working out is if you stop seeing him. Period."

"You mean even as friends?"

"Yes. And if you can't do that . . ."

"What?"

"You have a choice to make. Me or him."

Island Food & Spirits
by
Hayley Powell

This holiday my brother is hosting our annual Christmas Eve dinner; and as I do every year, I am going to make my favorite dessert, chocolate bourbon pecan pie. I only bake these pies once a year for two big reasons! First, I love this dessert so much that I will eat a whole pie in one sitting, which does my waistline no favors. Second, these pies are made with bourbon and I just can't rationalize putting all that bourbon in a pie that is already loaded with calories when I can simply add it to a glass of Diet Coke, heralding much better results when it comes to my diet!

Last year it was my turn to host, so I took the three days off before Christmas Eve to make my pies and do some much-needed house cleaning, present wrapping, and preparing the Christmas Eve dinner.

I had just sat down with a cup of coffee in front of the TV (one has to caffeinate in order to motivate one's self) when the phone rang. I should have expected something to come up on my precious days off, as something always does. And I was right. It was the high-school nurse calling to inform me that Gemma was running a fever. The flu was going around the school like wildfire, so I was asked to come and pick her up immediately.

Now, don't get me wrong. I love my daughter. But for those of you with kids, you can sympathize with me when it comes to having a moody teenager. Add a fever and chills into the mix and you have a disaster in the making.

I grabbed my car keys and winter coat and slipped into my boots while noting what extra remedies I would need to pick up at the Rite Aid, since I knew our medicine cabinet was pretty bare. Then, bracing myself with a big sigh, I headed out the door to the car and off to the high school.

With my daughter finally bundled into the backseat of the car and complaining loudly of how achy and awful she felt (why didn't the school ever get an epidemic of laryngitis?), we finally began the fifteen-minute journey home and my cell phone rang again. I glanced at the number and my heart sank. It was my son's junior high school. And sure enough, on the other end was the school nurse requesting that I come and pick up Dustin right away, as he seemed to be suffering from flu symptoms.

Well, as every parent knows, when two teenagers are down sick with the flu, there is only one word that best sums up what any hardworking mother experiences over the next few days— torture!

I said a quick prayer to myself as I headed to Dustin's school to pick him up and steeled myself for the tough days ahead. I am acutely aware as to why I never went to nursing school after high school like some of my friends. I just don't have that kind of patience!

As expected, the first day was filled with an endless stream of "Mom, I'm hot!" "Mom, I'm cold!" "Mom, can I have soup?" "Mom, I can't eat this soup!" "Mom, can I have toast?" "Mom, why isn't there strawberry jam on my toast?" "I hate strawberry jam!" I was already reaching my breaking point.

By the end of the second day, I was physically exhausted from running up and down the stairs, catering to their every need, but still trying to maintain a sweet smile on my face. It was the Christmas season, and I knew a positive outlook was my best shot at making it through this crisis.

In between my Florence Nightingale duties, I was also trying to plan a menu, prepare food, wrap gifts, scrub the bathroom, polish the floor, and dust the furniture for Christmas Eve. I kept my eye on the prize: a big piece of my chocolate bourbon pecan pie. I did have a minor meltdown on the third day. I screamed up the stairs at the kids that if I heard one more whiny "Mom!" the flu wasn't the only thing they were going to have to deal with. That shut them up pretty quick.

I collapsed on the couch and closed my eyes for a brief moment of rest. All of a sudden my cell phone, which was lying on the coffee table in front of me, began buzzing nonstop. I tried meditating to ignore it, but about a dozen text messages were coming through at a furious pace. It was my kids upstairs obeying mother's orders not to yell, but choosing, instead, to communicate through their smartphones for their immediate needs.

I jumped up off the couch and raced upstairs and, though not proud of myself, ranted and raved and threatened to cancel Christmas if I didn't get at least five minutes of peace and quiet. I must have yelled pretty hard because my head began pounding, so I stormed off to my bedroom to lie down for a spell.

The good news is the kids felt much better by the time the Christmas Eve dinner rolled around. The adults sang cocktail-infused "Santa-tini" Christmas carols all through the night. There were yummy smells of turkey and ham and stuffing wafting in from the kitchen, and gales of laughter as everyone toasted and sang, full of happiness and good cheer.

At least that's how I *thought* it was going. I could only imagine the fun that everyone was having downstairs as I huddled, shivering, under a stack of blankets in my bed. Yes, I had caught the kids' flu and was so sick that I couldn't even make it downstairs to join the festivities.

It was only later, the following morning on Christmas Day, that I managed finally to drag myself out of bed and downstairs to have a piece of that chocolate bourbon pecan pie. It was the only thing I could think about. Unfortunately, all I found were two empty pie plates on the counter and a note propped up beside them that said, *Your Best Chocolate Bourbon Pecan Pies Yet! Love, the Gang*

I hope you all have a merry Christmas this year. I know I will. And to make up for missing last year, I will be having an extra "Santa-tini" or two and making three chocolate bourbon pecan pies. One *just* for me!

"Santa-tini" Cocktails

Ingredients

2 ounces chili-infused vodka
2 ounces good chocolate liqueur

Cocoa powder
Cayenne pepper
Whipping cream
One small chili pepper

Mix some of your cocoa powder with a pinch of cayenne and rim a chilled martini glass with it. Add the vodka and chocolate liqueur to a shaker filled with ice and shake it well, then pour into the martini glass. Top with the whipped cream and place your chili pepper on top of that. A guaranteed hot time will be had by all!

Now, let's combine two of my favorite treats, bourbon and chocolate, but in a pie! What could possibly be better than that?

Chocolate Bourbon Pecan Pie

<u>Ingredients</u>
1 piecrust of your choice, home-
    made, store-bought, etc.

<u>Filling</u>
3 eggs
1 cup packed dark brown sugar

½ cup light corn syrup
½ cup dark corn syrup
½ cup your favorite bourbon
2 tablespoons melted butter
½ teaspoon salt
1½ cups pecan halves divided in half
¾ cup bittersweet chocolate baking
    chips divided in half

Place your crust in a pie dish and flute your edges. Set aside until ready to use.

In a large bowl, beat eggs, brown sugar, corn syrups, bourbon, butter, and salt until blended. Stir in one cup of the pecans and a half cup of the chocolate chips. Pour into your ready piecrust and top with remaining pecans and chocolate chips. Bake in a 325-degree preheated oven for 50 to 60 minutes or until crust is golden brown and filling is puffed. Cool completely, slice, serve, and enjoy!

Chapter 32

"Look, Hayley, I've gone over the facts of this case about a dozen times and nothing makes sense," Bruce said, sitting behind his desk the following Monday as he bit into a grilled meat loaf sandwich on a whole wheat roll he had picked up at the Epi Sub & Pizza Shop on Cottage Street.

Hayley sat opposite him on an uncomfortable metal chair in his tiny, stuffy office at the *Island Times*. "But that doesn't mean you close the book on it. There has to be something we're all missing."

"Would you mind opening the door a bit more?" Bruce said, wiping some stray ketchup off his cheek with a wadded-up napkin.

Hayley turned to see the door already half open. "Why?"

"I just want to make sure everyone knows we're simply having a professional conversation about a local murder investigation and that nothing inappropriate is going on in here."

"I'm sure they know that, Bruce."

"Sometimes people get the wrong idea."

"You mean after what happened at the Christmas party?"

"Do you *have* to bring that up?"

"Is that the reason you're so nervous to be alone with me?"

"No, of course not."

"Come on. You were never concerned about us talking in your office alone before that incident. I thought we decided to forget about that whole office-party thing."

"Just crack the door open some more, would you, please, Hayley?"

Hayley sighed, reached over, grabbed the handle, and opened the door all the way before calling out, "In case anyone out there is wondering, Bruce and I are having a strictly professional, work-related dialogue about his next column. Is everyone clear on that?"

There was a single "yeah" from the sales office. Everyone else was out to lunch.

"Thanks for that," Bruce said, frowning.

"Let it go, Bruce. I did the morning after it happened."

Hayley suspected that the silly groping incident was far more magnified in Bruce's mind because it brought up some unresolved feelings he might still have for her, but there was no way she was ready to delve into that discussion, given the drama she was currently juggling with Aaron and Lex.

"I'm not even sure what to write about in my column anymore. I'm as stumped as the police are."

"There are questions you can raise, Bruce. For instance, Sergio found a lit pipe in Garth Rawlings's hand."

"So?"

"So, if someone is smoking a pipe, doesn't that suggest he was casually minding his own business right before he was killed?"

"Yeah, I guess."

"And if Sabrina's findings are to be believed—that Garth suffered massive internal injuries, which was what killed him—how does that square up with him smoking a pipe? That would mean the killer had to get inside the locked warehouse somehow, beat him to death, then take the time to light a pipe and put it in between his fingers before fleeing the scene! It's a ridiculous scenario!"

"What if someone bludgeoned him outside the warehouse, attacked him on the street, but he was still alive after they left, and he managed to stumble back inside and lock the door, but then died from his injuries before he had the chance to call for help?"

"That still doesn't explain the lit pipe! Wouldn't you call 911 *before* you took the time to light up a pipe and smoke it?"

"It sure is a head-scratcher. I'll give you that," Bruce said, polishing off his sandwich and tossing the napkin, the wrapped wax paper the sandwich came in, and a crumpled brown bag into the wastebasket next to his desk.

"Sergio examined the pipe. The only finger-prints he found belonged to Garth Rawlings. So Garth lit that pipe himself *before* whatever happened to him happened."

"Okay, so what do you want me to do?"

"Just keep the story alive. I don't want this case to be swept under the carpet. I want whoever is responsible to know we're not letting this go, and eventually we're going to nail him."

"You mean Nick Ward."

"Yes."

"You are one hundred percent certain it's him?"

"Yes."

"Even though there isn't a shred of evidence that implicates him?"

"Yes."

"So you're relying on your woman's intuition?"

"That's a sexist term, Bruce. I prefer 'gut instinct.'"

"Fine. Whatever. I'll keep writing about the case. But if you ask me, this is one mystery that is going to remain unsolved."

Hayley took that as a personal challenge.

She stood up and stepped outside the office. "Thank you for that very enlightening review of the case, Bruce. You're a crackerjack crime reporter and I am happy to report to everybody within earshot that there was not even a mild flirtation going on during our constructive conversation."

Hayley heard giggling coming from the sales office.

Bruce came out from behind his desk and angrily slammed his door shut.

Hayley had not taken her lunch hour yet, so she closed out her computer, threw on her winter jacket, and headed to her car. She drove directly over to the building that housed Garth Rawlings's kitchen warehouse. She wasn't sure why. She just thought walking around the outside of the building once or twice might tell her something she may not have thought of previously. She knew there were no windows for an assailant to enter through. The only way inside was through that locked door. When she parked her car out front, she noticed that Lex's construction office next door looked closed up and deserted. She assumed the guys were probably out doing a contracting job at a local residence. The yellow police tape draped across the front door of Garth's office had finally been removed by the police, indicating Sergio felt there was no further need to scour the inside for clues.

Hayley got out of her car and circled around the building.

Nothing appeared out of the ordinary.

She walked back to the front of the warehouse.

She felt a chill.

Not from the cold wintry air.

It was more like a feeling.

As if someone was watching her.

She scanned the area.

No sign of anyone.

She was definitely alone.

Maybe Bruce was right and this case would just remain an unsolved mystery.

She started crunching through the hardened snow back to her car; then a heavy wind gust blew through and she heard a rattling sound.

Hayley pivoted to see the door to Garth's office bang against the hinges.

That wouldn't happen if the bolt had been slid securely in place.

Hayley raced over and turned the knob.

Sure enough. Someone left the door unlocked!

She opened it and poked her head inside. "Hello?"

No answer.

She quietly entered, shutting the door behind her.

She decided that this would be her last chance to find anything that would shed some light on what really happened that fateful night. And if her final search of the crime scene turned up nothing, she would be done investigating.

After nearly thirty minutes of wandering around the kitchen, her last-ditch, spur-of-the-moment fishing expedition was officially over.

She found nothing.

Absolutely nothing.

Bruce was right.

Garth Rawlings's death was going to be an unsolved mystery perhaps featured on a couple of true-crime shows, like the Investigation Discovery network or CBS's *48 Hours Mystery,* but otherwise soon forgotten.

She was about to turn to leave, when a bag was suddenly thrown over her head and arms of steel encircled her, pinning her arms to her side. The attacker lifted her violently up off the ground. She struggled mightily in his grasp as he half carried, half dragged her over to the far end of the warehouse before releasing her with one arm and wrapping the other around her neck in a choke hold while reaching for something. She heard some kind of door open; and before she knew what was happening and could tear the bag off her head to get a look at her assailant, she was shoved inside a bitter-cold space. Her head smacked against something hard. She grabbed at it and it felt like a big slab of frozen beef.

She knew exactly where she was—the walk-in freezer that Garth kept his food stored in so it wouldn't spoil.

She finally managed to rip the bag off her head just as the door slammed shut, enveloping her in darkness. She ran over and pounded on it, but she knew in her heart that it was hopeless. The person who threw her in here was already gone.

Hayley reached for her cell phone.

No bars.

No signal.

No way to call anyone for help.

It was only a matter of time before she would succumb to the harsh freezing temperature and the lack of oxygen.

Someone had left her here to die.

Chapter 33

Panicked, Hayley banged on the steel freezer door for almost five minutes, screaming at the top of her lungs for help, but to no avail. There was no one outside. She felt so helpless. Her lips quivered and her whole body shivered. She hugged herself in a vain attempt to keep warm. She was angry she didn't fight back harder against her attacker. Deliver a swift kick to his shins. Maybe he would have loosened his grip long enough for her to get away. But that was all hypothetical. The reality was she was stuck in here and she was now in a very serious and deadly situation.

She used the light from her cell phone to look around. There were just stacks of frozen meats and vegetables and cartons of ice cream. A couple of hanging slabs of beef were there. Nothing she could use to aid in any kind of escape. The freezer door was sealed up tight. Her phone was already flashing its low battery signal. Once her phone was dead, she would be in total blackness, left all alone with her last thoughts before eventually succumbing to hypothermia.

She sank to the floor and hugged her knees. There was nothing for her to do. She wondered who would find her, how long it would take. Her kids would call Sergio when she didn't come home. Sergio would contact Aaron. There would be a thorough search around town: the *Island Times,* Drinks Like A Fish, all of the places she normally frequented. Sergio would sweep her house and office for clues, but he wouldn't find anything suggesting she was at Garth Rawlings's kitchen warehouse. The last person she spoke to was Bruce, and she gave no indication where she was going when she left him—only that she was taking her lunch hour. Then Sergio would check all the local restaurants that were open this time of year. And would turn up nothing. No one would have seen her. She drove over to the warehouse almost on a whim. That meant someone had to be following her and was afraid of what she might find here.

How long? How long would it take before someone finally opened the freezer and found her frozen corpse? Days? Weeks? Months? The only person who used this place was very much dead.

She wanted to close her eyes.

Fall into a deep sleep.

At least, then, she would finally escape this arctic hell.

Her eyelids were heavy.

Her fingers were numb.

She hugged herself more tightly.

It wouldn't be long now.

Hayley fought the urge to close her eyes, but the idea of relief from her surroundings was overpowering.

She was giving up.

Her last thoughts were of her children.

And how much she loved them and would miss them.

And then everything went black.

She wasn't sure how long she was out before she felt a pair of hands grabbing her coat.

She was weak.

Disoriented.

Confused.

Unable to move.

Like a deadweight.

Someone dragged her slowly across the floor.

When her eyes fluttered open, they hurt from a blazing fluorescent light. She brought her hand to her face, covering them until they could adjust to the harsh light.

She finally managed to focus on someone standing over her, a woman, holding a stack of blankets. When she knelt down to wrap Hayley in them, trying to bring her body temperature back up, Hayley saw her face clearly.

"Tiffany . . ."

"How the hell did you lock yourself inside the freezer, Hayley?"

Hayley coughed. Her body was still spasming from the shivering cold.

"I didn't. . . . Someone . . . put me there—"

"What? Are you serious? Who?"

"I don't know. . . ."

Hayley was slowly coming back to life.

She checked her hands for frostbite, but they looked okay.

Tiffany scooted to the kitchen and made some hot coffee and cranked the heat in the warehouse to eighty degrees. After about twenty minutes Hayley started to feel a little better.

"We should get you to the hospital so they can check you out," Tiffany said. "Can you walk?"

"No, I'm fine, Tiffany. I don't need to go to the hospital. How did you find me?"

"The building's owner called this morning and said if I cleared out Garth's belongings by New Year's Day, he would let me out of the lease. So I dropped by to take a quick inventory and see what kind of moving job I was going to be faced with. Then I went to rent a U-Haul and decided to start with the freezer first, and there you were balled up on the floor, passed out."

"If you hadn't come along . . ."

"You would have frozen to death. Yes, I saved your life. You see? Even adulteresses can have a good side."

Hayley nodded. "Thank you."

"Are you sure you don't want to go to the hospital?"

"Yes. Tiffany, when you got here, did you see anyone else around?"

"No. No one suspicious anyway. Just one of Lex Bansfield's crew, but he works right next door, so it wasn't exactly out of the ordinary."

"Which crew member was it?"

"The foreman, I think. Nick something."

"Nick Ward?"

"Yes. Him."

"What was he doing?"

"He was getting in his truck as I pulled up. I waved at him, but he didn't see me. He looked like he was in a hurry. Do you think he was the one who put you in the freezer?"

"I can't say for sure, but right now I'm betting on it."

Hayley climbed to her feet. She stumbled and swayed a bit, and Tiffany held her arm to steady her.

"I need to go—"

"Look, Hayley, we haven't exactly been the best of friends lately, and I wasn't quite prepared for you to dig so deep into my personal life, but I'm worried about you."

Hayley stumbled toward the door that led outside the warehouse.

"Where are you going?" Tiffany asked.

"I need to get inside Lex's workshop and look around."

"You *need* to see a doctor!"

Hayley limped out the door, leaving Tiffany to start her inventory, and crossed to the entrance to Lex's half of the warehouse. She tried the handle. It was locked. Frustrated, she jiggled it again.

"You could just ask me to let you in," a man's voice said from behind her.

Hayley whirled around.

It was Lex.

He was climbing out of his truck as he struggled with his crutches.

"Lex, I know you're angry with me, but I just need five minutes inside your workshop. If I don't find anything, I promise I will let the whole thing go."

Lex laughed. "Don't make promises you can't keep."

He noticed her gripping the door handle to keep her balance.

"Are you all right?"

"Yes. Please, will you help me?"

He ambled over to her, using his crutches, while fishing a ring of keys from the pocket of his corduroy pants. He inserted one of the keys into the lock and swung open the door.

"After you."

Hayley straightened herself and marched inside, taking great pains not to let on that she had nearly died twenty minutes earlier.

Lex flipped on all the lights and followed

Hayley as she poked around, checking for clues. "Where is Nick Ward's desk?"

Lex pointed to a small metal table and chair in the corner. There was no file drawer or pencil holder or even a stapler nearby.

"Nick's not one for paperwork. He prefers banging nails and sawing wood. He spends more time out in the field than he does here."

Hayley nodded and carefully scanned the workshop from top to bottom.

"What are you trying to find?"

Hayley shrugged. "How one man could kill another man when neither of them was in the same room."

"That's crazy."

She was just about done when suddenly she spotted something.

On the wall opposite Nick Ward's desk.

A few inches above another metal desk and chair.

"Who sits over there?"

"My intern, Hugo. Why?"

She walked over and examined it.

It was putty or some type of caulking.

"What happened here?"

"What are you talking about?"

"This. It looks like some kind of hasty repair job."

Lex shuffled over and stood behind her, looking at the dried paste. "Beats me. Never noticed it before. Maybe it was here when we moved in."

"Did you paint the walls when you rented the place?"

"We did. They were pretty scuffed up."

"So this has to be a relatively recent repair. And this is the wall you share with Garth's kitchen next door, am I right?"

"Yeah. So? What are you getting at Hayley?"

"Come on."

She led Lex back out of the workshop, not as fast as she would have liked, since she was still woozy from being in cold storage and Lex was following her on a pair of crutches.

She hurried back through the door into Garth's side of the warehouse, with Lex trying to keep up.

Tiffany was in the kitchen, stacking plates and saucepans she had laid out on Garth's long stainless-steel worktable.

"Excuse us, Tiffany, we just need to check something."

"Oh, hello," Tiffany said, noticing Lex.

He gave her a distracted half smile.

Hayley charged over to the far wall and started feeling it with her hands.

"Hayley, there's no way Nick somehow killed Garth Rawlings when Nick wasn't even here," Lex said, sighing impatiently.

"Here. Look at this," Hayley said, pointing to a small, neat hole in the wall opposite the kitchen area.

"So you think this place has termites?" Lex asked, snickering.

"This is the exact same spot on this side as the patched-up hole in your workshop."

"I'm not following."

"Hugo knew what happened. He slipped and said Garth was shot. And it was Nick Ward, I strongly suspect, who killed him."

"What? How?" Tiffany asked, scurrying over to join the conversation.

"He pulled the trigger on the other side of this wall, and the bullet came through this hole into the kitchen and struck Garth as he cooked over here at his workstation."

"But the coroner said someone beat him to death. She never said anything about him being shot," Tiffany said, examining the neat hole in the wall.

"You have to admit, Hayley, that poses some-what of a problem with your theory," Lex said.

"She's wrong. She has to be," Hayley said, grabbing her now-working cell phone. "I have to call Sergio."

Chapter 34

"That doesn't make any sense," Sabrina said huffily, marching away from Hayley and Sergio, her high heels clicking on the tiled floor of her medical lab. "Now, if you excuse me, I have a lot of work to do."

"Sabrina, wait. I'm convinced Hayley is onto something here. Would you at least take a look at the body one more time before the burial and see if you missed a bullet?"

Sabrina straightened her white lab coat and threw her chin up in the air as she stared daggers at Hayley. "I can't believe you are doing this to me again! Is it your life's mission now to ruin my reputation? My God, Hayley, I thought we were on the road to being friends again. I confided in you and fed you information on this very case, and now you're going to turn it all against me?"

"This has nothing to do with you, Sabrina. This is about getting Garth Rawlings the justice he and his family deserve," Hayley said calmly, trying hard not to antagonize Sabrina more than she already had.

"Please, Sabrina. . . ," Sergio said, a puppy dog look on his face. "One more examination, just to be sure."

But not even his charm and South American good looks were going to work on her. Sabrina was refusing to budge.

"No. It's impossible."

"Sabrina, nobody's trying to make you look incompetent," Sergio said.

"I can't do it," Sabrina said.

"I can always get a court order," Sergio said, quickly losing patience.

"No, I mean I *literally cannot* examine the body. He was cremated yesterday."

Hayley gasped.

It was like a blow to the solar plexus.

"What? How? Who?" Hayley sputtered.

"His wife," Sabrina said.

Tiffany!

Hayley turned to Sergio. "Maybe Tiffany knew her husband had been shot and wanted to get rid of the body quickly in order to make it impossible for anyone ever to discover the truth, so she ordered her husband's body to be cremated."

"Tiffany did no such thing," Sabrina said, folding her arms and shaking her head at Hayley. "She was simply executing the wishes of the deceased, who clearly stated in his living will that he did not want to be buried."

"Does she have the ashes in her possession?" Hayley asked. "Maybe we can find a piece of the bullet there or in the oven, where the body was cremated."

"The ovens are hot enough to destroy metal fragments," Sabrina said, desperate to put this matter to rest. "We're done here."

"What do we do now?" Hayley asked Sergio.

"Take one more look at the autopsy photos," Sergio said, pivoting to face Sabrina, whose mouth was already open and ready to protest. He raised a hand for her to keep quiet. "I'm chief of police here, Sabrina, and it's part of your job to assist me in any open investigation. I have yet to close the case on Garth Rawlings—so, until I do, you are obligated to provide me with any information I request."

Sabrina mulled over his words for a few seconds, ultimately deciding she didn't have much of a choice. She turned swiftly on her heels and marched over to a filing cabinet on the other side of the lab.

High heels *clicking, clicking, clicking.*

"They haven't been uploaded to the computer yet, so you'll have to settle for the hard copies."

She heaved a big sigh as she yanked open the top filing drawer and snatched a manila folder out before making a big show of slamming the metal door shut again. Then she hurled the folder down on top of a desk, forcing Hayley and Sergio to walk over to her instead of her bringing the photos to them. She was at the point where she would no longer go out of her way to help them.

Sergio picked up the folder and flipped it open, going through the autopsy photos, one by one, before handing them off to Hayley to examine.

"What is she, your deputy now?" Sabrina asked, adding a healthy dose of sarcasm.

They ignored the comment.

Sergio's eyes fixed on something in one of the photos. "What's that?"

Sabrina wrested the photo from his hand and gazed at it. "What? I don't see anything."

Sergio pointed with his finger. "That."

"That's the liver," she scoffed.

"Yes, but look at that black dot. What is that?"

"It's liver damage, probably from the beating."

Sergio's finger moved across the photo. "And what's that?"

"The intestines. I'm not here to teach you a class on the human anatomy!" Sabrina bellowed.

"Hear me out, Sabrina," Sergio said. "I heard about a similar case once up in Toronto. If Garth was shot—"

"He wasn't," Sabrina said emphatically.

"Okay, but for the sake of argument, let's just say he was."

"He wasn't."

She wasn't about to give an inch.

"Sabrina, would it really hurt just to hear what Sergio has to say?" Hayley asked as gently as possible.

"Fine. Whatever. Okay. Hypothetically, he was shot."

"Now, what if the bullet entered somewhere down here, near the scrotum, and tore up through him?" Sergio asked, tracing the trajectory with his finger. "Couldn't it cause roughly the same damage as blunt-force trauma?"

This caught Sabrina off guard. She remained silent as she thought it over. Her face was a mask of professional indignation. However, there was a crack in her veneer. A few seconds of doubt showed in her eyes.

Still, she was holding firm.

The wait for her response was interminable.

Sabrina shrugged finally. "I suppose so. *If* he was shot. But I stand by my autopsy results. Garth Rawlings's injuries were consistent with a savage beating."

"In a locked room that showed no signs of a struggle while casually smoking a pipe," Sergio said before thrusting the photo in Sabrina's face and pointing at the black spot on Garth's liver. "Take another look, Sabrina. Isn't that a bullet hole right there?"

Her lips quivered as she glanced once more at the photo, and then, a slight, almost imperceptible, nod.

"Yes," she whispered.

"Thank you," Sergio said, relief in his voice.

"I am *so* going to get fired over this," Sabrina said under her breath.

Hayley tried to put a comforting arm around her, but Sabrina ducked away and dashed out of the lab in tears.

Chapter 35

Hayley stood outside the interrogation room, straining to hear what she could, as Sergio questioned Billy Parsons, who had just returned from his Massachusetts shrimping job earlier that morning. She was now convinced beyond a doubt that it was Nick Ward who shot Garth Rawlings through the wall of the warehouse and killed him. However, without the murder weapon or a viable witness, there was no way Sergio could prove it enough to warrant an arrest.

The plan now was to get one of Nick's coworkers, either Billy or Hugo, to turn on him, to tell the truth of what really happened that night. Hugo was a scared kid, whom Nick had successfully intimidated into keeping his mouth shut. Billy was now their best bet. He was a bit surprised when Sergio called him and asked him to come into the station and make a statement, especially since he had already told everything he knew about the incident at the scene. Billy was an agreeable man, though, and certainly wanted to stay on the chief of police's good side, so he offered to come in and go over the facts one more time.

Although the door to the interrogation room was closed and their voices were muffled, Hayley could make out most of what the two men were saying.

"Not sure what else I can tell you, Chief," Billy said calmly. "Like I said before, me and the guys were just kicking back, drinking some beers, and didn't hear anything until the sirens. That's when we walked outside to see what was going on."

She heard some faint *clicking*.

Sergio was obviously typing on a computer. He was writing up Billy's statement as it was happening.

"So you swear you've told me everything? You're not forgetting any details?"

"No, sir."

"You were drinking alcohol that night, and we both know that can sometimes make your memory a little fuzzy."

"Trust me. I remember everything, Chief. I may have slammed down three or four beers, but I'm a big guy and it takes a lot more than that to get me drunk and sloppy."

"Okay, then," Sergio said. "If that's everything, let me just print out your statement and have you sign it."

There was a *whirring* as the printer spit out a

piece of paper. Hayley heard Sergio's chair squeak as he stood up to retrieve the statement.

A moment of silence as Hayley assumed Billy was scribbling his signature and handing the piece of paper to Sergio.

"Is that all, Chief?"

"Looks good. You can go now, Billy. Thank you."

Billy's chair squeaked as he stood up.

Hayley was about to dash down the hall to avoid Billy catching her eavesdropping at the door, when Sergio spoke again.

"Wait. There is one more thing."

"What's that, Chief?"

"The coroner reexamined the autopsy photos and has changed her conclusion about Garth Rawlings's death."

"Oh?"

"Yes. Mr. Rawlings was shot."

Another moment of silence as Hayley pictured the blood draining from Billy's face.

"Shot?"

"That's not all. We found a patched-up hole right in the office where you were drinking with the boys. That's where the bullet entered the wall. And wouldn't you know, we found the exit hole on the other side in Garth Rawlings's kitchen, a few feet from where he dropped dead."

"I don't know what you're talking about—"

"Of course you do, Billy. You were there. You know exactly what happened, and I think you better tell me. Right now."

More silence.

Hayley pictured Billy shaking his head in defiance.

"Go ahead. Mussel up on me."

"Excuse me?"

Clam up. Sergio is mixing up his shellfish.

"You can always get yourself a lawyer and stick to your story, but here's the problem. Eventually the real facts are going to come out. And when they do, I have this."

The signed statement! Of course! Sergio is a genius.

The police chief might not have mastered the English language, but he was one hell of a law enforcement officer.

"You see, Billy, signing a false police statement is illegal. You could get serious jail time."

"Say what?"

"I got the judge on speed dial. I can have the warrant in a couple of hours. But I don't want to do that to you, Billy, because my gut tells me you weren't the shooter. Tell me who was and I will rip up this report."

"Nick! It was Nick!"

Billy wasn't wasting a second.

"We were just fooling around. We'd only had a few beers. We weren't drunk, but Nick pulled out his pistol and was waving it around, trying to get a rise out of Hugo. He said he wanted to toughen him up and teach him how to shoot. He pointed the gun right at the poor kid, who was just sitting at his desk. I thought the boy was going to piss his pants—he was so scared. Nick thought the safety was on, but it wasn't. The gun went off and the bullet whizzed right past Hugo's ear."

Garth had been at war with Lex's crew over their noisy shop machines.

The walls were extra thin.

The bullet went straight through.

"We . . . we never dreamed anyone got hurt, let alone—"

"Killed by the bullet."

A long pause.

Hayley heard sniffling.

And whimpering.

Billy Parsons was crying.

"Hugo freaked out and Nick had to slap him hard across the face to calm him down. He tossed the kid another beer and we went back to drinking until we heard the sirens. Nick poked his head out first and saw what was going on. Rusty Wyatt told him Garth Rawlings was dead. That's when he put two and two together and warned us to keep our mouths shut and not say a word and just to follow his lead. When we all read in the paper that the coroner thought Garth died from a beating, we breathed a huge sigh of relief. But I haven't been able to stop thinking about it. It keeps me up at night. I should've spoken up sooner."

"Do you have any idea where Nick may have disposed of the gun?"

"*Disposed of it?* No way. He'd never get rid of it. It's a family heirloom. Goes back in his family generations. He may have hidden it somewhere in his house, but he sure as hell would never, ever part with it."

It made sense.

In Nick's mind nobody was ever going to find out Garth Rawlings actually had been shot, given what the coroner and the papers were saying. So, why toss out a prized possession if there was no danger of it ever connecting him to any crime?

That gun was the key to pinning Garth Rawlings's murder on Nick Ward.

Chapter 36

Sergio gave Billy Parsons a stern warning not to contact Nick Ward and alert him to the fact that the police were onto him. Sergio needed time to secure a police warrant to search Nick's house for the gun that killed Garth Rawlings. Billy knew the chief had that false police report to hang over his head, so he promised not to say a word. At this point Billy was more concerned with saving his own skin than protecting his good buddy.

Or so Hayley thought.

Sergio dismissed Billy, and Hayley watched him fly past her, not even noticing her standing outside in the hallway. He wiped his brow with a dirty, stained handkerchief as he scurried out the front door of the police station and into the night. Sergio put a call into the judge for the warrant, which would take at least a couple of hours to be issued.

Hayley checked her watch.

It was already half past five in the afternoon.

She prayed there would be no delays; because if Nick got word about what was happening, he would surely go to any lengths to get rid of the gun.

Suddenly there was pandemonium in the station as a call came through the dispatch radio about a major three-car pileup outside town, near the Trenton Bridge. A local woman hit a patch of ice with her Chevy Malibu and spun out of control, sideswiping a Ford pickup truck and a Prius. No fatalities, but there were reports of injuries. Sergio grabbed his coat and raced out the door, his deputies Donnie and Earl on his heels. The search warrant was going to have to wait.

Hayley heard the sirens screaming as they sped away to the scene of the accident. There was nothing left for her to do but to go home and wait for news from Sergio after he had a chance to surprise Nick Ward with the warrant and search his house. She walked outside to the parking lot and hit the button on her remote to unlock her car; then she heard a man's voice a few feet away from her. She glanced around and spotted Billy sitting in his Range Rover, parked a few cars away from hers. The driver's-side window was open partway and he had his cell phone clamped to his ear.

"They know everything, Nick! You've got to get rid of the gun or you're going down for murder. Do you hear me? Call me back the minute you get this message! I'm going to try to text you."

Billy started tapping out a message on his phone.

Hayley crouched down between her car and the one parked next to hers to avoid being spotted by Billy. She couldn't believe it. Billy had lied about keeping his mouth shut. And with Sergio on the outskirts of town dealing with the car accident, there was no way to stop Nick from disposing of the gun that would pin him to the murder.

Hayley's mind raced.

She had to do something.

Billy had gotten Nick's voice mail.

That was a good sign.

At least she had a little bit of time before Nick checked his messages.

She waited for Billy's Range Rover to pull out and drive off before she jumped in her own car and drove straight over to Nick Ward's house on Ledgelawn Avenue. She knew exactly where he lived; several years ago Nick had bought six boxes of Girl Scout cookies from Gemma and they had personally delivered them to his door.

Nick's house was a modest two-story structure painted white with black shutters. As a contractor he kept the property in immaculate condition, since basically it was an advertisement for his work. Nick had divorced seven years ago. His wife claimed irreconcilable differences, but rumors were he had knocked her around for years until finally she stood up to him and said enough was enough. But that was just idle gossip. Still, given recent events, and seeing what a bully Nick could be, Hayley was prone to believe the stories.

Hayley was surprised to see so much activity on the block. There was hardly any street parking and she watched as people poured into Nick's house, which was lit up with Christmas lights. She heard Madonna's version of "Santa Baby" playing from inside. Nick was hosting a Christmas party. That would surely explain why he hadn't answered his cell when Billy called to warn him.

She parked her car a couple of blocks away and hurried down the sidewalk toward Nick's house, blending in with a crowd of merrymakers who were heading into the house for Nick's soiree. The place was packed.

The guests Hayley arrived with shook off their coats and made a beeline for the open bar, which was serving spiked eggnog and assorted spirits. Hayley followed suit, but she kept a watchful eye out for Nick.

She scanned the living room.

No sign of him.

She wandered over and glanced in the kitchen.

He wasn't there either.

That's when Santa Claus, with a big sack of presents tossed over his shoulder, came marching down the staircase. "Ho, ho, ho! Merry Christmas!"

It was Nick.

No wonder he hadn't checked his voice messages or texts.

He was too busy playing Santa Claus.

A handful of children hovered in the living room near the fireplace. Their eyes lit up with wonder at the sight of Santa, and they clapped their hands wildly. Nick sauntered over to them. A couple of them grabbed his leg, hugging him, while two more jumped up and down excitedly. Nick began doling out presents to the tots as their beaming parents looked on.

This was Hayley's chance. Nick was going to be busy for a while. Here was the perfect opportunity for a quick search.

She rushed upstairs to see if she could find the gun. She started with a guest room that Nick had converted into a small office, furnished with a desk and a computer. The drawers were pretty much empty, except for a few bills and tax papers.

Against the opposite wall was a gun rack. Hayley carefully inspected each firearm, but they were all rifles. No pistol.

She then made her way into Nick's bedroom, closing the door behind her, and checked his dresser drawers. There were just socks and under-wear and a small stack of white t-shirts.

She crossed to the closet. Mostly work boots, an assortment of plaid flannel shirts, and a few pairs of jeans and khaki slacks folded on the shelf.

She was about to leave and go back downstairs, but then she heard the doorknob to the bedroom jiggle. She scooted into the closet and quietly shut the door behind her as two people entered the bedroom.

"Are you sure Nick won't mind?" a woman's slurred voice said.

"Baby, he's never going to even know we were here. Relax," an equally drunken male voice cooed.

Hayley opened the closet door a crack to see the couple fall back on the bed in a fit of giggles. The man slipped his hand through the woman's bright red blouse and began caressing her breasts as she reached down to work the zipper on his pants.

Oh, dear God.

They were about to have sex.

And Hayley was going to be the captive audience.

She slid down to the floor and wrapped her arms around her knees, hoping this would not take too long. She didn't want to be stuck in the closet all night.

Through the crack Hayley watched in horror as the woman yanked the man's pants down as he lay on top of her, giving Hayley the perfect view of a full moon. She averted her eyes to the floor, where they settled on a shoe box, just to her left, tucked back in the corner of the closet.

She reached over and pulled off the top. Resting in the middle of some white tissue paper was a gun.

A pistol.

Hayley knew instantly she had just found the weapon that had killed Garth Rawlings.

Chapter 37

As the inebriated couple fumbled with one another on top of the bed, the man wheezing and thrusting, the woman moaning and gasping, Hayley reached up and plucked one of Nick's flannel work shirts off the hanger. Slipping her hand through the sleeve, she used the shirt to pick up the gun, being careful not to get her own prints on it. She wrapped the rest of the shirt around it and held it until the couple on the bed finally finished. The man rolled off the woman and collapsed on his back. Hayley spied the woman smiling, satisfied. The man closed his eyes and fell instantly asleep, snoring loudly. The woman, offended that her partner wasn't as anxious as she was for some postcoital pillow talk, violently shook him awake. He grunted and snorted and finally came to his senses. She shoved him off the bed and ordered him to put his clothes back on and get her a drink. The man was spent, but he did his best to do as he was told.

Once the woman checked herself in the mirror, wiping some smeared lipstick off her chin, the couple finally retreated out the door and back downstairs to join the party.

Hayley waited a few moments, making sure the coast was clear, before slowly opening the closet door. Tucking the gun wrapped in Nick's shirt under her arm, she crossed past the now-disheveled bed and headed to the bedroom door. Before she even had a chance to reach for the knob, the door swung open, nearly banging her in the head.

Standing in the doorway was Santa Claus.

Or, at least, a nightmarish version of him.

This Saint Nick had a menacing look on his face, his eyes wild with rage.

Hayley took a step back as Santa pushed his way into the bedroom, slamming the door shut behind him.

"I thought I saw you slipping up the stairs," Nick growled. "I don't remember inviting you to my Christmas party."

"I had no idea this was an invitation-only party. I thought you were having an open house and I just wanted to stop by and wish you 'Merry Christmas.'"

"Really?" Nick said skeptically, leering at Hayley.

His eyes went right to the balled-up shirt tucked underneath Hayley's arm.

"You trying to steal one of my shirts?"

"I was cold. I was just going to borrow it while I'm here."

Nick lashed out, grabbing one of the sleeves that was dangling, and ripped it away from her. The shirt unraveled and the gun clattered to the hardwood floor.

They both briefly stared at it.

Then Nick raised his eyes and stared at Hayley. "You know."

He advanced upon her.

Slowly.

He quickly glanced back to make sure the door to the bedroom was firmly shut.

Hayley moved away from him, her eyes searching for some means of escape.

"Damn it! I thought I had taken care of you, once and for all," Nick said, spitting out the words, his face a mask of fury.

"By locking me in the freezer?"

"I was so sick of you snooping around and badgering Hugo!"

"You were afraid if I kept at him, I might get him to crack, so you decided the best thing to do was to put me on ice permanently."

"Why couldn't you have just let it go, like everybody else? We were so close to getting away with it and putting it all behind us."

"Not 'we,' Nick. *You!* This is on you. *You* pulled the trigger. *You* were the one who killed Garth Rawlings!"

Hayley ducked to her right.

Nick lunged at her.

Then in a flash she ducked to her left, faking him out.

She managed to get past him; but before she reached the door, he was on top of her, throwing his beefy arms around her, pinning her against his chest.

"Sergio knows where I am! He's probably on his way over here right now!"

"You're bluffing! If Chief Alvares knew anything at all, he wouldn't have let you come here on your own!"

Nick hurled Hayley onto the bed with all his might.

She landed on her back, bouncing up and down on top of the mattress. She scrambled away from him and hit her head on the headboard.

Nick unbuckled the shiny black belt around his Santa suit.

Hayley shuddered at the thought of what possibly could come next.

He reached up underneath the red coat and yanked out the large, fluffy white pillow he was using to create the illusion of Saint Nick's ample stomach.

Hayley suddenly knew what Nick was planning to do. She opened her mouth to scream. Nick jumped on top of her in an instant.

The last thing she saw was the self-satisfied sneer on his face as he pressed the pillow over her face and began smothering her.

Chapter 38

Hayley struggled desperately, kicking and clawing, but Nick was too powerful. As she thrashed around violently, he managed to keep her pinned down and the pillow clasped firmly over her face. She couldn't breathe. She knew it was only a matter of minutes now before she would get light-headed from lack of oxygen and lose consciousness.

Just like when she thought she was going to die in the freezer, Hayley thought of her children and how horrific it would be for them to find out they had lost their mother so close to Christmas. She couldn't bear the thought of them going through that. It just made her fight harder.

But Nick was twice her size. And twice her strength. She was not going to win this one.

Suddenly she heard a man yell, "Nick, what the hell are you doing?"

Within seconds Nick loosened his grip and

then let go of her completely. Someone was hauling him off her. There were sounds of a scuffle: two men punching each other. One let out an earsplitting war cry. It sounded like Nick.

Hayley threw the pillow off her face and gasped for air. She turned her head to the side just in time to see Nick scoop up one of Lex's crutches that had fallen to the floor during the melee. He raised it up to bash it into Lex's skull, but Lex was too fast for him. He delivered a roundhouse blow to Nick's right cheek.

It was a sickening, crunching sound. A tooth flew out of Nick's mouth as he spun around and dropped to the floor.

Dazed.

Barely conscious.

Lex grabbed the shiny plastic black belt Nick had used to tie around the waist of his Santa suit. He flipped Nick over on his stomach and pulled his arms together, using the belt to tie his hands. He left him there, writhing on the floor, and hobbled over to the bedside to check on Hayley.

"Are you okay?" He placed a gentle hand behind her neck and helped her sit up.

She nodded, still gulping in air. "Lex . . . ," she panted. "How did you know?"

"I didn't. I just came by to confront Nick about the damaged wall, maybe strong-arm him into confessing. I had no clue he was throwing a Christmas party. Someone downstairs said she saw him heading upstairs, so I came up to find him and just walked in on him trying to . . ."

Hayley stood up, but she was still woozy, and Lex had to steady her. "We better call Sergio and tell him what happened."

Nick was on the floor, groaning. "It was an accident. . . ."

Lex was already on his cell phone, calling the police station.

Hayley walked over and stood over him.

He flopped around a bit like a desperate trout on the deck of a fishing boat. "I never meant to hurt anyone. . . ."

"Maybe you didn't intentionally kill Garth," Hayley said, feeling no sympathy. "But you lied and you covered it up, and that's just as bad, if you ask me. Plus you tried to kill *me* twice. You'll always be a murderer in my book."

Hayley watched as Nick groaned some more and struggled against his bonds, but it was half-hearted because he knew in his heart that it was over. He was going to prison for a long time.

Sergio left Officers Donnie and Earl to deal with the car accident and raced back to town in his cruiser to place Nick Ward under arrest. After scolding Hayley for charging into a dangerous situation without any backup, he tossed Nick in the back of the squad car and spirited him off to jail.

Hayley found Lex leaning against the flatbed of his truck, staring up at the stars as she was heading back to her car to go home to her kids.

His face was pale. His shoulders sagged. The crutches were propped up next to him.

She walked over to him; and when his eyes met hers, she gave him a comforting hug.

"He wasn't just my employee. He was my friend. I trusted the guy with my life. How could he have done such a horrible thing? How could I not see it?"

"It's not your fault, Lex. You can't blame yourself."

She could tell he was tormented. Nothing she could say was going to make him feel better. It was going to take time.

All she could think to do was give him another hug. He latched onto it like a lifeline. He held her there, tight in his arms.

Perhaps a moment too long.

His embrace felt warm. It felt safe to be in his big arms again.

Finally she let go.

He leaned in, savoring the moment, with his lips puckered.

Hayley reared her head back a bit too fast to avoid the kiss.

That stopped Lex cold.

And it was at that moment that he finally knew and accepted it.

Hayley had made her choice.

His arms dropped back down to his sides and he forced a smile. "Merry Christmas, Hayley."

"Merry Christmas, Lex."

Chapter 39

The following day was Christmas Eve. Hayley was anxious to leave work early in order to spend the night with her family. Hayley was looking forward to a quiet, noneventful holiday. Her brother, Randy, was going to host a dinner on Christmas night, so Hayley could spend Christmas Eve with her kids.

During lunch she received a call from Sabrina asking if she would join her for a cocktail at Drinks Like A Fish. Hayley tried to beg off, but Sabrina was insistent, promising it would only be for one round and that she would be home in plenty of time to cook dinner for her kids and do any last-minute wrapping and decorating. Hayley agreed; and after wishing Sal, Bruce, and the rest of the *Island Times* staff a happy holiday, she drove over to her brother Randy's bar.

The bar was surprisingly full for Christmas Eve. Randy had left early to have a romantic dinner with Sergio at home, so his crack bartender, Michelle, was on duty, serving the customers. Hayley spotted Sabrina at a corner table away from the bar. Hayley waved at her and crossed over to join her.

"Thanks for meeting me, Hayley," Sabrina said softly, twirling the lemon from her vodka tonic around the inside of her glass.

"No problem. What's up?"

"I want you to be the first to know. I'm resigning as county coroner."

"Sabrina, no!"

"I've had a good run. I think it's time for some new blood."

"But you're so good at it—"

Sabrina raised an eyebrow.

"I'm not joking, Sabrina. Everybody makes a mistake."

"I've made several the last couple of years and in very high-profile cases."

"I am so sorry if I played any role in your decision. I never meant for you to quit."

"Rest assured this has very little to do with you."

"Then what?"

"I'm just tired of carving open dead bodies. I want a new challenge."

Her words sounded hollow. She wasn't exactly being forthright. They made eye contact and Sabrina instantly saw the doubt on Hayley's face.

"Jerry's leaving me," Sabrina said, taking a swig from her vodka tonic.

"What?"

"Told me this morning over breakfast. Can you believe it? I told him I was burned out and needed some time off, and maybe he could get a part-time job to help pay our bills for a few months. And before I even had the chance to take a bite of my blueberry waffles, he was asking for a divorce."

"Oh, Sabrina, I am so, so sorry."

"He prattled on about how the magic was gone, how we had grown apart, but that's just a lot of crap. He was using me. Do you know how many dead carcasses I've carved up these last few years to support his career as an artist? I am such an idiot."

Hayley reached over and squeezed Sabrina's hand. "You're not the idiot. Jerry is."

"I feel like such a failure. My first marriage to Matt went down the toilet. And now I've lost Jerry."

"You haven't lost anything. You've gotten rid of deadweight. And now you're free. This is the first day of the rest of your life. You can do and be anything you want to be."

"You sound like a fortune cookie."

"Yes, I know. I eat way too much Chinese food."

They smiled at each other.

Sabrina continued to grasp Hayley's hand, and she looked down at the table as she spoke. "I know we've had our differences over the years, Hayley, and I may not have been as nice to you as I could have been in high school. . . ."

That was a humongous understatement, but Hayley wasn't about to spoil the moment by pointing it out.

"And maybe lately I've been feeling threatened by you and your success. . . ."

Success? What success? Successful people can pay their winter heating bill.

"But from this point on, I want to start fresh. I want us to be friends," Sabrina said, finally raising her eyes to meet Hayley's tentatively. "I don't have a lot of friends." She had no idea how Hayley was going to react to this "Come to Jesus" moment.

Hayley grinned. "Well, if you really want to be my friend, then you should know the most important thing friends always do for me."

"What's that?"

"Order me a drink."

Sabrina laughed and then signaled Michelle.

Chapter 40

Hayley left Sabrina and was pulling into her driveway by 6:30 P.M., which was plenty of time to whip up a nice dinner for the kids. She hadn't spoken to Aaron, so she was unaware of his plans or if he was going to spend part of the evening with them.

She saw the Christmas tree lights blinking through the window as she got out of the car and walked up the porch steps and inside to the kitchen.

She was surprised to smell a turkey roasting in the oven as she entered the house. She could also see a hot apple pie cooling on a rack, which was sitting on top of the stove.

"Gemma?"

"In here, Mom."

Hayley wandered into the living room to find Gemma, Dustin, and Aaron sitting on the couch, drinking eggnog, and watching a cheesy Hallmark holiday movie on TV. Something with Andie MacDowell and one of the handsome guys from that old show *Ugly Betty*. Hayley had seen the movie before. It was about a small-town family on the verge of bankruptcy who were going to be evicted from their home by an evil bank on Christmas Day and how the six-year-old son writes to Santa Claus asking for help—and, lo and behold, he actually shows up.

It didn't matter.

Hayley was more interested in what was happening right here in her living room.

Aaron was hanging out with her kids.

And there was a holiday feast ready to be eaten in her kitchen.

"Can I ask what's going on here?"

"Aaron cooked dinner. We were just waiting for you," Dustin said, eyes glued to the flat-screen television.

"I've been racking my brain trying to come up with what to get a gourmet chef for Christmas and it finally dawned on me."

Hayley folded her arms and looked at Aaron with anticipation.

"And what's that?"

"A night off from cooking."

"Smells good, doesn't it?" Gemma said, taking a sip of eggnog from her mug. "I helped with the sweet potatoes."

"And I ran to the store to get the apples for the pie—so, technically, I helped too," Dustin was quick to add.

Hayley took off her coat while Aaron stood up and bounded into the kitchen to pour her a cup of eggnog. He was back in a flash.

"I added a special ingredient to ours," he said, winking, as he handed it to her.

Hayley took a small sip and nearly choked on the 90-proof bourbon.

"That's certainly a strong Christmas spirit," Hayley said, coughing.

"The kids told me opening their Christmas stockings is a family tradition around here, so I made sure to fill them up with goodies I bought at the store today," Aaron said proudly.

Hayley glimpsed over to the fireplace and saw three red stockings with white furry trim hanging from the mantel, each embroidered with a name.

Mom. Gemma. Dustin.

"Aaron, I feel terrible. I didn't know you were coming over tonight. I would've gone out and bought you a stocking."

"Oh, don't worry about that. The kids have that covered."

"What do you mean?"

"They already gave me a gift. Best one I could ever imagine."

Hayley reacted with surprise. "Really? What did they give you?"

"Permission to spend the night."

Aaron pinched her butt cheek and dashed off to the kitchen.

"I've got to check on the turkey."

Hayley laughed.

This was going to be one Christmas for the books.

Island Food & Spirits
by
Hayley Powell

With all the events that unfolded during this holiday season, it was no surprise I finally collapsed in my bed after coming home from Christmas dinner at my brother Randy's house. I quickly fell into a deep sleep and had the craziest dream. It was in the future. Twenty years or so. And I am happy to report I looked pretty darn good. Very few gray hairs. Not too many wrinkles. I guess that's why they call it a dream.

I was married again. That was my first shock. My husband and I were sitting in our living room and waiting for our guests to arrive on Christmas Eve. We were sharing a lovely bottle of Off the Vine wine made from our very own Bar Harbor vineyard, which we had purchased some years back. Yes, how fitting I became a winemaker. The extra yearly income was a nice boost to our lifestyle—and, best of all, we had loads of wine at our disposal to share with family and friends.

The first to arrive at the house was Liddy, one of my oldest friends, and still one of my two BFFs, who had scored a huge multimillion-dollar sale on a mansion on the island that once had been owned by a former reality-TV producer a few years back. The commission had allowed her to retire finally and see the world and collect pieces of art. She had recently brought back her latest acquisition from her travels to show off at the party. Not a painting—rather, a stunningly handsome young man from Costa Rica. "Young" being the operative word. I wasn't sure if he was old enough to drink the wine we were serving.

Next to arrive was my other best friend, Mona, with a few of her grown children who still lived on the island. Mona was carrying a newborn baby in each arm, but I am relieved to say they were her grandchildren. Mercifully, Mona had passed menopause years ago. I was starting to lose count of the grandchildren her offspring were constantly providing for her, but she was thrilled and proud of each and every one of them.

Next was my brother, Randy, who still owned his bar, Drinks Like A Fish, which had become so popular he bought two more properties and now had three highly successful Bar Harbor watering holes for the locals and visiting tourists to frequent. Randy, of course, was still with his husband Sergio, who was as handsome as ever (although Liddy's boy toy gave him a run for his money). Sergio was still the chief of police for Bar Harbor. Poor Officer Donnie! Sergio's second in command was waiting patiently for Sergio to hand over the reins to him, but my brother-in-law loved his job so much that he wasn't ready for retirement just yet.

My son, Dustin, soon arrived. He looked to be in his early thirties and had grown quite tall and very handsome. Hanging onto his arm was a lovely woman, his fiancée, Destiny.

Mona's grandchildren eagerly ran to Dustin, since he was bearing free copies of his latest, successful video game, a futuristic James Bond-type adventure, which, of course, I never understood. To no one's surprise he had become a popular video game designer in California, where he and his future bride resided.

Last, but not least, the door flung open again and in breezed my daughter, Gemma, who had grown into such a beautiful woman! (Mothers are always biased, I know.) I'm proud to admit she had followed in her mother's footsteps, or at least a small footprint of it. Gemma had chosen not to go to vet school, but had moved to New York City and was now a well-known food writer. The restaurant world clamored for her to come try out their delicious creations in hopes they would get a glowing review in the newspaper and her online blog. But, of course, in true Gemma fashion, she was a tough critic, with a fierce reputation, in the close-knit but competitive group of top-ranked food writers. She rarely gave rave reviews. You had to knock her off her feet. If you did, then your restaurant was suddenly on everybody's radar and reservations became near impossible to get. My husband and I, however, dined at most of them, thanks to my power-house daughter's connections.

I would like to take at least a sliver of credit for her impeccable palate. But whenever I did, I would get the same withering look she used to give me when she was a teenager. "Oh, Mom!"

Following behind her was her ador-ing businessman husband, who thought the world of his food critic wife and my equally adorable two twin grandsons, Jack and Daniel. Some-where in their names I feel there is a loving nod to their grandmother there.

Gemma also had become quite the cook in her own right. She was carry-ing my husband's favorite, her sweet potato casserole, which she had made for him our very first Christmas after we were married. He looked forward to it every year since. As soon as Thanksgiving was over, he would start sending her little reminders not to forget to make her sweet potato casse-role. Now it was a running joke be-tween the two of them. They had become very close over the years.

Suddenly I was jolted awake by shouting downstairs. The kids were arguing over who was going to get the last piece of pie in the fridge. It was only the day after Christmas. They had another whole week at home before the end of the holiday break. But I knew somehow I'd get through it. As I climbed out of bed and put my robe on, I had one nagging thought in the back of my head. It was that dream set in my future Christmas. As I headed downstairs to referee my kids' wrestling match, I couldn't stop thinking about it. Who in the world would have ever thought I would end up marrying *him*?

Merry Christmas to everyone, and as you toast New Year's Eve and Day, don't forget to grab yourself a favorite bottle of wine from one of your local vineyards. Plus, this year at your own Christmas dinner, be sure to try one of our family favorites: a Christmas sweet potato casserole.

Powell Family Sweet Potato Casserole

<u>Ingredients</u>

5 to 6 good-size sweet potatoes peeled, boiled, drained, and mashed (enough to make 3 cups)

½ cup melted butter
⅓ cup milk
¾ cup white sugar
1 teaspoon vanilla
2 eggs, beaten
Pinch of salt

Topping
5 tablespoons melted butter
⅔ cup brown sugar
⅔ cup flour
1 cup chopped pecans

Preheat your oven to 350 degrees. Mash your sweet potatoes and add the melted butter, milk, white sugar, vanilla, beaten eggs, and a pinch of salt. Stir until well blended together. Pour into a shallow baking dish.

Now for your topping: In a bowl combine the melted butter, brown sugar, flour, and pecans. Using your fingers, mix together to make a crumbly topping, then sprinkle the mixture over the sweet potatoes. Bake in the oven for 25 to 30 minutes until the top is a golden brown. Cool for 10 minutes. Serve and enjoy.

Merry Christmas!

Recipe Index

Please read on
for an exciting sneak peek of
Lee Hollis's next Hayley Powell mystery
DEATH OF A CUPCAKE QUEEN
coming soon from Kensington Publishing!

Chapter 1

Sabrina Merryweather was not the kind of woman you kept waiting for long. And Hayley was panic-stricken that she was already almost a half hour late meeting her for an after-work cocktail. This explained how the back left tire of Hayley's Kia ran up over the curb as she tried to quickly parallel park outside her brother Randy's bar, Drinks Like A Fish.

Hayley had been delayed at the office by an irate caller complaining about his name being misspelled in today's *Island Times* "Police Beat" column.

Seriously? You want accuracy in the report of your Driving Under the Influence conviction? Unbelievable.

Hayley checked her watch as she jumped out of the car and slammed the door shut. She dashed forward but was slung back suddenly by something snagging against her shoulder blade. She had been in such a hurry that she didn't notice she had shut her bag inside the car. The leather strap attached nearly dislocated her shoulder. Hayley lost her balance and landed butt first on the pavement, her arm still dangling from the now limp strap.

Hayley composed herself and casually glanced around to make sure no one had seen her embarrassing pratfall.

No such luck.

A couple of gum-chewing skateboarders, in shorts hanging low enough to see the label of their Jockey underwear, nudged each other with their elbows and guffawed at Hayley, who was now using the strap to pull herself up on her feet. She hit the unlock button on her remote, slowly opened the car door, and daintily removed her faux Fendi bag, which had been trapped inside.

As the snickers and giggles a few feet away persisted, Hayley brushed herself off, locked her car again, and marched inside the bar, head held high.

God, it's only Monday.

She found Sabrina sitting alone at a table next to the wall, sipping a cocktail, a bright smile on her face. Whatever happy pill she was on, Hayley wanted a prescription. *Pronto.*

Sabrina had left her post as county coroner months ago after her husband had filed for divorce. She resigned in order to reassess her life and figure out where she wanted to go from here. Since that time Hayley hadn't seen much of her at all. Which, to be truthful, wasn't such a bad thing considering Hayley had never been all that fond of her former high-school nemesis in the first place.

Although Sabrina's memory of her astonishingly bad behavior back then was fuzzy at best, Hayley had a far more clear-eyed picture of Sabrina's past cruelty. But after seeing a self-help segment on the *Today* show about how letting go of grudges helped you live longer, Hayley tried her best to forgive and forget.

Or at least forgive.

Forget? Never.

When Sabrina called Hayley earlier in the day to suggest they meet for a drink and catch up after she got off work, Hayley just didn't have the energy to come up with an excuse not to go. She just said yes. One drink.

After all, she'd be lying if she said she wasn't at least curious to know what Sabrina had been up to all these months. She had heard rumors. One person said Sabrina took a trip to see the "Seven Wonders of the World," but got waylaid at the Pyramids in Egypt with a stomach virus before giving up and coming home, having seen only one wonder. Another said she was launching her own medical practice again in Bangor, which was one hour north of the island. There was also the "Debbie Downer" who insisted Sabrina had never fully recovered from her divorce and was holed up in her house, crying over her leftover frozen wedding cake, like some demented, haggard, jilted bride from the Charles Dickens novel.

Hayley knew that last one was an outright lie, because the Sabrina who was beaming from ear to ear as she sat down across from her was a far cry from the emotional car wreck some of her detractors were making her out to be.

"Hayley, you must have a sip of this peanut butter cup martini. It is so decadently delicious, you will just die!" Sabrina cooed as she pushed the glass by its stem over in front of Hayley.

"Let's hope not," Hayley said, lifting the glass and taking a tiny sip.

There was no arguing her point. The drink was orgasmic.

"Kudos to your brother for another to-die-for cocktail recipe," Sabrina said, retrieving the glass back from Hayley and downing another gulp as she closed her eyes and savored the taste.

Hayley noticed a half-empty bottle of Sam Adams on the table. "Is someone else joining us?"

Sabrina popped her eyes back open and nodded, excited. "Yes. A friend. He's in the men's room."

"I see. And he's just a *friend*?"

A spurt of giggles escaped from Sabrina's lips. She turned her face slightly away like an embarrassed schoolgirl. Hayley didn't remember Sabrina being so coquettish and demure. Suddenly she had gone from Dickens to a full-fledged Brontë heroine.

"Well, now you've certainly gotten my attention," Hayley said, smiling as she signaled to her brother behind the bar to bring over her usual Jack and Coke.

Randy gave her a wave and then grabbed a bottle of whiskey off the shelf.

"Is he local? Is it someone I know?" Hayley asked Sabrina, who was now dragging her fingertip across the rim of her martini glass, gathering up the chocolate that lined it, and then sliding her finger into her mouth and licking it off.

"No. I met him when I was visiting my sister in San Diego a few months ago. We were having dinner in the Gas Lamp district and he jogged by. Our eyes met, but he kept going. It was a fleeting fantasy on my part. How could this strapping hunk of a man ever be interested in me? But then, without warning, he double-backed and introduced himself. My sister asked him to join us, and he did! We've been inseparable ever since!"

Hayley glanced up to see a young man, not far past the legal drinking age, walking from the restrooms back toward their table.

This couldn't be him. He was striking: dark-skinned, black hair, probably half Latino. Plus he was covered in tattoos from what Hayley could see. His arms, the back of his hands, and what Hayley could see of his smooth bronzed chest through his open silk white shirt were inked.

He wore thick black glasses and had two perfectly round holes in his earlobe. He was a sight to behold. Hayley normally wasn't a big fan of body art and piercings. But this kid, this lean yet muscled Adonis, wore it so well.

When he smiled, it was as if the whole bar was suddenly bathed in a heavenly light.

Hayley's heart fluttered. Not because she was attracted to him. This was male beauty in its finest form and she was just appreciating it.

Oh, who am I kidding? Of course I'm attracted to him!

However, he was almost young enough to be her son.

He stopped at the table and massaged Sabrina's shoulders. She melted at his touch. Her face turned crimson and out came another girlish giggle.

"You must be Hayley. I've been anxious to meet you. Mason Cassidy," the Adonis said in a deep baritone voice.

Hayley stood up and held out her hand, but Mason brushed it away and enveloped her in a tight hug. She could feel his rock-hard chest as he squeezed her body into his.

After releasing her from his iron grip, Mason gave her a playful wink. "Sorry. I'm a big hugger."

Oh, this kid is good.

Hayley suddenly found herself giggling. It was contagious.

He took a seat at the table. His bright smile still blinded both of them.

Randy nearly walked into an adjacent table as he delivered Hayley's cocktail, his eyes glued to the handsome stranger. Somehow he managed to set it down in front of her without spilling too much of it.

"Thank you, Randy," Hayley said.

Randy never once looked at her. He was staring at the painted god with a laser-like focus. "Can I get you another beer?"

Mason picked up the bottle and examined it. "I'm not even halfway through yet. Are you trying to get me drunk?" He winked at Randy, whose knees nearly buckled.

"Why? What would happen if I got you drunk?"

"Thank you, Randy. I think we're fine for now," Hayley said, placing a hand on his hip and giving him a subtle yet forceful send-off.

"Just yell if you need anything, and I do mean *anything*!" he called out as he walked back behind the bar.

"For heaven's sake, Randy, you have a husband!" Hayley called after him.

"I know! I'm happily married, but that doesn't mean I'm dead! There's no harm in window-shopping, even if I'm not going to buy anything!"

"So you two met in San Diego?" Hayley asked.

"Yes, she swept me off my feet," Mason said, cupping the back of Sabrina's neck and pulling her close so he could plant a sweet kiss on her cheek.

"Mason works as a high diver at SeaWorld. He swims with porpoises. How sexy is that?" Sabrina said, squealing so high that Hayley was surprised their glasses didn't shatter.

"Wow, that's very impressive," Hayley said. Truly impressed.

"Yes, he trained as an acrobat and even worked in a couple of those Cirque du Soleil shows in Las Vegas. So you can just imagine how limber he is when it comes to you know what!" Sabrina said, now lowering her voice to the point where it was almost Kathleen Turner husky in order to make her point.

"Yes, I can. So there's no need to explain—"

"Neither of my fuddy-duddy former husbands had the tactile grace that Mason brings to the bedroom. Hell, Jerry sprained his back just coming from the toilet to the dresser, where he kept his condoms. We hadn't even started yet!"

Mason nuzzled Sabrina's neck with the tip of his nose. "You are so cute."

"You know, Hayley, I never would have met Mason if I hadn't quit my job as county coroner. That was the best decision I have ever made."

"I'm so happy for you, Sabrina. Really, I am."

In fact, there was a slight pang of jealousy deep inside Hayley.

Not that she wasn't blissfully happy dating the handsome town vet, Dr. Aaron Palmer. *Not at all.* Aaron was certainly a keeper. Her relationship with him was an unexpected gift that she treasured.

But like her brother said, she wasn't dead.

Mason Cassidy, with his caramel complexion, suave manner, and lovely features, was certainly fun to look at and admire.

Good for Sabrina. She deserved a little happiness after two ugly divorces.

Sabrina clasped Mason's hand and turned to Hayley. "You know, I seriously considered skipping out on our high-school reunion this year, even though I've been on the planning committee. I just couldn't bear the thought of my former classmates judging me and whispering behind my back about my two failed marriages and collapsed career. But now, with Mason by my side, I think I'm ready to face anyone. Even those mean bitches who were so rotten to us during high school, right, Hayley?"

Hayley was speechless. *Rotten to us?*

Sabrina was the kind of ultimate mean girl who literally had inspired Rosalind Wiseman's *Queen Bees and Wannabes,* the best-selling guide to adolescent torture!

Hayley nodded, deciding it was best not to poke a hole in Sabrina's happy mood.

"I am ready to introduce the new Sabrina Merryweather to the world in all her glory! I can just feel it! This reunion is going to be history-making!"

Sabrina had no idea just how on the mark she was with her comment. Their twentieth high-school reunion was certainly going to make history.

Only not in the way she imagined.

Showing off her hot, new, young boyfriend was soon going to take a backseat to a dead body turning up even before the class president's welcome speech was over.